Mystic Connecticut: A Woman's Hundred Year Journey to Heaven

Bryan James Lockett

Life's Journey
Publishing Co.
Mystic

Please visit www.bryanlockett.com

"But even if you should suffer for what is right, you are blessed. Do not fear what they fear; do not be frightened."
1 Peter 3:14

For my grandmother Elizabeth Lockett, whose poem "Journey Through Time" inspired this novel. Rest in peace.

To my beautiful wife Elena; my constant companion, conscience, and best friend.

To my parents Jim and Betty who are always there for their children…and grandchildren…and great-grandchildren!

To my daughter Jackie who possesses all the potential for greatness anyone could ask for.

To my daughter Beth; a wonderful mother with the steadfast determination to carve her own way through this world.

Special thanks to cover artist Shirley Karkow who brilliantly captured the essence of this novel.

And of course to all my friends and the reviewers who have provided invaluable input to make this tribute as passionate and powerful as possible.

Acclaim for Bryan James Lockett's

Mystic Connecticut:
A Woman's Hundred Year Journey to Heaven

"... this book deserves to be read and re-read. And there are not many such books in my world. I've always judged a good book by its ability to create enough suspense that one is willing to re-enter the world of its characters to "live again" through them. This book has that capacity."
Pastor Bob McCoy, Groton Bible Chapel

"Bryan James Lockett has attempted an ambitious undertaking with "Mystic Connecticut: A Woman's Hundred Year Journey to Heaven." Weaving history with fiction, the mundane with the ethereal and great tragedy with great joy, Lockett offers a story that is at times fully engaging and immersive… As a storyteller, Lockett commands attention."
Joan Radell for the Post Road Review

"Find a piece of your own pain, regret, joy and sorrow in Elizabeth's story and then step into her triumph and discover something you didn't think possible."
Pastor Brad Whipple, Seaport Community Church, Groton, CT

"Literary enthusiasts will find that the endearing story, "Mystic Connecticut: A Woman's Hundred Year Journey to Heaven" is a moving testament - one that in some way could be the life story of each of us. The joys and pains of being a child, of growing up and losing loved ones. A celebration of the waxing and waning of life's seasons in all of its fullness, and then finally death and the great beyond."
Albert Williams, Literary Critic and author of "Haunted Heritage and Other Stories"

©2009 by Bryan James Lockett
All rights reserved. No part of this book may be reproduced, stored in a retrieval system or transmitted in any form or by any means without the prior written permission of the publishers, except by a reviewer who may quote brief passages in a review to be printed in a newspaper, magazine or journal.

Second printing.

All characters appearing in this work are fictitious. Any resemblance to real persons, living or dead, is purely coincidental.

ISBN: 978-0-615-46151-9
PUBLISHED BY LIFE'S JOURNEY PUBLISHING CO.
Mystic

Printed in the United States of America

Journey Through Time

Elizabeth Lockett (1914-2000)

Memory takes me again and again
To my childhood of yesteryear.
Life was a doorway forever ajar
To a future all simple and clear.

Summers of sunshine-Autumns of gold;
Spring ever-welcome and bright.
Darkness of winter-dreary and drab-
'Til the Lord painted everything white.
Arms I could run to in moments of grief;
Days that were carefree and gay.
When did the bitterness enter my world
To scatter my sunshine away?

Was it the loss of a loved one's smile,
Or a friend turned into foe?
Burdens so heavy-why did they come,
Never again to go?

Where shall I go to find solace now?
Not in this world of strife!
Perhaps in a Heaven somewhere above
I will learn the meaning of life.

But even the heavens have had to adjust
To the maddening journey through space.
Highways lead on to vast cities of steel,
And the Devil has set the pace.

Now I am rich in material things
And pretend to be reconciled.
But I would relinquish all that I own,
For the dreams that I dreamed as a child.

Yes, the twilight of life is upon me now.
But before the darkness draws near,
Let me return down the Roadway of Time;
To my childhood of yesteryear.

Preface

Sweet smells of honeysuckle and wild grapes snaked through the vehicle exhaust as the jogger turned onto Old North Road. The first warm sunny day of spring is as magical as winter's first snowfall; and the world was alive again! The jogger heard the low groan of a SEAT bus behind him; the bus no doubt waited for by the oldster sitting alone on the bench up ahead. The jogger's toe caught a frost-heaved patch of sidewalk and he swore as he flapped his arms in an attempt to prevent sprawling face-first. As he regained his footing, the jogger saw the old lady grab her purse and lean forward preparing to stand. She pushed up with her hands, but instead of standing erect she actually rolled forward in slow motion - melting rather than falling onto the concrete.

The jogger was upon the woman in an instant and knelt beside her as the SEAT bus labored past. "OWWWW, help me! Somebody help me!" screamed the hyperventilating woman. The ancient figure writhed and twisted in an effort to sit up, but each movement seared more than the previous.

Bird seed spilled from the woman's purse during the fall, a good bit of it embedding in her cheek when she impacted the sidewalk. "Its okay, you're going to be fine. Let me help you up. What's your name?" The jogger placed one hand under the woman's neck and cupped his other behind her frail shoulder.

The soothing voice and confident hands comforted the woman and her yelling subsided. "Elizabeth," gasped the woman.

"Alright Elizabeth, we're going to get you up now. Ready? One…two…" On "three" the Samaritan gently lifted the woman's upper body off the ground, initiating a fresh round of hollering at which the jogger promptly returned the woman to the sidewalk. The jogger's heart melted as tears welled in the woman's terrified eyes. "I'll be right back; I'm going to get help. There's a house right here," said the jogger as he pointed to the small house behind the bench.

The woman's eyes puddled with tears that spilled onto her cheeks as she clenched the jogger's wrist. "Please don't leave me. You have to help me up, I just tripped. The ducks are waiting for me; I go to the Village every Sunday to feed them."

"I know, let's get you up then." The jogger brushed the woman's thin gray hair from the birdfeed-crusted road rash on her face. "I think it's your hip. I have to-"

"DON'T YOU DARE SAY THAT! IT'S NOT MY HIP! I HATE YOU! They'll put me in Bayside! Get away from me!" The woman screeched venomously as she thrashed the jogger.

The outburst flabbergasted the jogger but he kept his hand under the woman's head as she lay back sobbing. A moment later a Buick pulled onto the shoulder of the road and asked the jogger what was happening. The driver didn't have a cell phone, but told the jogger he would drive to Pequot Medical Center a mile away and have an ambulance sent. The jogger, obviously having no medical training, agonized through the woman's swearing and berating for ten minutes until the ambulance arrived. The jogger briefed the EMTs on the situation and continued on his way, no longer enjoying the first magical day of spring.

Bayside

Red lights danced atop the ambulance as it transported Elizabeth to Bayside Elder Care Facility from Pequot a week after her hip replacement. Elizabeth cursed losing the final thread of independence she still possessed. She'd called Seaside Gardens home for over a decade. She had few visitors, fewer friends, and no family. Her tiny three-room quad in the senior citizen housing complex provided privacy, what independence she could manage, and a tremendous amount of solitude in which she nurtured her bitterness.

The instant she crumpled to the ground waiting for the bus she knew her hip gave out, and with no one to care for her that meant no more Seaside Gardens. She'd seen it hundreds of times throughout the years. The idea of spending her final days in a nursing home sickened Elizabeth.

The ambulance slowed to a smooth stop in front of Bayside. Although it was Easter Sunday, when the insurance folk say your stay is up, that's it. The rear door opened as the driver joined the EMT riding with Elizabeth. "You doing okay? We're going to wheel you out now." The driver pulled the gurney from the back of the ambulance and released the rolling carriage assembly. The EMTs flanked Elizabeth and rolled her toward the facility entrance.

"Hold on ma'am, we've got to back up a second." The gurney reversed direction as the automatic double doors opened in front of them. A stocky female orderly pushed a gurney similar to Elizabeth's from the building toward a van with a Groton Human Services emblem on its door. A white sheet fully concealed the large dead man laying beneath it. "Out with the old, in with the new, huh boys?" asked the woman as she approached Elizabeth and the two EMTs. The two men lowered their heads as the woman continued past them. The EMT who rode with Elizabeth whispered to her. "I'm sorry about that ma'am. Her name is Dora; we've heard stories about her." The man's apology fell upon deaf ears as a shockwave riveted Elizabeth's body. Even as Elizabeth assumed the pain must be emanating from her newly acquired titanium hip, she dismissed the idea. The jolt equilaterally seized her entire being, causing her to bolt upright at the waist. The invasiveness consumed Elizabeth instantaneously, and diffused just as quickly. Elizabeth welcomed death as her upper body returned to the gurney.

A year later Elizabeth realized that the shock that night was not the gift of death, but rather the gift of eternal life.

Elizabeth's throbbing hip provided her the unwelcome realization that she was not dead. As the EMTs wheeled Elizabeth into the lobby of Bayside, the smell of old people, bleach and urine wrenched her stomach and nearly made her vomit. Dora returned to the EMTs and, after the requisite transfer signatures were complete, recklessly wheeled Elizabeth to her room. Dora manhandled Elizabeth from the gurney to a bed and left Elizabeth, cackling as she slammed the door shut behind her.

Opposite Elizabeth's bed sat an unoccupied bed dressed with once-white sheets and a coarse blanket. Two nightstands, a couple chairs, yellowed pictures of lighthouses, and a door most likely leading to a bathroom comprised the remainder of the small room.

In short, all the hell on earth Elizabeth expected a nursing home to be. Elizabeth lay back and rested her head. As her eyes began closing, they snapped back open in a panic. Elizabeth frantically scanned the room. On the floor beside her bed she finally saw it; the box of personal items that she asked be collected from Seaside Gardens while she was in the hospital.

Pain seared through her hip as Elizabeth leaned over and tugged at the box top. Soft rays of light just now snuck into the room on either side of the window blinds. The sun's amber fingers gently lapped the gilded cover of her family Bible which lay at the top of the box. The Bible's original content was insignificant to Elizabeth; she'd lost her religion too many years ago to count. But the Bible itself provided Elizabeth's only link to her childhood of yesteryear; the final beacon of light in her long dispirited life. Someone had crammed her clothing in the bottom of the box. On top of them lay her reading glasses, her purse and an envelope containing the few precious photographs she'd kept through the years. Comforted that her few earthly possessions lay at her side, Elizabeth pulled the blanket over her head as darkness consumed her.

Elizabeth could not imagine the eternal impact that the Book she so easily dismissed would have on her in the months to come.

"STOP CALLING ME BABY!" shouted little Elizabeth.

William Newton lowered the newspaper that concealed his face so he could view the intruder. Unshaken, his wife sipped her morning tea. The two glanced at each other and then back at their daughter. The seconds ticked by like hours for the small child. Her mother finally broke the silence. "I beg your pardon dear. Did you want something?" Although born in New England, Clara's brogue and auburn hair attested to Irish descent.

Like a ball of black twine the girl's sweaty unkempt hair framed her square red face. Her tiny fists clenched the handle of a chicken feed pail. The bottoms of her denim bib overalls were rolled up to her knees and chicken litter caked her boots. At four years old, the girl portrayed quite an imposing figure. "Stop calling me Baby! My name is Elizabeth!"

William set down his newspaper. He and his wife had told their daughter since she was old enough to understand that she had to choose her own name. His left hand rose to his face, partially covering the grin that blossomed at the corners of his lips. He slowly scratched his stubble as he scrutinized his daughter. "Well...*Elizabeth*. That's a fine name you've chosen for yourself. But can I ask you a question? Did you have to bring that corn meal all the way from the barn to tell us?" Once said, William could contain himself no longer. He exploded into laughter and slapped his knee as tears formed in his eyes from laughing so hard. With the faux gravity of the situation relieved, his wife joined his outburst.

Furious at her parents' laughter, Elizabeth dropped the pails and stormed out of the house. She marched toward the chicken coop, anger overriding any concern about being punished for the mess she'd just made. Halfway across the back yard she heard the screen door bang closed. Despite promising herself she wouldn't turn around, fear got the best of her as her mother's footsteps quickly overtook her own. She turned and looked up at her mother, surprised to see a smile instead of a hand coming down to administer a licking. "I'm sorry Ma'am."

Clara's hand cupped her daughter's face. "I think we'll let it slide, this time. Of course, you're marching right back in there to clean it up. But Bab-...Elizabeth, I want to talk to you about something. You're going to be five next year and you'll start going to the school with me. I think it's time you start dressing, and acting, like a young lady."

"But Mother, I like farmin'. I want to be a farmer like Father." Her mother's raised eyebrows told Elizabeth not to pursue the subject any further. Elizabeth sighed. "Yes ma'am. But can I at least *help* take care of the animals?"

Her mother's eyebrows didn't lower. "Your father has Jacob to help him." Jacob drifted into town a few years earlier, when he was barely an adult himself. He had been the Newton's only steady farm hand ever since. Finally Clara raked her hand through Elizabeth's nappy hair. "Well, even the two of them have a hard time keeping up with chores. I suppose you could help - *sometimes*."

§

As mother and daughter hugged in a world a million years past, someone knocked gently on the door.

"Mrs. Newton? Mrs. Newton, are you awake?"

Elizabeth frowned. *What kind of question was that?* "Wrong room, I don't need anything."

"I volunteer here Mrs. Newton. May I come in?"

Elizabeth tugged the blanket off her face and turned toward the door. The knob turned and the door eased partially open. Elizabeth watched a young woman's face poke inside the room. The woman called Elizabeth's name again as she stepped inside. "May I come in? I'm here to welcome you to Bayside." The young woman shuffled toward Elizabeth's bed. Unkempt hair blossomed beneath a knit stocking cap. Her eyes never lifted to make eye contact with Elizabeth. She wore jeans and a light jacket, and an oversized bag draped her shoulder. "I'm Nancy Nichols. I brought some things you might need. I have soap, shampoo, toothpaste." Nancy's hand disappeared inside the bag as she began placing the items on a small table. Nancy glanced at Elizabeth. "Can you hear me?" Nancy took a step closer and for a moment Elizabeth thought she was going to reach out and shake her. Elizabeth prepared to howl like a banshee if the woman laid a hand on her. Elizabeth choked back giggles at the thought of scaring the pants off the young visitor.

"Are you okay?" asked Nancy. Elizabeth enjoyed Nancy's discomfort. "I'll go get help." The young lady kept her eyes glued to Elizabeth and walked backward, as if something very scary might happen if her eyes diverted from the old woman lying in front of her.

Nancy groped for the door behind her when Elizabeth's raspy voice slapped the weight from the room. "Crosswords!"

Nancy jumped at the unexpected sound, causing her to reel against the door and slam it shut behind her. "I'm, I'm sorry, no. I didn't say any cross words. I'm Nancy-"

Elizabeth held up her hand. "I know; you're Nancy Nichols the candy striper; congratulations," sighed Elizabeth. "I need crossword puzzles."

Nancy's face flushed as she groped for the door knob and quickly disappeared into the hallway, closing the door behind her.

Elizabeth almost smiled at the sight of the flustered uncomely girl. Almost.

Elizabeth cursed her fate. She was hungry and had no food. She was thirsty and had no drink. Her hip throbbed and she had no medicine. But what was absolutely unbearable was that she had to use the bathroom and had no idea how to get there. The door to the bathroom was a mile away near the room's entrance. The medical technicians at the hospital administered some initial physical therapy, but Elizabeth knew she couldn't yet walk without assistance. She loathed the idea of using a walker, but with one she knew she could amble about. Without one she didn't stand a chance. Her discomfort escalated to sharp pain across her bladder. Elizabeth considered relieving herself in bed. After all, she thought, that's what people do in here. She actually tried at one point, but her subconscious wouldn't let her.

Finally Elizabeth turned over and forced her legs over the side of the bed. She pushed herself toward the edge until gravity took control, drawing the rest of her body off the bed and landing on her knees with a slight thud. After briefly collecting herself, Elizabeth grasped the mattress and tried to pull herself erect. She stood on her strong right leg while weightlessly resting her left foot on the floor. Just getting to that point required tremendous effort, causing sweat to bead on Elizabeth's brow. Suddenly her focus shifted from *going* to the bathroom to *getting* to the bathroom. Elizabeth squared off with the lavatory. Using her hands, she positioned her left leg in front of her right. On three, she kicked off with her right foot and shuffled it past her left. Fatigue set in quickly as she repeated the process two more times. If she could reach the table she would be over half way there and could rest. Elizabeth shuffled again, this time nearly losing her balance. Sweat seeped through the top of the hospital gown and Elizabeth gasped for air. One big step should do it. Elizabeth grabbed her left thigh and again placed her leg in front of her. With great effort she pushed off with her right leg, her foot landing two feet shy of the table. Her knee buckled and she couldn't control her forward momentum. Elizabeth launched her arms toward the edge of the table to prevent crashing to the floor, with the terror of breaking her other hip flooding her mind. She fell too hard to catch herself. Her elbows folded like accordions as her forehead smacked against the edge of the table and Elizabeth toppled to the floor.

Elizabeth stared at the ceiling. Seconds ticked by like minutes; minutes like hours. Soon thoughts of *going* to the bathroom replaced *getting* to the bathroom, and the cycle began again. Elizabeth cocked her head and looked behind her. Only five feet to the lavatory. Elizabeth pushed with her legs and scooted herself backward with her elbows. Ten minutes later her head slid onto the tiled bathroom floor. As Elizabeth contemplated how to get on the toilet, the hallway door crashed open. A buxom woman backed into her room from the hallway, dragging an aluminum walker behind her.

"Okay honey, time for PT, then chow." The woman stopped at the sight of the empty bed. She scanned the room and finally spied Elizabeth lying on the floor. "Oh my Gawd you crazy ol' fool! What in the world ails you? Look at you, blood runnin' down your face and everything!" The woman ran to Elizabeth and knelt beside her. She wiped the stream of blood from her forehead and asked if Elizabeth could hear her. Elizabeth nodded. "I'm alright. I just have to use the bathroom."

The woman placed a meaty arm beneath Elizabeth and plucked her off the floor. "Lawdy child, next time use the buzzer on your headboard. You like to gave me a heart attack seein' you lyin' there like that. And if anybody asks, you cut your head in the amb'lance, you hear?" The woman plopped Elizabeth on the toilet and told her to take care of business.

When Elizabeth finished, the woman hoisted Elizabeth off the toilet. "We *was* gonna start PT, but you're not up for it today. And you sure ain't up for walkin' to the dining room." The woman half-dragged, half-carried Elizabeth to her bed. She snorted toward the toiletries on the table. "That crazy girl bring this stuff? Something's wrong with that skeeza - ever since her mother died. And DON'T get up again by yo'self else you won't be gettin' no chow. You might be a hundred, but you ain't in charge around here! I'll bring your dinner later, but don't get used to it – I ain't no maid!"

That must have been funny, because the woman repeated herself and cackled as she left Elizabeth alone.

Father Digiacomo

Elizabeth flirted with restless sleep after spending her first full day at Bayside without food or drink. Her forehead stung, but the cut appeared worse than it was. Her hip throbbed, but not much more than the rest of her body after all the crashing around a day earlier. All things considered, thought Elizabeth, it could have been much worse. And she *didn't* relieve herself where she shouldn't!

Elizabeth was light-headed from lack of food. Something from the previous afternoon crossed Elizabeth's mind - the woman told her to use the buzzer on her headboard. Elizabeth craned her neck around and spotted an intercom mounted to the headboard. She pushed the call button and waited for a response. And waited. And waited some more. Elizabeth wondered whether she stood a greater a chance starving waiting for the intercom to be answered or waiting for the woman from yesterday to return with her dinner.

Elizabeth dozed and her dreams returned to her family's North Stonington farm. "I'll see you at school Mother," Elizabeth called. Elizabeth rode the carriage to school with her mother for two years. Finally her mother gave in to Elizabeth's pleadings to let her walk to school by herself. By cutting through Beaver Dam Hollow, Elizabeth rationalized, she could leave home later – and therefore help Father and Jacob with the animals before school. Elizabeth missed the animals so much since her mother occupied nearly all Elizabeth's free time with more domesticated instruction. By age seven, Elizabeth could sew, churn butter, preserve jam, bake bread, pickle beets, cucumbers, and pretty much anything else her father could grow. And Elizabeth hated it! Despite her domiciliary resentment, Elizabeth enjoyed spending time with her mother and learned the tasks quickly. Because of this, her mother occasionally indulged Elizabeth's tom-boyish indiscretions.

"Father, the chickens are fed. Can I help Jacob feed the hogs?"

William Newton considered his daughter for a moment before responding. "Look Little Me," as William was fond of calling Elizabeth. "The thing is, you're turning into a young lady and I'm not so sure you should be doing these types of chores anymore. Why don't you run along to school now?"

Elizabeth stared disbelievingly at her father. She knew her father loved her working with him. "But father," she started.

"Get along now, and don't dally either."

"Yes sir." Elizabeth turned and walked toward the Hollow, not understanding what just happened. As she rounded the barn and disappeared from her father's sight, Jacob trotted up behind her. "Hey there pretty girl, where you going? I been waiting by the pigs for you."

Elizabeth continued walking. "'Lizabeth, wait up." Jacob placed his hand on Elizabeth's shoulder and spun her around. "Did you like the necklace I gave you yesterday? You didn't tell anybody, did you?" Jacob saw that Elizabeth was upset. "What's wrong Sunshine?"

Elizabeth cried as she relayed the discussion with her father. Through her tears, Elizabeth thought she saw fear cross Jacob's face. The look quickly transformed into sympathy, and Elizabeth assumed she mistook Jacob's initial reaction. "Well, don't worry about it Sweetheart. He's just a little grumpy today is all. Here, I brought you some penny candies. 'Sweets for the Sweet.' Okay, 'Lizabeth, you better run along now. I'll see you after school."

Jacob was gone when Elizabeth returned home from school and her parents refused to discuss the matter. "He's gone, and that's all you need to know," her father told her.

"You made him leave! I hate you!" screamed Elizabeth as she ran upstairs to her room. Elizabeth sobbed for days, missing her "special friend."

§

Elizabeth awoke as the residue of her dream's youthful naiveté faded. She was weak, famished, and dehydrated. And furious! Elizabeth spotted the walker just out of reach at the side of the bed. By finagling her right leg she tipped the walker over toward her. She uprighted it and sat up on the edge of the bed. Grasping the handles Elizabeth slid off the bed, awkwardly transferring her weight to her right leg. Once erect, Elizabeth clumsily shuffled toward the bathroom. Without too much agony she reached the sink. Elizabeth lowered her head and sipped from the faucet. Tap water never tasted so good to the dehydrated old woman. Careful not to drink too quickly, Elizabeth took several small gulps. The cool liquid instantly sparked life to Elizabeth's parched body. She drank again, more greedily this time, and considered resting on the toilet before venturing into the hall. She dismissed the idea, however welcoming it might be, not certain if she could get up again.

Through no small feat of maneuvering, Elizabeth opened the door and shuffled out of the room. The hallway dead-ended to the left, and opened to a large room to the right. Elizabeth began her trek down the corridor, growing fatigued but more confident as she progressed. She scanned the Community Room. A dozen old folks watched television, played cards, read, and gossiped. A priest sat alone by the gas fireplace. Elizabeth likened him to a vulture waiting for an injured prey to die so he could begin feeding.

Elizabeth heard glass clanking. A counter ran along the far side of the room, with a large roll-up window at its end. A man worked methodically behind the service window. Elizabeth made her way to the window, the man behind it never making eye contact with her as he stacked cups and glasses from the dishwashing machine. Elizabeth stood silently for a moment until she could not take it any longer.

"I'd like some breakfast," demanded Elizabeth.

"Breakfast was over an hour ago," replied the man. Elizabeth banged her walker against the counter. Finally the man looked at her and shrugged.

Elizabeth glared at the man. "Give me some food or I'll kick you where it counts."

The man did a double take and studied Elizabeth. She still wore her hospital gown and had nothing on her feet. Straw hair matted her head in some places, flew helter skelter in others. Sweat from her walk ran down her face, turning the crusty blood from her wound into a pink paste that streamed down her cheek.

A huge white smile lit up the man's jet black face. "You know, I just bet you would at that. Hold on a minute." The man disappeared from sight and returned with a plate of scrambled eggs and home fries. He placed the plate on the counter as Elizabeth continued staring at him. "What? You want more? I can get you more."

Elizabeth tapped the walker's handles with her thumbs. When the man didn't understand, Elizabeth looked down at her walker. The man's eyes followed her gaze and he finally got it. "Oh, right - walker! Umm...hang on." The man took back the plate and emerged a moment later from a door next to the service window carrying Elizabeth's food. He set the plate down on an empty table and tried to hold Elizabeth's arm to help her to the chair. Elizabeth shirked the man's hand and plopped down in the seat. The man asked if Elizabeth needed anything else. Elizabeth snorted and looked at her breakfast. The man muttered under his breath as he returned to the kitchen.

Elizabeth's starved body was beyond the point of hunger. Her small stomach didn't growl. She was numb with malnutrition and her hand shook as she fought to steady the fork. The first two attempts yielded egg on her lap. Elizabeth fought the urge to lay her head on the table and shovel the food directly from the plate into her mouth. She sensed the other occupants of the room staring at her, and didn't want to give them anything else to talk about. She managed to get most of the third forkful into her mouth and swallowed it without chewing. After eating half her eggs, Elizabeth's stomach felt as though it would burst. Her dizziness subsided, and she contemplated the impending journey back to her room. The small murmur that occupied the room when she entered died as Elizabeth stole the room's attention. For the first time Elizabeth considered her appearance and a bitter half-smile touched her lips.

Elizabeth rested for a few minutes and painstakingly stood up from her chair. She ignored the greetings and offers of help as she left the Community Room. Half way down the hall her stomach gurgled, adding a sense of urgency to her labored progress. She prayed that she would make it to her bathroom in time; or at least into her room and out of sight. Just as Elizabeth began believing she would indeed reach her room in time, a horrible thought crossed her mind: *What if the door is locked?* Her hand shook as she reached for the doorknob. With relief beyond words, the knob turned and the door opened inward. Elizabeth shuffled to the bathroom and pulled the door closed behind her.

Elizabeth rested for a short while after completing her business. When she entered her room from the hallway her body was covered with sweat from the arduous task of walking with her new hip. Now that she rested, she cooled quickly and became quite chilly. Elizabeth placed her hands on the sink and her walker and pulled herself upright. When Elizabeth opened the bathroom door and entered the main part of her room, her heart skipped a beat and her breath caught in her throat at the unexpected sight of a large figure seated in the chair beside her bed. The priest Elizabeth spotted in the Community Room smiled at Elizabeth's start.

"Holy Cow! Business isn't good enough, you have to scare people to death now?" asked Elizabeth. Angry, fatigued and cold, Elizabeth ambled across the room. She lay on the bed studying the priest. His burly frame barely squeezed into the chair, and, even seated, Elizabeth judged him well over six feet tall. The priest was old. His salt and pepper hair fell nearly to his shoulders, and the slightest traces of red dotted his beard. Even through the Priest's beard and wrinkles, the good humor caused by Elizabeth's fright danced like fireflies at the corners of the large man's mouth.

"Please forgive me, I didn't mean to startle you. Elizabeth, isn't it?" When Elizabeth didn't reply, the Priest continued. "I'm Father Digiacomo."

Elizabeth studied the large man. "Digiacomo huh?" snorted Elizabeth. "Italian my *behind*! As big as you are and with that red beard, you're an Irish Mick if I ever saw one."

"Concerned about my name, are you? As they say Elizabeth, 'a rose, by any other name.' Well, you know the rest. I'm afraid I have to apologize for the welcome you've received at Bayside."

"Don't apologize. I'm not here to be welcomed, or rehabilitated, or enjoy the 'twilight of my years.' I am here to die Father. Just like you. Just like all the other walking ghosts over there," Elizabeth jerked her head toward the Community Room. Elizabeth didn't let on that her little show of theatrics actually produced a pretty nasty crick at the base of her neck. Compensating for her neck spasm, Elizabeth shifted her head and body in unison as she turned away from her visitor, fully covering her head with the blanket. "I would see you to the door Father," spoke Elizabeth from her veiled darkness, "but as easily as you found your way in, I'm sure you can see yourself out just fine."

Elizabeth lay in black silence. Her mind reflected on the priest's visit and resisted yielding to sleep. How could someone as old as Father Digiacomo (*which of course*, thought Elizabeth wryly, *made her ancient*) still think that life contained some purpose other than converting oxygen to carbon dioxide? Particularly someone who, by nature of his profession, earned his livelihood amidst so much grief and despair. Elizabeth witnessed a lot, *too much*, in her hundred years, and couldn't remember the last time anyone's actions surprised her. So if Father Digiacomo could escape life's adversities by ignorant bliss, more power to him.

The first discontinuity of coherent thought, the harbinger of sleep, interrupted Elizabeth's deliberations. She was warm now, and comfortable. Images flashed through Elizabeth's ruminations. Disjointed scenes of her family's farm appeared like a reel to reel movie projector showing symbols and numbers before the film begins.

Elizabeth possessed an arsenal of haunting nightmares, and fought sleep when hints of them invaded her consciousness. But dreams of her childhood provided Elizabeth's only respite and she welcomed them like a warm crackling fire on a frigid night. As sleep eventually consumed her, flashing images of yesteryear transformed into three dimensional reality - even if only for a brief period of borrowed time.

Daniel

The clock on the classroom wall moved painfully slow. At ten years young, Elizabeth excelled at schoolwork but hated every minute spent inside the classroom. Elizabeth spotted Buckboard in the playground. He normally waited patiently until the bell rang and Elizabeth emerged from the small school's front door. Today, however, Buckboard was clearly agitated. He circled toward Beaver Dam Hollow, raced to the path on which he and Elizabeth walked to and from school, and then dashed back, beckoning Elizabeth.

Elizabeth was helping her father with chores after church services a year earlier. Sam Pritchard's two-horse team pulled his buckboard up the lane to William Newton's farm. Elizabeth joined her father and greeted Sam Pritchard, who made periodic deliveries. "Ho! Tch, Tch!" shouted Sam as he drew in the reins to halt his team. "Morning William. Miss Newton." After bowing to Elizabeth, Sam's considerable girth dismounted and extended a beefy hand to her father. Elizabeth spied the ever-present bottle of rum in Sam Pritchard's now vacant seat.

William wiped his brow and sighed. "Pritchard, you know Clara doesn't like me doing business on the Sabbath. What have you got for me today?" asked William.

"Yes sir, I appreciate a man who likes to get right to the point. I always admired that about you William." Pritchard walked to the rear of his buckboard and dropped the tailgate. "Your feed, of course, and I brought some of Cobb Tyler's smoked sausage. I know you jerk your own, but you can't beat Cobb's. He's got some Indians he uses, and you know he don't pay them crap…uh, excuse me Miss. You know he don't pay them much, so I can let you have some for a song."

Pritchard grabbed a corner of the canvas and flipped it off the back of his rig. In between a dozen bags of cornmeal and chicken feed stood a bare-bones brown mutt. With a long string of jerked sausage hanging from each side of his drooling mouth, the young dog couldn't have looked prouder. Elizabeth laughed at the sight, and even her father couldn't help cracking a grin.

"Well Pritchard," started William, "I have to admit it looks like that sausage comes pretty highly recommended."

The dog's tail wagged feverishly. William's grin gave way to laughter at the sight of Pritchard's normally pink face turning deep crimson. Before anyone could react, including the buckboard stowaway, Pritchard's hand shot out and grabbed the mutt by the scruff of its neck. The dog yelped as Pritchard heaved him over his head and slammed him on the ground behind the wagon. As the mutt wriggled to gain his footing and escape, Pritchard's huge boot kicked him square in the ribs, knocking the animal another ten feet from the wagon. Elizabeth screamed. Pritchard was at the yipping dog in an instant, froth flying from the enraged man's mouth. Pritchard bent his right leg back to deliver a blow that surely would have crushed every organ in the emaciated dog's young body. As Pritchard launched the death blow, William tackled him, sending them both reeling through the air. William landed on top, engulfing Pritchard in a bear hug with his massive arms. "That's enough! You hear me? Let it go!"

Pritchard fought to free himself with all his might, spit flying from his beet red face. "I'll kill him! Let me up!"

William's vice-like grip held fast, and after a moment Pritchard succumbed to exhaustion. "Okay, okay. Let me up."

William slowly relaxed his grip and stood up, dusting himself off. Elizabeth ran to the dog.

Pritchard stood up, brushing at his pants. Reluctantly, he tore his eyes from the dog. "Who's gonna pay for that jerky then? I'm telling you William, I'm either handing Tyler the money for the sausage or that mutt's hide."

William's eyes never left the fat man's. "I'll pay for it," said William as he unloaded the feed bags from the buckboard.

The buckboard was unloaded by the time Pritchard regained his breath and joined William. "I still think I ought to skin that mutt," said Pritchard, his face again turning violet.

William pulled out his billfold. After paying for the feed and sausage, William told Pritchard he should take a ride and cool off. Pritchard muttered as he climbed back to his seat, immediately removing the cork from his bottle.

"Pritchard," called William. "Don't ever step foot on my property again."

Pritchard mumbled something unintelligible as he whipped his team into action, leaving a dusty plume in his wake.

Elizabeth sat on the ground, stroking the injured mutt. Her father answered the question that Elizabeth didn't have to ask. "Well, if he's staying here, he needs a name."

A smile lit up Elizabeth's young face and melted her father's heart. "You don't know his name, Father? It's Buckboard." The bond between Elizabeth and Buckboard was instantaneous, and the two became inseparable.

When Elizabeth spotted Buckboard dancing excitedly outside the school, she closed her book and raised her hand. When Mrs. Wheeler acknowledged her, Elizabeth asked to be excused. The teacher glanced at the clock and told Elizabeth that whatever the emergency, she could surely wait ten minutes for the bell. Elizabeth stood up. "But, Mrs. Wheeler, I -"

"Miss Newton, please sit down! Do I need to ask your mother to step in for a moment?"

"No ma'am," sighed Elizabeth as she returned to her seat. The seconds slowly ticking by tortured Elizabeth as Buckboard continued dancing. Elizabeth wiggled in her chair until the bell finally rang. Mrs. Wheeler glanced at Elizabeth, intentionally delaying (in Elizabeth's opinion) class dismissal. When she finally released the students, Elizabeth bolted out the door.

She ran toward Buckboard, but as she neared him he darted up the path toward the hollow. "Wait Buckboard! WAIT UP!" The dog dashed back to Elizabeth, and then charged ahead again, clearly urging Elizabeth to follow. Although it was only mid-afternoon, it was November and already the sky was turning a fuzzy gray. Elizabeth crashed through the brittle fallen leaves coating the forest floor. Within a few minutes the two were deep in the hollow and Elizabeth had difficulty keeping up with Buckboard. Running full speed and nearly out of breath, Elizabeth rounded a blind turn in the path and nearly tripped over Buckboard. As she bent down to pet him and catch her breath, Buckboard bounded off the path into the woods, glancing over his shoulder to make sure Elizabeth followed. Without hesitation, Elizabeth took off after Buckboard. After running another hundred yards Elizabeth saw Buckboard standing like a sentry at the edge of a meadow.

Dusk swallowed the hollow quickly, and by the time Elizabeth caught up with Buckboard she realized she didn't recognize her surroundings. She knelt, wheezing. As she tried to set her bearings straight, Buckboard began whining and spinning in circles. "What is it Buckboard? Come here," called Elizabeth. Buckboard joined Elizabeth and nudged her with his snout. "What's wrong?"

Buckboard stood motionless. The woods grew eerily silent; the air weighing heavily on Elizabeth's shoulders. The hollow's secretiveness pierced Elizabeth's ears with its vacancy. Buckboard's hackles stood at full attention as a low, throaty growl erupted from deep within his chest. That was when Elizabeth first heard the noise.

A soft, nearly imperceptible moan penetrated the unbearable emptiness that engulfed the woods. Now the hair on the nape of

Elizabeth's own neck prickled as she fought to deny the sound. Clamping onto Buckboard's neck, Elizabeth's ears strained for some hint of the sound to return. Just as she was about to discount the first moan, an agonized cry pierced the night. Elizabeth and Buckboard's eyes locked on each other before Elizabeth screamed. "RUN!"

§

Elizabeth's orientation instinctively returned as she catapulted off the ground and beat feet back toward the path, certain that at each step fingers from some undead soul would reach out from the darkness and clench her throat. Elizabeth didn't stop running until the clearing at her farmhouse provided a relative light at the end of the dark tunnel that was the hollow. Buckboard nipped at her heels the entire time. Elizabeth was oblivious to the fact that the dog attempted to quell her racing and lead her back to the frightful meadow. Elizabeth collapsed when Beaver Dam Hollow spit her out, finally providing relief to her small pounding heart.

Eventually Elizabeth stood and began walking. Still terrified, she rounded the barn that obscured her view of the house. William Newton leaned over a tailgate, surrounded by a dozen men carrying torches. A couple hounds ran free in the farmyard, a half-dozen more yelping anxiously at the ends of their masters' leashes. Elizabeth pushed through the men to reach her father. Maps of Great Fox Swamp, Lantern Hill, and Beaver Dam Hollow were spread out on the truck's tailgate. "Jed," said William, "you, Jim and Tom take your treeing walkers to Wyntechog Road and work down Lantern Hill. Not up, but down. Lost kids don't go up hills, got it?" Jed nodded and turned from the truck. His hounds sensed the excitement and howled as Jed barked for Jim Cliff and Tom Harvey to go with him.

Elizabeth's heart still raced and normal breath hadn't yet returned when she tugged on her father's coat tails. William focused on the maps and didn't notice. Elizabeth yanked again and called to her father. William turned and glanced down at his daughter. "Not a good time Liz." William thought to dismiss Elizabeth, but gave her a second look. "What's wrong, are you alright?"

Elizabeth panted, on the verge of tears. Her young heart raced like a thoroughbred, terror still encompassed her, her always-happy-to-see-her father seemed mad at her, and all the men and dogs at her house scared her. "Father," panted Elizabeth. A ghost... in the Hollow. Buckboard took me to it. I *heard* it! "

Williams look of concern turned to irritation. "Elizabeth, get on inside and help your mother with dinner."

"But Father -" protested Elizabeth. William silenced his daughter with a glance. Elizabeth dropped her head and plodded toward the house. Through the window, Elizabeth watched horses and trucks carry the remaining men and dogs down the lane. Clara told Elizabeth that Daniel Stanton had been missing since the previous day and the men were organizing a search party. Elizabeth remembered that Daniel wasn't at school, but it wasn't unusual for boys to miss school, especially around harvest season.

"A little late getting home from school, aren't you?" asked Clara. Based on her father's reaction when told of Elizabeth's ghost, the girl decided not to share it with her mother.

"Mrs. Wheeler kept us late today. She is so *mean!*"

As Clara scolded her daughter for being disrespectful to an adult, and especially a fellow teacher, the farmyard lit up from the lights of an approaching vehicle.

William Newton jumped from the cab before the truck completely stopped and ran to the house, taking all four steps to the rear stoop in a single bound. "Elizabeth!" hollered William as the back door slammed open.

Elizabeth wasted no time. She had no idea what was happening, but knew it couldn't be good. She sprinted to the stairs and was halfway up when her father yelled again, this time from the landing at the bottom of the stairs. "Elizabeth! Get down here!"

Elizabeth froze in her tracks as renewed fear sparked every nerve in her body. "Tell me about the ghost you heard," ordered her father.

Elizabeth nearly peed her pants. "I'm-I'm sorry. I didn't hear a ghost. I was kidding."

William raised his hands and fought to control his excitement. "Its okay, I'm not mad. Just tell me what happened in the Hollow?"

Elizabeth's mind worked overtime. She thought if she spoke again of the ghost she'd get a licking she wouldn't soon forget. But the same fate awaited her if she disobeyed her father's order or lied to him. As Elizabeth considered her conundrum, William ascended the steps. He placed a comforting hand on Elizabeth's shoulder and looked into her eyes. "Can you take me to where you heard the ghost?" asked William. Elizabeth nodded. "Okay then. Get Buckboard and meet me out back."

Minutes later Elizabeth, Buckboard, William, Joshua and Zachary Cheseborough, and their two Black-and-Tans entered the Hollow. The hounds raced ahead silently like shadows of death, hunting in expanding arcs searching for scent of the lost boy. The rest of the party stayed to the path until Buckboard started yipping, beckoning the men and girl deeper into the woods. William motioned to Joshua, who called to his hounds. "Hooo-Way! Hooo-*Waaay*!"

A minute later the dog-phantoms raced past, their stealthy legs galloping through the autumn debris. Seconds later one of the hounds cried out. A moment later they both barked with increasing crescendo. With anxious fervor the hounds worked the faint trail until a single sound quieted the woods. As though from the bowels of hell, a solitary howl erupted from Zeb, Joshua's large male hound. The bellow started low, its intensity gradually overtaking the yapping coming from the hound's sister. The howl continued, claiming undeniable dominance over the Hollow. The solitary wail lasted a full minute and sent chills up the rescuers' spines. Fighting against relinquishing ownership of the night, Zeb's full cry continued until his lungs nearly collapsed.

Joshua's voice broke the new, heavier silence that smothered the forest like a windless snowstorm. "Zeb's got him. Come on!"

The men crashed and flailed through unseen briars as they raced toward Zeb, whose full cries were now joined by his sister's.

Elizabeth couldn't keep up, but followed the torches as Buckboard urged her along. By the time Elizabeth joined the men they had already torn away the ground cover and rotted boards that covered a long-abandoned well in the middle of the meadow she and Buckboard were at two hours earlier. Joshua held his lantern over the well's opening and peered down the black hole. Zachary, the smallest of the three men, secured one end of a horsehair rope around his waist while William looped the other end around his own body.

Zachary lay on his stomach at the black hole's opening. William wrapped the rope around his wrists and pulled it taut with his great fists. Zachary eased his body over the edge of the well and descended into the abyss head first. William crept toward the well in unison with Zachary until his descent stopped. The two hounds circled the well, crying frantically. From the well's obscurity, Zachary shouted. "I got him, pull us up. *Hurry*!"

Joshua set down his lantern and joined William. The two men backed away from the well, straining to pull their load from the murky depths. Zachary's feet appeared first, and William kept the rope tight as he and Joshua moved forward and each grabbed a leg. The earth ripped Zachary's stomach as the two men pulled him from the ancient shaft. The instant Zachary's body lay on firm ground, William and Joshua scampered to the breach and groped along Zachary's arms until they found Daniel's armpits. They each grabbed one and dragged Daniel's limp form from the well.

Adrenaline pumped through the three men's veins as they turned Daniel's filthy body over. The boy's femur protruded from his thigh and muck caked his torn, blood-soaked pants. Lacerations ran across the boy's face and skull. His right ear dangled from the side of his head. No one said a word as the three men and Elizabeth stared at Daniel. Joshua and Zachary crossed their hearts and William bowed his head. A moment later Elizabeth cried out. "He's alive!" Elizabeth pointed to the mangled boy's eyes which had just opened.

Daniel softly moaned and tried to reach for his shattered leg. "Come on," shouted Zachary, "Let's get him to your house

William." Zachary and Joshua positioned themselves and lifted the boy.

"No, the school's closer. Take him there. I'll go get my truck and pick up Doc Allyn and meet you there. C'mon Elizabeth." William picked up a torch and ran back to the path with Elizabeth and Buckboard trailing behind. Back at the farm, William raced to his truck and told Elizabeth to stay with her mother and tell her what was happening.

The following day William called to Elizabeth when she and Buckboard returned from school. "Sorry I was short with you last night. Halfway down the lane what you said finally sunk in. Daniel's going to be fine...well, after a while anyway. He was out hunting squirrels. Curiosity got the best of him and he fell in that old well. Doc Allyn said he'd have been dead by midnight if we didn't find him. Tell you the truth 'Lizabeth, I was gonna go in the Hollow up at Wyassup and wouldn't have made it to the well till morning. If then. Anyway, thought you'd want to know about Daniel." Elizabeth beamed as she went to the barn to feed the chickens.

Two years later Daniel Stanton stole Elizabeth's first kiss.

Eight years after that Elizabeth read the New London Day's headline about Daniel: "NATIVE SON DIES ON GERMAN BATTLEFIELD."

Bible Disease

Following her curt dismissal of Father Digiacomo, Elizabeth slept soundly. She dreamed of her favorite place, but as usual her dreams were accompanied by the nightmares Elizabeth considered her life. As memories of Daniel faded from her mind's eye, Elizabeth allowed consciousness to defeat sleep. Instinctively she eased her hand beneath the covers to massage her hip, which normally howled upon wakening. Despite its abuse from the previous two days, her hip felt tender but not pained. Judging by the soft light pouring in the window Elizabeth figured it to be late afternoon; which meant she didn't miss dinner. Having teased her body with its first real meal in days, however slight it may have been, Elizabeth's stomach now screamed for food.

Elizabeth eased her legs off the bed and cautiously planted herself behind the walker. Once stable, Elizabeth pointed herself toward the bathroom. She paused at the table and placed the toothbrush and toothpaste left by Nancy Nichols in the pocket of her gown. A hundred years old or not, Elizabeth still possessed most of her teeth; a fact in which she took no pride or satisfaction. After completing her business, Elizabeth pulled herself erect and stood before the bathroom's sink. She hadn't brushed her teeth in several days and the filminess of her mouth disgusted her. Elizabeth fumbled removing the toothpaste cap but finally managed to squeeze the tube's contents onto her brush. Elizabeth lifted her head and when her reflection in the mirror stared back at her she nearly jumped in shock. She looked *hideous*! Her thin straw-like hair looked like a wheat field ravaged by fire. The maroon blood-sweat from her wound covered half her face and trailed down her neck. The skin covering her neck stretched tightly over her protruding collar bones, and her body listed to the right to compensate for her recent surgery. Additionally, her neck was slightly cocked from the pulled muscle she gave herself while putting on her little show for the priest. Following her initial revulsion, Elizabeth grinned. She never doubted that her life would come to this. As Elizabeth finished brushing her teeth, the door banged open and the woman who promised her dinner a day earlier stood before her.

The woman briefly studied Elizabeth. "Sit your butt down on that commode! Yeah that's right; I know what you did this morning. You trying to make me look bad? Let's clean your skinny self up."

When Elizabeth hesitated, the woman bear hugged her from behind and plopped her on the toilet seat. After running water from the faucet over a wash cloth, the woman grabbed the back of Elizabeth's head with one hand and stabbed the wash cloth at Elizabeth's face and neck with the other. The dried flaky blood felt like sandpaper under the woman's aggressive hand. Finally satisfied, the woman stole a towel from the rack and dried Elizabeth. "I don't know what we gonna do about your hair." After a moment, the woman wrung the wash cloth out over Elizabeth's head, the water soaking her hair and dripping down her face and neck. Rough fingers coursed through Elizabeth's hair, taming it against her scalp. "Well Sugar, that's as good as it's gonna get. You got any clothes?"

Elizabeth stared vehemently at the woman and nodded toward the room. The woman left the bathroom and returned carrying a pair of slacks, a blouse and slippers. She reached behind Elizabeth and tugged the cord securing her gown. She slipped it off Elizabeth and let it drop to the floor. Sitting naked before this woman, Elizabeth's final shards of dignity vanished. After manipulating Elizabeth's legs and sliding the pants in place, the woman placed the slippers on Elizabeth's feet. Next she grabbed the shirt and placed Elizabeth's arms through the sleeves. "I didn't see no bra in that box. But then again," said the woman as she pointed to Elizabeth's breasts, "I don't think *they're* really going to be upset about that." The woman cackled as she buttoned Elizabeth's blouse. "Now you listen to me. You better think twice before you go leaving your room looking like a chainsaw massacre again. You hear me?"

"I hate you," seethed Elizabeth through clenched teeth.

"And I don't care!" replied the woman. "Now go get you some dinner. Physical therapy is over." As the woman slammed the door closed, Elizabeth heard her shrill cackles echoing down the hallway.

Elizabeth's eyes became misty. *Why couldn't this just end?* Once Elizabeth recognized her self-pity, she exorcised it as if it was a demon. She dabbed her eyes with her fist and pulled herself off the seat. Her hip throbbed from being manhandled, but the pain was bearable. Elizabeth again studied herself in the mirror. "She was right," muttered Elizabeth. "That's as good as it's going to get."

Relying less on her walker than the previous day, Elizabeth shuffled down the hall toward the Community Room. Dinner was in full swing, and a loud buzz permeated the air as Elizabeth entered the room. Nearly a hundred seniors ate and gabbed, and two waitresses brought coffee and juice to the patrons. A middle-aged woman holding a clipboard greeted Elizabeth.

"You must be Mrs. Newton," stated the woman as she made a check mark on her clipboard. "You're the last guest. We were getting worried; I was going to send someone to check on you."

"That's *Miss* Newton," corrected Elizabeth.

"Very well then," replied the woman as she scribbled something on the clipboard. "I'm Mrs. Nedbetter, Bayside's Activities Director. Let me show you to your table." Mrs. Nedbetter walked ahead of Elizabeth, slowly enough for Elizabeth to keep up. The hostess stopped at a table with six other seniors and pulled back a chair for Elizabeth. Mrs. Nedbetter introduced Elizabeth as Bayside's newest centurion. Elizabeth remained silent when the other diners welcomed her.

"*Miss* Newton," said the hostess, "help yourself to the entrees on the table and Daphne will be right over to take your drink order. Be sure to stop by at nine o'clock in the morning for the daily activity agenda. And don't hesitate to let me know if you need anything." Mrs. Nedbetter patted Elizabeth on her shoulder and circulated among the other tables.

Elizabeth felt the stares as she sipped from the water glass at her place setting. A man sitting opposite Elizabeth broke the silence as Elizabeth scooped a pile of pasta onto her plate. "So Miss Newton, do you have a first name?"

Elizabeth answered as Daphne placed a glass of iced tea in front of her.

"Well, Elizabeth," continued the man, "what's a swell dame like you doing in a joint like this?"

Elizabeth studied the other residents sitting at the table. Two women and two men appeared to be in their eighties, and one man looked to have been born around the time of the Flood. The man who spoke to Elizabeth had a sarcastic smile that Elizabeth correctly assumed never left his face. Elizabeth sipped her tea and replied. "I came here to die. Like you."

One of the women gasped and the other muttered "*Sweet Jesus*" under her breath. The ancient man to Elizabeth's right slapped his knee and whistled. "Plenty of fire left under that hood. What I wouldn't give to be a hundred again!"

The man who asked the question grinned slyly. "You can pull that *bitterness* crap with the young folk Elizabeth. But we've all been through it, *life* that is, so you're not impressing us any. Anyway, I can tell you got the hots for me. And I don't mind saying that I'm no stranger to the ladies around here, so meet me at the fireplace after lights out." The man raised his eyebrows twice and winked at Elizabeth, making little kissing motions through his toothless gums.

Despite the mental anguish in her room only moments earlier, Elizabeth had difficulty concealing her laughter at the obscenely comedic gesture. She looked down to conceal her face, lest her grin be observed by the other members of her table. One of the women scolded the fresh old man while the antique to Elizabeth's right slapped his knee again and burst into a fit of laughter.

Elizabeth kept her face buried as she inhaled pasta. She finished her iced tea and squirmed in her chair to give her room to stand up. Daphne appeared from nowhere. "Here, let me help you," said the waitress. Elizabeth brushed Daphne's hand away.

"I'm fine," replied Elizabeth as she squared herself behind the walker. Daphne excused herself as she left to attend other patrons.

"That's an understatement, Toots! Don't forget, see you after lights out."

Elizabeth didn't acknowledge the comment. She departed the Community Room and journeyed back to her room. As Elizabeth reached for the doorknob she sensed someone approaching from behind. Father Digiacomo opened the door and followed Elizabeth into her room.

"Sorry Father," said Elizabeth. "There's no business for you here. Hopefully soon." Elizabeth crossed the room and laid on her bed.

Father Digiacomo resumed his position in the bedside chair. "I'm not so sure about that, Elizabeth. Believe it or not, I actually help people before they die as well as post-mortem. You look like you could use some help."

Elizabeth stared at the Priest. "You're right Father. I could use some peace and quiet. So if you don't mind?"

Father Digiacomo rummaged through Elizabeth's box and withdrew the Bible. "Well, you certainly could use some peace. However, I don't think the quiet would serve you much right now. This is a lovely Bible. Oh, I hope you don't mind; I saw it when you drifted off to sleep earlier this morning. How did you come upon it?"

Elizabeth reflected on the day she came into possession of her family Bible.

"How long has your wrist been like this?" asked Doctor Allyn.

Elizabeth massaged the plum-sized knot on her left wrist. "It started about two weeks ago. It doesn't hurt, but it keeps growing. Now it's so big that I can barely bend my wrist."

"I've placed hot compresses on it, and cold compresses," added Clara Newton. "And yesterday when Elizabeth came home from school it appeared twice the size it was the day before. That's why I asked William to have you come over."

Doc Allyn pressed, pulled and rotated Elizabeth's wrist. At fourteen years old, Elizabeth was much more concerned with the unsightliness of the growth on her arm than any medical implications. The doctor "mmm-ed" and "ahaa-ed" a couple times. Finally he pushed back his chair to mark reaching a conclusion. "Can you get your family Bible and bring it here, Mrs. Newton?" asked Doc Allyn. "I'm afraid our young patient here has a nasty case of Bible Disease."

"Oh my goodness!" exclaimed Clara. She dashed from the room and returned an instant later with the Newton family Bible, all five pounds of it. "What is Bible Disease? Is it serious?" Clara looked at Doc Allyn as though he was about to perform an exorcism on her only daughter.

The doctor gently extended Elizabeth's arm and laid her hand palm downward on the kitchen table. "Oh, don't fret. I think she's going to be just fine. LOOK AT THAT ELEPHANT!" yelled Doc Allyn pointing out the kitchen window. Elizabeth's head jerked over her shoulder in the direction the doctor pointed. Before Clara could react, Doc Allyn raised the Bible over his head with both hands and sent it crashing down upon Elizabeth's wrist. Elizabeth screamed. Clara tried to scream but couldn't. The doctor placed the heavy Bible on the table and massaged Elizabeth's wrist. The lump disappeared, the skin slightly loose from being stretched.

"Sorry 'bout that," apologized the doctor. "Just seems to work better if I don't tell what I'm going to do before I do it. Sometimes the blood just gets stuck and needs a little help getting along. The Bible is most folk's biggest book; that's why they call it Bible Disease. I better run along now. Let me know if it comes back."

"Probably not," muttered Elizabeth under her breath.

"What's that, Dear?" asked the doctor.

"I said thank you," corrected Elizabeth.

Clara Newton had still not fully collected herself by the time Doc Allyn left.

That evening William Newton called Elizabeth into the parlor. "Your mother told me about your experience today. She and I talked about it and figure you earned this." William handed the Bible to Elizabeth. "It's been in our family for nearly a hundred years, and every Newton birth, death, and major event is recorded in here. Little Me, this Bible has been through fire and rain, through good times and bad. You know that we believe the Lord is with us always. He may seem distant, especially when times are difficult. But everything that happens is for a glorious purpose, although it is not for us to understand. You will endure atrocities in your lifetime, but every one of them can make you a better person – if you *choose* to. We trust you'll take care of it. Run along to bed now."

"I say, how did you come upon your Bible?" repeated the priest.

Father Digiacomo's voice jarred Elizabeth from her reverie. "I found it. Stole it from a church."

"How very odd," replied the priest. "You stole a Bible that records your own birth."

"I earned it, that's how I *'came upon it'*. And a fat lot of good it did me. Goodnight Father Digiacomo."

"Your Bible might still help you more than you can imagine. If you can fit it into your schedule, you might try opening it again."

Elizabeth didn't reply, the harshness of her previous response still stinging even her own ears. Sleep again relieved Elizabeth's sullenness before she heard the priest leave her room.

Ocean House

"I still don't think this is a good idea," Clara Newton told her daughter.

"Mother, I'll be fine. We've been through it all before. I'm going with Tessie, and she's been there plenty of times. She even stayed at Benjamin's family's estate, which is only a couple blocks from the Ocean House. Benjamin is picking us up at the Westerly Station, and he'll be with us all night."

"All night?" challenged her mother.

"I know the rules, Mother. We'll leave the Ocean House by eleven o'clock, Benjamin will take us to his parent's house, and we'll catch the ten o'clock train tomorrow morning. I'm starting college next month; I think I can take care of myself for one night. Besides, you don't want the beautiful dress you made me go to waste. Look! Here comes Tessie now." Elizabeth pointed to an old jalopy entering the dirt parking lot at the Mystic Train Station.

"It's just that you've never spent the night out of the state before."

"Mother, I've never been out of *North Stonington* before. See you tomorrow!" Elizabeth grabbed her suitcase and pecked her mother on the cheek as she jumped from the truck. "Love you!"

Clara watched Elizabeth run toward her friend, the sweet plume of innocence trailing behind her.

§

"I am so excited!" shouted Tessie. "I can't wait to show you around up there. *Everyone* will be at the Summer Ball tonight. Most of the people who summer at Watch Hill are leaving next week, and Benjamin said this is *the* party to be at. To be *seen* at. And I don't have to tell you that plenty of eligible bachelors, *rich* eligible bachelors, will be there. Elizabeth," said Tessie, warmly grasping Elizabeth's hand, "I know you don't believe me, but you are very beautiful. Any boy, any *one*, would be lucky to have you."

A warm chill ran up Elizabeth's spine to her neck. She finally broke eye contact with Tessie. "Well, you know I have to leave by eleven."

Not seeming to notice the relief that the broken silence provided Elizabeth, Tessie replied. "Of course, no problem. Plus," continued Tessie in a whisper, "Benjamin told me that he has a big surprise for me tonight. I could just burst!"

"You don't mean…?"

Tessie wrapped her arms around Elizabeth and the two young women jumped up and down in unison, tears streaming down Tessie's face. "I think so!"

Elizabeth and Tessie reminisced about their childhood, and Tessie told of the mansions at Watch Hill, most of which, she informed Elizabeth, belonged to good friends of Benjamin's family.

A shrill steam whistle broke the otherwise tranquil afternoon, signaling the New London train nearing the station. The girls gathered their bags and joined the other passengers on the boardwalk platform.

Embarking on their adventure thrilled Elizabeth. This really was the first time she'd been out of North Stonington. The girls quickly found their seats after boarding the train. A moment later the whistle blew and the train took off. The rhythmic chugging quickly became background noise and Elizabeth kept her eyes glued to the window. The train navigated marshy coves that marked the boundary of Long Island Sound. Hugging the coast east of Mystic, the train seemed to leave civilization. As the train entered Pawcatuck, Elizabeth's world seemed even further away. The train tracks cut through the ancient forest, plunging the passengers into darkness even in mid-afternoon. The thick canopy of vines plucked gingerly at the railroad cars.

The forest thinned as the train emerged from its swampy path and entered Westerly. Elizabeth reveled at the sights of the first city she'd been in. Horses, carriages, and automobiles lined the sides of the cobblestone streets. People crowded the vegetable stands, bakeries, cafes and taverns. Tessie shouted as the train approached Westerly Station. "Look! There's Benjamin!" Tessie reached across Elizabeth and waved frantically out the window. "C'mon, let's go!"

Tessie and Elizabeth grabbed their bags and joined the other passengers disembarking. The bright sun forced Elizabeth's eyes closed as she emerged from the train. When Elizabeth reopened them, the reality of the adventure overcame her. Ecstatic, Elizabeth tried to blaze every sight into her memory. Tessie took her hand and pulled her along the platform. Benjamin wrapped his arms around Tessie, and Elizabeth shyly turned away as they kissed.

Tessie smiled. "What's the matter? We're not children anymore. Maybe we'll find someone for *you* to kiss tonight. I think Benjamin already has someone in mind." Tessie turned back to her boyfriend. "Benjamin, this is my best friend, Elizabeth."

Benjamin extended his arm and firmly shook Elizabeth's hand. "I'm Benjamin Copp. It's a pleasure to meet you. Tess told me you were gorgeous, but I had no idea. I have a friend I want to introduce you to later. Ready ladies?"

Benjamin took the bags from Elizabeth and Tessie and the threesome crossed the gravel parking lot to Benjamin's car. With the luggage stowed in the rear, Benjamin opened the passenger door for Tessie and Elizabeth, then returned to the driver's side and got in. "Ever been in a car like this Elizabeth?"

Elizabeth was beside herself. "I've never *dreamed* of a car like this."

Benjamin beamed. "You ladies just happen to be driving in the finest automobile ever manufactured. Liz...can I call you Liz? Liz, this is a Pierce-Arrow Model Sixty-Six. Eight-hundred and twenty-five cubic inches of solid power screaming under the hood with a -"

"Stop bragging and drive!" ordered Tessie.

"Ah-ooga, ah-ooga!" Benjamin honked the horn to clear a path as he eased the car onto Main Street. After a short drive they turned onto Granite Street and houses quickly became sparse. Fresh sea breeze filled the air as they neared Watch Hill. Elizabeth's mouth was agape watching the oceanfront mansions tick by like candy. Benjamin pulled off the road onto a gravel drive leading to the largest mansion yet.

"This isn't...?" began Elizabeth.

"'Fraid so. Tanglewood, my family's summer home. It's really not as big as it looks. Besides, you get used to it. My grandfather started a couple businesses in New York that made him filthy rich. Now he has this vision of creating a dog park in every town. You know, a place where people can bring their dogs to play and socialize with each other. He's daft," said Benjamin, circling his finger around his ear. "Anyway, being a rich playboy isn't all it's cracked up to be. You know, trying to remember all the maids' and butlers' names, women throwing themselves at me. It can all be very taxing."

Tessie jabbed Benjamin in his side and scolded him.

"Just kidding!" Benjamin stopped the car in front of a sweeping veranda that disappeared around both sides of the mansion.

"Sweetheart, can you take our bags inside? I want to show Elizabeth around back." Without waiting for an answer, Tessie pushed Elizabeth from the car and grabbed her hand. "Come on, I've got to show you this!"

Tess towed Elizabeth across the yard toward the rear of the mansion. As they crested the hilltop estate, the Atlantic Ocean came into view in all its glory. The waves crashing against the surf filled Elizabeth's ears as she inhaled the fresh salt air. Seagulls flew to and fro, and Elizabeth watched a particularly large gull drop a clam shell onto a jetty from mid-air. As the shell smashed against the rocks, the gull swooped upon and picked through the broken pieces for to get at the clam. Two other gulls nipped at his tail to horn in on the bounty. Elizabeth couldn't contain herself any longer. She broke free from Tessie's grip and dashed down the slope toward the water. Elizabeth kicked off her shoes as she ran; the sun scorched white sand burning the bottoms of her feet. Oblivious to the pain, Elizabeth continued running and hollering with glee as she plunged into the ocean. Then seventy-degree water temperature momentarily stole her breath as she heard Tessie yelling at her.

"You are CRAZY! Get out of that water; I have a swim suit you can borrow. *Elizabeth*! Oh, heck with it!" Tessie took of her shoes and trounced in the water toward Elizabeth, her dress floating in a wake behind her.

The two young ladies frolicked in the water for over an hour - laughing, splashing, riding the waves, flailing at the small stripers feeding in the shallows.

"Come sink with me!" shouted Tessie as she waded toward shore.

Puzzled, Elizabeth followed and joined Tessie just beyond the water's reach. The two friends stared at the horizon as a wave flooded the beach. As the wave receded, the water's force sucked the sand from beneath the girls' feet. They laughed gaily, the laugh that only the innocent can laugh. As they awaited the next wave, they heard Benjamin shouting.

"Okay children, playtime is over. We'd better start getting ready for the ball." Reluctantly, Elizabeth and Tessie collected their shoes and trudged up the beach.

"What do you mean, 'you can't wear that dress'? My mother spent over a month making it just for tonight. Besides, I think it's *beautiful*." Elizabeth and Tessie changed for the ball in the guest room Benjamin led them to.

"It *is* lovely Elizabeth," replied Tessie. "And it's perfect if you're going to a Grange Hall social. I went to the Fourth of July Ball at the

Ocean House. Believe me, if you wear that dress you'll be the only person under forty with a corseted waist."

Elizabeth considered. "Well, I don't want to stand out. Not *that* way anyhow. But it doesn't matter, that's all I have to wear."

"Not to worry. I thought I might have to bail you out." Tessie ducked into the dressing room and returned an instant later concealing something behind her back. "Now close your eyes." Elizabeth heard Tessie rustling with something in the room. "Okay, you can open them."

Elizabeth opened her eyes and laughed when she saw the narrow red skirt laid out on the bed. "You must be joking! Where's the rest of it?" asked Elizabeth.

"I know it's not what you're used to, but just humor me. It's a hobble skirt, an original Paul Poiret. Benjamin wanted to buy me one for the ball. Let's just say that I...convinced him to buy me two."

Elizabeth blushed at the thought. "You are insufferable! You win, I'll try it on. But no promises."

Tessie slipped into her skirt and was applying makeup when Elizabeth emerged from the dressing room. The tight-fitting skirt truly showed off Elizabeth's magnificent figure. Tessie turned to look when Elizabeth entered the room and dropped her makeup on the vanity. "Oh, Elizabeth." Tessie stood up and crossed the room, grasping Elizabeth's shoulders. "You are gorgeous. I'd better keep a close eye on Benjamin tonight. Oh, one more thing; pull up your skirt."

Elizabeth froze. "Pull up my skirt?"

"I have to tie this cord around your legs. Otherwise you'll end up splitting your skirt. Benjamin's cousin Deborah split her skirt at the Fourth Ball. Everyone *still* talks about it! Come on now." Tessie knelt in front of Elizabeth and pushed her skirt up to her thighs. She fastened a velvet swath around her legs to prevent her from taking too long a stride, and then slowly pulled Elizabeth's skirt back in place. "It takes some getting used to, but you'll be fine."

"But I can barely walk! And I can never tell my mother I didn't wear the dress she made me, so I'll have to lie to her for the first time."

Tessie smiled. "I know, isn't it wonderful!" Without warning, Tessie planted her lips firmly against Elizabeth's. "We've got to go; Benjamin is waiting for us downstairs."

Elizabeth stood speechless as Tessie disappeared down the hallway. Her face still flushed, Elizabeth followed Tessie down the grand staircase a moment later.

§

Elizabeth entered the parlor and saw that another young man joined Benjamin and Tessie. "Elizabeth," said Benjamin, "this is Theodore Haas. Theodore will be joining us tonight." Theodore stared with open admiration at Elizabeth.

Theodore broke the trance and crossed the room to Elizabeth. "A pleasure, Elizabeth." Theodore kissed Elizabeth's hand. "Something I don't understand, however," said Theodore turning to Benjamin. "I thought you said Tessie's friend was a farmer. Now, I don't get to the country often mind you, but I am *positive* that this ravishing young lady standing before me is definitely not a farmer."

"Don't mind Theo, Elizabeth," said Benjamin. Benjamin turned and, pointing with a concealed finger at Theodore, tipped his fingers toward his mouth to insinuate his friend had been drinking.

Theodore noticed Benjamin's mimicry and smiled. "Not yet," he said patting something concealed in his waistband. "But soon."

"Are you ladies ready?" asked Benjamin.

Elizabeth and Tessie nodded. "Its lovely outside," commented Elizabeth. "Shall we walk to the Ocean House? Tess said it's only a short walk from here."

Benjamin grimaced and shook his head, leading the way outside toward the Sixty-Six. Tessie rolled her eyes as she waited for Benjamin's response.

"What? And deprive everyone the opportunity of casting their eyes on the finest automobile-"

Tessie cut Benjamin short with a jab to his side. The foursome loaded into the Arrow, Tessie claiming her place beside Benjamin and conveniently leaving the back seat to Elizabeth and Theodore.

Fresh air laden with salt from the Atlantic blew gently on the young men and women. The car rounded a bend and the oaks dissipated. The Westerly Ocean House emerged from the forest like a giant white monolith.

Benjamin spied Elizabeth's astonishment in the rear view mirror. "Amazing, isn't it? My grandfather helped build it in eighteen-sixty-eight. Five stories, one-hundred-fifty-four rooms. Only open ten weeks a year, mostly for us summer residents."

Elizabeth soaked in the enormity of the Victorian hotel. She had never seen any building that immense, nor anything that compared to its glamour. Benjamin pulled into the valet lane as two men opened the passenger doors and helped Elizabeth and Tessie from the vehicle. Benjamin slipped something to one of the valets when he walked past, and the four of them ascended the stairs to the sweeping veranda overlooking the ocean. A slow waltz spilled outside from the ballroom, and Elizabeth inhaled deeply, savoring the finest moment of her life and wishing it would never end.

"Shall we?" asked Theodore, breaking Elizabeth's reverie. Theodore took Elizabeth's hand and escorted her into the hotel's foyer. Imposing oil portraits adorned the soaring walls and exquisite settees and antique tables decorated the marble floor. Extravagantly dressed men and women of all ages sipped cocktails and nibbled on hors d'oeuvres. Elizabeth basked in the radiance of the energized crowd.

Theodore guided Elizabeth to the already-crowded dance floor. Elizabeth's mother taught her the foxtrot and waltz, and practiced with her for weeks prior to the ball. Once Elizabeth adjusted to the limitations her tight dress and velvet swath imposed, she glided across the floor like she'd been ballroom dancing her entire life. Theodore and Elizabeth danced together like poetry in motion, causing the other dancers to leave them a wide berth so they could be admired. Elizabeth felt the eyes upon her, and beamed with jubilation.

After dancing for an hour, Theodore whispered that he could use a breath of fresh air. For the first time Elizabeth noticed that her heels were killing her and she let Theodore lead her outside to the veranda. Theodore steered Elizabeth through the crowd with his hand on the small of her back, sending chills up Elizabeth's spine. The evening had cooled since they arrived at the Ocean House, and a comfortable breeze caressed Elizabeth's face. The full moon reflected brightly off the crystal-white beach sand and Elizabeth watched the white caps crash against the jetty.

Even on the crowded veranda, Elizabeth and Theodore faced each other undeniably alone, together. Following a terribly awkward silence, Theodore asked Elizabeth if she would like a glass of punch. Disappointed, and fearing the moment had passed, Elizabeth replied that she would love one. Theodore turned and hesitated. Suddenly he spun back toward Elizabeth.

"You are so beautiful!" Theodore pressed his warm lips firmly against Elizabeth's, drawing her to him. Elizabeth returned Theodore's kiss briefly before he broke their embrace. "I'll be right back!" Theodore turned and walked toward the foyer. Halfway through the crowd Theodore jumped in the air and shouted with joy.

Elizabeth couldn't imagine anyone ever being more jubilant than she was at that moment. Theodore was wonderful, and the thought of waiting for his return grew unbearable. Overcome with exhilaration, Elizabeth felt so alive and energized. She maintained her composure as she navigated the veranda and descended the steps to the white sand. Once hidden from most of the party-goers, Elizabeth quickly untied the swath securing her legs and kicked off her shoes. She ran hard and fast toward the beach head, feeling the cool firm sand that grew wet from the incoming tide. She ran in the moonlight, hearing the band's music fade in the background. Though she only ran for a couple minutes, she was already a quarter mile from the Ocean House. Elizabeth didn't want to worry Theodore and, having exhausted her overcharged energy, let the spent waves massage her feet while she caught her breath.

As Elizabeth grudgingly tore her gaze from the horizon, she detected movement from the tall sea grass behind her. A large figure rushed from concealment and hurled itself at Elizabeth, knocking them both to the ground. The man punched her head and ripped her dress, kicking her legs apart as he buried Elizabeth's face in the surf.

The man reeked of alcohol as he shoved his face against Elizabeth's. "I get one of you rich whores every year. Time to feel a real man!"

Elizabeth kicked and clawed her assailant. Sandy saltwater flooded her mouth and lungs when she tried to scream. The seconds passed like hours as the man beat her to the brink of unconsciousness. Still Elizabeth fought and squirmed to escape, but her efforts were no match for the man's brutal pounding to her face and body. Just before merciful unconsciousness consumed her, the man entered her, shredding her virginity with stabbing pains that haunted Elizabeth for the rest of her life.

Ode to a Lake

by Elizabeth Lockett

Have you ever walked by the side of a lake at the sunset of a day
And witnessed the merging of water and sky in a colorful display?

All amber and russet and flame and gold to herald the purple of night,
And you bow your head here in Nature's shrine, humbled and awed at the sight.

Though you've sometimes doubted the presence of God 'midst life's burdens and
grief and pain,
Now you lift your head and the glory fades, but you can go on again.

The beauty of sunset over the sea is lost in the waves' wild moan,
And a river goes on at the end of the day - still trying to find a way home.

But a lake is contented and tranquil and calm, just as the river should be.
No craving to venture to distant shores - like the ever-restless sea.

And if ever the burden of life has you down, and your God may seem far away-
Come with me as I walk by the side of the lake at the close of another day.

Nancy Nichols

Restful sleep was a commodity not often afforded Elizabeth. Nearly every night an ambulance brought someone to or took someone from Bayside. The sirens were normally silent, but the red lights atop the ambulance cast an eerie pulse throughout Elizabeth's room. Her new hip, to Elizabeth's chagrin, healed well and within a few days she moved about without relying on her walker. Elizabeth occasionally sighted her "physical therapist," but any therapy she received she administered herself.

After tossing and turning through the wee hours one night, Elizabeth needed to escape the confines of her room. She found the idea of venturing around the silent facility while everyone else slept appealing. Elizabeth drew a robe around her and left her room. As she entered the Community Room the duty receptionist briefly glanced up and then resumed her copy of "Evil Lurking." Elizabeth pulled up a chair in front of the fireplace. The gas flames burned softly and Elizabeth slipped into hypnotic reverie trying to clear her mind. *Father Digiacomo was right*, thought Elizabeth. *Solitude had never been Elizabeth's friend.*

Pots and pans banged around the kitchen and broke the early morning's tranquility. Elizabeth suddenly felt weary and longed for her bed. She pushed herself up and left the Community Room. As Elizabeth walked toward her room, the horrid woman who wheeled the dead man from Bayside the evening Elizabeth arrived walked toward her. *Dora*, Elizabeth remembered the EMT calling her. The woman stopped in front of Elizabeth.

"You're new here aren't you?" asked the squat woman.

Elizabeth grew wary and the hackles on her neck stood on end. Elizabeth nodded.

"I'll be seeing you soon then." A maniacal laugh erupted from the woman's throat. "Yeah, be seeing you *real* soon!" The woman's hideous laughter continued as she walked past Elizabeth.

Elizabeth's knees buckled causing her to slump against the wall. She watched terrified as the woman ducked into a supply closet, her insane laughter intensifying. Fear alone drove Elizabeth to stand up and continue to her room. She lay on her bed and sobbed herself to sleep.

§

Elizabeth slept through breakfast and didn't wake until well past noon. She lay silently in bed for several hours when someone knocked on her door. Elizabeth's heart jumped in her throat thinking it might be Dora. She pulled the covers over her head for protection. The knocking continued.

"Hello? It's Nancy Nichols, may I come in?"

Elizabeth never thought she would be happy to hear the volunteer's voice. "The door is open, of course."

Nancy gently pushed the door open and entered the room. "Sorry I haven't been back sooner. Something came up and I couldn't come. I brought you some crosswords. Different kinds, you know, like word games and stuff." Nancy fished a few magazines from her satchel and placed them on the table. Elizabeth perked at the sight of the magazines. Crossword puzzles were her most loyal companions for half a century.

Elizabeth studied the young woman. "Why are you here?"

Nancy froze at the unexpected, direct question. Under Elizabeth's gaze, she finally replied. "My mother told me that I should get out of the house and make some friends. Ever since she got sick I've taken care of her. I didn't even finish school. She wasn't happy when I told her I registered with Sunshine for Seniors - I guess that's not what she meant by getting out of the house."

"Thanks for the history lesson. So why are you in *my* room?"

"They sent me here. You must have signed up with Sunshine or they wouldn't have sent me."

Even through her knit cap, frumpy coat and downcast eyes, Elizabeth realized that Nancy wasn't as uncomely as she initially perceived.

"I assure you that I never registered with Sunshine for Seniors," said Elizabeth.

"I'm so sorry; there must have been some mistake." Nancy's face flushed as she turned to leave the room. If Nancy needed a sign that she should go through with her secret evening plans, that was it.

The door burst open as Nancy reached for it and slammed into her side. The woman who manhandled Elizabeth and helped her off the bathroom floor appeared in the doorway and checked Nancy's shoulder as she entered the room.

"Whatchu doin' here, fool?" Without waiting for an answer, the woman crossed the room and stood at Elizabeth's bedside. "That's right, didn't think I'd find out, huh? Dora told me you ratted me out and told her I haven't been doing PT with you. You better be careful who you stab in the back." The woman stooped down and placed her face even with Elizabeth's. "I'm gonna tell you this one more time. We do PT every day for one hour. Do I make myself clear?"

The woman's yellowing bloodshot eyes bulged from her head. Elizabeth sickened as she recalled her own fear when she crossed Dora the previous evening. "Go to hell."

The woman grabbed Elizabeth cheeks and pressed her mouth to Elizabeth's ears. "Don't mess with me. Final warning." The woman shoved Elizabeth's face aside and stormed toward the door. She stopped short of leaving and glared at Nancy. "You didn't see none of this, got it? And don't come back here no more!" The woman left the room, slamming the door behind her.

§

Heavy seconds passed before either woman spoke. Finally Nancy broke the silence. "I'll go tell someone," she said as she reached for the door.

Elizabeth stopped her. "Don't bother. When I can't take care of myself there's no reason left to live." *Did I just say that?* Elizabeth asked herself. *Reason to live?*

"I'll be going then. Sorry I bothered you." Nancy shouldered her satchel and turned to leave.

"Wait! You're here now. Hand me the crosswords."

The shaken girl picked up the magazines and crossed the room. When she held them out to Elizabeth her coat sleeves rode up her forearms, exposing a wide gauze bandage encircling her wrist. Elizabeth noticed but glanced away. Nancy withdrew her arm as soon as Elizabeth took the magazines.

"I brought some pens too." Nancy's left arm darted for her satchel. Reconsidering, she placed her bag on Elizabeth's bed and removed a pack of pens with her right hand. Obviously self-conscious about her bandage, she handed the pens to Elizabeth and pointed to the opposite side of Elizabeth's bed. "Is that why you're so strong? Because you're religious?"

Elizabeth's eyes followed Nancy's finger to the Bible that Father Digiacomo must have left on her bed. "Not at all. Why should I fear death? Aren't I already in hell?"

The two women stared at each other. After a minute a wrinkled smile grew across Elizabeth's face. Nancy burst out laughing and, to Elizabeth's surprise, so did she.

When the laughter subsided, Elizabeth told Nancy that she needed some rest. Although what she really needed was to start her crosswords. "When are you coming back?" Elizabeth noticed Nancy's hesitation. "You are coming back, aren't you?"

Nancy faltered, as though working through a difficult decision. She didn't plan on returning to Bayside. Didn't plan on returning anywhere after that night. "I can come on Thursday, if that's okay."

Elizabeth saw Nancy's thought process and the relief that crossed the young woman's face when she replied. "Yes, Thursday is fine. That woman who was just here?"

"LaShawna," offered Nancy.

"Whatever. What she said and did to you? Don't *ever* let anyone treat you like that."

Nancy left the room and Elizabeth reached greedily for the first magazine.

Ethan

Clara Newton entered Elizabeth's room a short while after Doctor Allyn left. "Did the doctor tell you?" she asked.

Elizabeth stared past her mother out the window. The bruises had turned from purple to blue to yellow and finally faded. The cuts on her face and lips had scabbed, and the scabs slowly flaked away leaving virgin pink skin in their places. Elizabeth didn't begin college at Avery Point that fall, and had barely left her room following the night at the Ocean House.

"He didn't have to," Elizabeth replied.

Clara stroked her daughter's hair. "You're father is beside himself. He hasn't eaten, doesn't sleep. He's working before dawn and doesn't come in until after all the lights are out. When he finds out…"

"It's not my fault," sobbed Elizabeth, thinking that it was *all* her fault.

"But that dress! What were you thinking? Well, it doesn't matter now. Doc Allyn knows someone from the hospital who can take care of this. He's going to bring him over next week."

"Thou Shalt Not Kill," recited Elizabeth.

Clara reeled back and slapped Elizabeth across her freshly healed face with all her might. "Don't you dare blaspheme in this house! You listen to me! I told you going to that ball was a bad idea. You are not going to shame our family. You are going to take care of this, end of discussion."

"You can hit me all you want. Do you think you can hurt me after what happened? I'm sorry for what happened, but I'm going to have my baby."

Clara pulled her arm back to strike again and then reconsidered. "You're a smart girl Elizabeth. Do you want to ruin your life because of what happened? And what about your father and me? Do we deserve this? I suggest you think through this before your father gets home."

Elizabeth watched her mother leave the room, feeling no better or worse than before Doctor Allyn told her she was pregnant.

Hours later the headlights from her father's truck bounced along the farm's driveway. Through the house's post and beam construction and plaster walls, Elizabeth heard the crescendos of the ensuing heated discussion and her father's hollering but couldn't decipher any of the words.

The following morning Clara tapped on Elizabeth's door and entered her room. She held a plate of sizzling bacon and eggs and had a renewed calmness about her. Clara placed breakfast on Elizabeth's night stand. "How are you feeling today?"

Elizabeth lay awake for some time before her mother came. Long enough to hear her father leave the house hours earlier. She stared at her mother, not knowing what to expect.

"I spoke to your father last night. He wasn't surprised by your decision, although it broke his heart. He has family in upstate New York. You and I will go there next month, before you start showing. We'll bring the baby home and raise it. The baby is your father's *sister's* child, and its father is dead. Do you understand?"

Relief spread through Elizabeth like wildfire and tears welled in her eyes. Elizabeth knew she was with child the moment she regained consciousness following the attack. She never expected her parents to allow her to carry the child, much less live in their house after the baby was born. Elizabeth planned on leaving home as soon as Doc Allyn made her condition official.

Elizabeth sobbed and sobbed, releasing all the emotions she'd repressed since that unspeakable summer night. "Mommy," cried Elizabeth with outstretched hands.

Clara leaned over her and hugged her daughter tightly, tears filling her own eyes.

§

William, Clara and Elizabeth Newton left their North Stonington farm well before dawn on All Saints Day. William didn't speak to Elizabeth and barely looked at his only child during the twelve hour drive to the outskirts of Schenectady. The corduroy roads jostled the passengers and rattled the fenders on the old Ford. The tension in the truck was so stifling that Elizabeth felt claustrophobic and nearly gasped for air by the time they finally arrived at her uncle's farm. The front light came on as the three walked toward the house. A large frame filled the doorway.

"Good to see you William."

Elizabeth's father shook his brother's hand. "I'm obliged to you Seth. This is Elizabeth, who you haven't seen since she was knee-high."

Seth Newton glanced at Elizabeth, and then clasped Clara's hand in both of his. "It's a pleasure to see you again Clara, despite the unfortunate circumstances."

"We can't thank you enough. I assure you we won't be a burden," said Clara as she averted Seth's lingering stare.

"To tell you the truth, the old place could use a woman's touch. It's been two years since my Sarah passed away. The fever."

"William told me, I'm so sorry," said Clara. "She was such a dear woman."

"Thanks. I've been getting by, but it's been tough. Anyway, Heidi Pepperschmidt, she's the midwife around these parts, will be by next week to meet you. You'll find your rooms upstairs. I'll bring your bags up later."

Taking their leave, Clara and Elizabeth climbed the stairs as Seth placed his arm around William and led him to the parlor.

§

Time passed at a snail's pace for Elizabeth. Her mother cooked the meals and cleaned the house, which had indeed suffered greatly since Sarah's passing. Seth instructed Elizabeth on the daily farm chores. Elizabeth frequently felt her uncle staring at her when they were alone and grew uncomfortable around him, prompting her to retire for the night immediately following the evening meals. She spent the days feeding livestock, cleaning the pens, milking the cows twice daily, collecting eggs and packaging most of them for her uncle to take to market. With harvest season past, there wasn't much left for Seth to do and he spent most days away from the farm, arriving home for dinner smelling of gin.

By December Elizabeth clearly showed her condition, although she had actually lost weight since arriving at her uncle's. The incessant chores and her lack of appetite caused her face to grow gaunt and her stomach to protrude as though malnourished. Her father planned on visiting at Christmas, and as the holiday approached Elizabeth grew more anxious. She missed her father so much, but he'd barely looked at her since coming home from the hospital.

Elizabeth's stomach was in knots Christmas Eve. The snow devoured the countryside like an ominous creature of white as time nearly stood still. She'd helped her mother prepare dinner, expecting her father to arrive late afternoon. Elizabeth, her mother and uncle waited until nearly nine o'clock, then ate without William. Seth retired to bed while Elizabeth and Clara cleaned the kitchen, preparing a plate and putting it aside for William. The two women moved into the parlor where Clara retrieved her yarn and needles. Elizabeth noted that the sweater her mother knitted was for a man.

Her mother hadn't yet made anything for the baby, although she knitted nightly since arriving in New York.

"Do you think anything has happened?" Elizabeth asked her mother.

The lantern's glow danced across Clara's pale face. "I'm sure your father is fine. He probably just got a late start. Besides, he's got to be very careful driving way up here in this storm."

Despite her mother's reassuring words, Elizabeth detected the concern in her voice. Elizabeth attempted to read her Bible by the dim light, but found herself too distracted to concentrate. "Father hasn't spoken to me since…since it happened. Do you think he will be…?" Elizabeth didn't know how to finish.

Clara rested her knitting on her lap and stared at her daughter. "Everything will be just fine once we get back home."

Headlights reflected off the falling snow and lit up the parlor. Clara carefully set her knitting ensemble by her side and smoothed her housedress as she stood. Elizabeth jumped from her seat and flung open the front door, allowing a freezing white cloud of snow to enter the house. The blizzard hid the vehicle from sight, but a moment later Elizabeth saw a large figure emerge from the snow and climb the porch steps, his head buried in his chest. As Elizabeth ventured on to the porch to wrap her arms around her father, the man looked up. It wasn't Elizabeth's father. Elizabeth jumped back, dread instantly consuming her.

"Evening Miss. Is Seth home?"

Elizabeth cried out. "What's wrong, is it my father?" Elizabeth's breathing became irregular and her stomach spasmed.

Clara pulled her daughter inside. "Please come in. Seth is sleeping, do you need him?"

The man stepped inside, pulling the door closed against the howling wind. "No ma'am. The General Store got a call from Connecticut about a Mister William Newton. Say, is that Seth's brother?"

Clara dropped to her knees and wrapped her arms around Elizabeth's waist. She began pounding on Elizabeth's legs, screaming. "It's your fault! It's all your fault! You killed him!"

The man caught the hyper-ventilating Elizabeth as she fell against the staircase. "Whoa! Whoa now! He's alright. He just called to say that he won't be able to make it, too much work to do. Said he'd send a message next month."

Clara's wailing subsided and her hands dropped to her sides. Elizabeth's white-knuckled fists clenched the banister until she felt the strength return to her legs.

The messenger glanced from Elizabeth to Clara and looked as though he'd rather be anyplace else in the world at that moment. "I'd best be going." The man backed out of the house, turned and ran across the yard until the blizzard swallowed him.

Clara collected herself and climbed the stairs. The two women never spoke of the incident.

§

By the middle of her pregnancy's third trimester, the twelve hour days took a heavy toll on Elizabeth. Her mother helped with the manual labor outside, and Elizabeth spent more time indoors cooking and cleaning. Elizabeth peeled turnips as Clara placed a ham in the oven. They didn't expect Seth for some time.

The knife thudded on the cutting board and Elizabeth shrieked in pain. Clara looked up as Elizabeth wrapped a towel around her finger.

"What is it?" asked Clara.

"I cut my finger." Elizabeth applied pressure on the towel to stop the bleeding.

Clara unfolded the towel and examined the wound. "You might need stitches."

"I think I'll be okay. It looks worse than it is." Elizabeth placed the bloody towel back around her finger as Clara picked up the knife and began paring the turnips.

Elizabeth stared at her mother before sitting. "Mother, how come you haven't knitted anything for the baby?"

"How do you know I haven't?"

"Because I do."

Clara held Elizabeth's stare for a long minute before replying. "You have more important things to worry about than what I knit."

"I've chosen a name for him," Elizabeth told her mother.

Elizabeth continued slicing the turnips. "Him?"

"It's a boy; I feel it. His name is Ethan."

Clara's hands trembled when she heard the name.

"What's wrong?" asked Elizabeth. "I thought you would be proud to have the baby named after your father."

Clara struggled to control her emotions. She washed the turnips and placed them in a pot to boil. Without saying a word, Clara left the kitchen. Elizabeth heard her mother sobbing as she climbed the stairs.

Elizabeth set dinner on the table when she heard Seth's truck barreling down the driveway. Clara looked peaked as she rejoined Elizabeth and poured milk in the glasses Elizabeth had set on the table.

Seth climbed the back steps and stumbled as he entered the mudroom. He missed the hook on the coat rack and his jacket tumbled to the floor. "And how are you lovely ladies doing this evening?" Seth scanned the kitchen. "No milk for me, honey. I'm all set," Seth told Elizabeth as he patted the half-pint bottle protruding from his shirt pocket. "Maybe we'll have a drink after dinner."

Seth slurred his words, and he walked in an arc to the table. "Let the master of the house sit at the head of the table, surrounded by his wenches." Seth laughed, spit flying from his mouth.

Elizabeth wanted to dart from the room, but knew her mother would be angry if she did.

Seth uncorked the bottle and took a long swig. "I never knew how good old Willie had it with you two women. My Sarah, she never lifted a finger helping me with the farm. And she didn't hold a candle to your cooking Clara. Makes a man wonder what else he's been missing out on." Seth's gaze passed from Clara's chest to Elizabeth's. "You know what, Lizzie? Sitting at that table you can't even tell you're preg-, oh excuse me, *with child*. Yes sir, some boy had a nice tumble in the sand all right!"

Elizabeth pushed herself away from the table and ran from the kitchen. She heard her uncle mumbling *"wassa matter, I's jus' kiddin'"* as she climbed the stairs two at a time, sending sharp pains through her abdomen. Once safely in bed, Elizabeth drew the covers tightly around her and sobbed herself to sleep.

Elizabeth awoke during the night to find her mother sleeping beside her. Nothing was ever said about the incident at dinner or anything that transpired following Elizabeth's sudden departure from the kitchen, but Clara slept with Elizabeth for the remainder of their stay in New York.

§

Winter slowly gave way to spring. The unseasonably warm temperature, combined with the discomfort of being at full term, prevented Elizabeth from sleeping. When she heard Seth leave the house she slipped out of bed. She eased down the stairs, carrying her belly in front of her. Elizabeth poured herself a glass of milk as she heard Seth crank the old Ford tractor to life in the barn. The unmuffled tractor engine's roar broke the morning silence and made Elizabeth homesick for her own farm - and for her father. With sowing season in full gear, Seth spent a lot more time at home. Fortunately, for now at least, Seth would be occupied outside most of the time.

Elizabeth sat alone at the kitchen table, rubbing her stomach. "I promise I'll never let anything happen to you, Ethan."

Suddenly Elizabeth's stomach convulsed and she doubled over in pain. A great torrent of liquid flooded from between her legs as she cried out. Elizabeth grabbed the table and tried to pull herself up. She was lightheaded and dizzy and she collapsed back in the chair. Elizabeth panicked. As with many first time mothers, Elizabeth was in denial about entering labor despite the fact that she was full term and she'd experienced all the signs the midwife told her she would when the time came. Elizabeth was certain she was losing her baby and began crying.

After several minutes Elizabeth's breathing returned to normal and her mind cleared. She got up from the table and was half way up the stairs when her second contraction struck. She fell to her knees and clutched her stomach, holding on to the banister to prevent her from tumbling down the stairs. Elizabeth's pain and fear were unbearable. She crawled up the remaining steps and down the hallway to her room. Sliding against the wall for stability, Elizabeth navigated the room and stood before her mother.

Clara Newton's eyes blinked open. The unexpectedness of someone standing at her side caused her to scream. That in turn caused Elizabeth to scream, triggering her third contraction. Clara saw Elizabeth's soaked nightshirt as she crumpled to the bedside. Clara sprang out of bed and threw the bed's linen to the floor. She placed her arms around her daughter and helped her to the bed. Clara saw the fear in Elizabeth's eyes.

"Everything is okay, it's time. How many contractions have you had?"

"Three," panted Elizabeth.

"How far apart are they?"

"I, I don't know. They started about five minutes ago."

Shock crossed Clara's face. "Five *minutes* ago? Where's your uncle?" The tractor's thumping sound answered her question. "I'll be right back; I'll send him to get Mrs. Pepperschmidt. Try to keep your breathing controlled."

Clara dashed from the room, donning her housecoat as she left. Minutes later Elizabeth heard the tractor rumble into the yard and turn off as another contraction assaulted her. Her mother bounded into the room, gasping for air.

"Seth's going for Mrs. Pepperschmidt. But Elizabeth, there might not be time. *You're* going to have to deliver this baby." Clara laid a pile of white linen and a knife on the night stand.

Terror seized Elizabeth at the sight of the knife and she struggled to prevent her mother from spreading her legs. "How could you?! You're going to kill my baby!"

Clara followed Elizabeth's gaze to the knife. "It's for the cord! Now lay back and relax. Oh my god, I see the head! Now when I say "push" you push with all your might. You understand?"

Elizabeth nodded as the greatest contraction yet consumed her entire body. From the deepest recesses of Elizabeth's mind she heard her mother screaming, *"Push, push, push, push*!" And Elizabeth did push, with every ounce of her being. She experienced two sensations: whiteness and her insides shredding.

Her mother's excited voice brought the world slowly back to Elizabeth. "The head is out. You're going to have to push again when the next contraction hits. Stay with me Elizabeth."

"I can't do this! I can't do it anymore!" Another wave hit Elizabeth and she heard her mother yelling in the background. Elizabeth pushed again and felt her entire insides being ripped from her. Fighting the desire to pass out, Elizabeth craned her neck and looked down the bed. Elizabeth's mind flashed red at the sight of the bloody purple baby in her mother's hand. "It's dead!" cried Elizabeth.

Clara reached for the knife and cut the umbilical cord. She patted the baby on the back and a weak hiccup followed by a cry erupted from the infant. Clara dabbed the inside of the baby's mouth with a cloth as he fought for his first breath of air. The skin quickly changed from purple to blue to pink, much to Elizabeth's relief. Clara wrapped the baby in a blanket and placed him in a bassinet by the bed. "I want to hold him," whispered Elizabeth. Another contraction sacked Elizabeth. "What's happening?" screamed Elizabeth. "I can't have another one!"

Clara resumed her position between Elizabeth's legs. "You're not. You need to push again."

Elizabeth agonized through two more contractions to deliver the afterbirth. Clara joined Elizabeth at the head of the bed. "You've lost a lot of blood and you're still bleeding; it's a very big baby. You need to lie very still until the midwife gets here."

Elizabeth lay back and slept. At some point someone fed her pills and worked between her legs, but she felt no pain. She drifted in and out of consciousness, and when she awoke her first sensation was her screaming breasts. They felt ready to burst, and the light nightshirt pressing against her flesh proved nearly intolerable. She hunched her shoulders to allow her breasts breathing room, but the strain sent daggers through her chest.

The small room was full of people. Clara sat at Elizabeth's side, and her uncle leaned against the doorway. As Heidi placed a cup of warm broth to Elizabeth's mouth, Elizabeth turned toward the bassinet. A strange couple stood beside it, their arms reaching inside.

"I want to hold my baby," whispered Elizabeth.

Everyone cast their eyes to the middle-aged couple at the bassinet. The woman spoke. "Of course." She drew her arms from the bassinet holding the newborn baby. Elizabeth reached for him, but the woman gently placed the baby on the bed beside Elizabeth. Elizabeth stared into her son's beautiful green eyes.

"Nearly nine pounds," said Heidi. "The delivery was fast, but very difficult. You lost a lot of blood, and the stitches can tear easily. You'll have to be very careful."

Elizabeth wasn't listening. She laid her son against her body, wanting him to feel her heartbeat against his. The baby nuzzled his head against Elizabeth's chest, vying for food. Elizabeth whispered his name over and over. "Ethan, Ethan, Ethan."

Suddenly a tremendous white light blinded Elizabeth. Terrified, she drew Ethan tightly against her body. When she refocused, she saw a man standing behind a large tripod with a camera mounted on top. A black cloth draped over the man's head from the rear of the camera. "One more. Smile!" Again the flash blinded Elizabeth.

Ethan began crying and the woman who brought him to Elizabeth took him back. "Thank you," said the woman.

Elizabeth tried to sit up, sending sharp pains shooting between her legs. "Wait, I want to lay with him. He's hungry."

Clara firmly pushed her daughter back to the bed. "The baby is fine. Get some rest now."

Elizabeth was too exhausted to protest. She felt fuzzy and her consciousness faded. In her morphine-assisted sleep, Elizabeth dreamed repeatedly about the savage attack at the Ocean House.

§

The bright spring sunlight filtered through the open window and beckoned Elizabeth from sleep. Despite the tragic circumstances causing her pregnancy, she felt compelled to have her baby-despite her parents' desire for her to abort the pregnancy. Even though she didn't call the baby hers, he was hers, and she raised him in her parents' house. Although both her parents were apprehensive about her having the baby, they both welcomed Ethan, and Elizabeth, with open arms. Buckboard's paws tapped against the plank flooring and he buried his snoot under the covers to cuddle beside Elizabeth. And Ethan is so...where is Ethan?

Elizabeth blinked the final shards of sleep from her eyes and awoke in bed at her uncle's farm. Buckboard of course had died two years earlier. She was alone in the bed and the house was silent. A feeling of instant dread overcame Elizabeth, and she bolted upright. Despite her medication, the pain seared through her internals. Holding onto the headboard for stability, Elizabeth slid against the wall until she reached the bassinet. Ethan was not in it. Calling her eyes liars, Elizabeth reached into the bassinet and lifted the sheet and light blanket as if somehow her baby was lost in them. She broke out in a sweat as panic consumed her. *Someone took her baby!*

The stitches tugged at Elizabeth's tender skin as she left her room and walked down the stairs. She smelled bacon and eggs and heard them sizzling on the skillet as she crossed the parlor. She entered the kitchen and saw her mother standing in front of the stove.

"Good morning Dear! You shouldn't be out of bed. Run along upstairs; I'll bring your breakfast."

"Where is Ethan?" asked Elizabeth.

Clara stood motionless with her back to Elizabeth. Finally she turned and faced her daughter. "Of course you couldn't keep it Elizabeth. That child's conception is not right in the eyes of the Lord. Anyway, a very nice, well-off couple adopted Eth- the baby. Very thoughtful, they are. They even left a picture of you and the baby." Clara nodded to the black and white photo on the table that had been taken while Elizabeth held Ethan in bed.

The room began spinning and Elizabeth leaned against the door frame. "I'll be able to see him then?" asked Elizabeth.

"Certainly not," replied Clara. "Your father and I thought it best that we not even know the couple's name."

"Father?" repeated Elizabeth. "Father knows what you've done?"

"Of course he does. It was his idea. I just wanted to have you sedated and be done with it months ago. But your father said if you had any idea that we planned an abortion you would run away and have that bastard in the streets. This is all really for the best. You will thank us for it one day."

Elizabeth put all the pieces of her parent's deceit together like a giant jigsaw puzzle. Her heart broke and she collapsed to her knees. "So I'm just supposed to go home like nothing ever happened?"

"Yes, Elizabeth. That is the whole point. Your father told everyone that we came to New York to help your uncle after he lost his wife. You will begin college in the fall and no one will ever know."

The room's colors gave way to gray as Elizabeth withdrew from consciousness. "I will," she whispered, too physically and emotionally defeated even to sob.

To a Little Brown Bird

by Elizabeth Lockett

In the kingdom of birds, you're the drabbest of all
Plain little bird of brown-
Do you not envy your fine-feathered friends?
What is your claim to renown?

You are not painted a Cardinal red-
You are not blue like the Jay-
Nor in full-dress suit like your penguin friend
In his icy home far away.

You can't speak out like the parakeet,
Brilliant in mind and in feather
Nor are you in tune like the lark and the dove
Blending their voices together.

You do not herald in the Spring
Like the robin with breast so gay
Nor soar like the pigeon into the blue-
A messenger bent on his way.

Pheasant and quail roam the meadow and field
Resplendent in colors galore.
And the pink flamingo strides proudly along
On some far-off tropical shore.

The peacocks strut through the gardens and parks
Spreading their beautiful wings
Each a professional work of art-
Elegant, arrogant things.

Far on his crag on the mountain top-
Mighty king on his throne
The eagle looks downward in cold disdain
Aloof, supreme-and alone.

Who is that creature in yonder tree
With great round luminous eyes?
Professor of Birdland, judging his class
The owl-subtle and wise.

Circling about in the far-off blue-
Swooping down on their prey.
Ominous creatures, buzzard and hawk,
Villains in bird-like way.

The golden canary bursts into song
In ever-enchanting voice-
Missionary from Heaven on High
For all to hear and rejoice.

But-do not envy your well-versed friends
Canary and parakeet-
They would surely relinquish their caged-in lives
To join you there in the street.

Or better yet-in a country lane-
Warmed by the rays of the sun
And pheasant and quail-in the Fall of the year
Are stalked by the man with the gun.

The red-breasted harbinger of the Spring
Must move on at earliest frost
And the homing pigeons, so skillful and swift
Is someday sure to get lost.

*Mystic Connecticut: A Woman's
Hundred Year Journey to Heaven*

Flamingo bird in your pink attire
You are not dingy and small
But it takes two long legs like two spindly sticks
To make you so stately and tall.

And our black and white friends in the far-off south-
We admit he is dressed very nice-
But who wants to spend his whole life through
Afloat on a cake of ice?

King Eagle must surely get lonesome at times
High on his rocky domain
And the Owl from high on his tree-top perch
Sees too much of turmoil and pain.

Hated and feared are the buzzard and hawk
Frightful, symbolic-and dark
But-what is the flaw of the peacock gay
As he struts along the park?

A beauty he is, we will not dispute
He is that "One in a Crowd"
But oh-what a voice when he opens his mouth-
Harsh, and discordant-and loud!

So-plain little bird-dig your worms-build your nest
Up in the old brown tree-
You have the greatest gifts of them all-
Contented-and ever free.

Word Games

    LaShawna Jackson burst into Elizabeth's room. She had not seen Elizabeth for a couple days and wanted to ensure she was still alive since LaShawna logged their physical therapy sessions on a daily basis. During her eight hour shifts, LaShawna typically spent the first and last half hour at Bayside. The hours between were spent in the city earning additional income through more licentious activities.
    "You still alive Bag of Bones?" shouted LaShawna.
    The room was deathly quiet. Elizabeth lay perfectly still on her bed. Her head was tilted to the side and her unmoving eyes pointed toward the ceiling. Her jaw was locked partially open. Her reading glasses were askew on her face, and the crossword magazine lay on the floor beside the bed. Even from across the room LaShawna saw the old woman's skin drawn tightly across her face, drool glistening at the corner of her mouth.
    "Hey!" yelled LaShawna. Elizabeth's rigid frame didn't budge. LaShawna stared at Elizabeth for a moment. "You better have just died last night!" LaShawna bolted from the room and slammed the door shut, hoping her daily logs hadn't yet been reviewed.
    LaShawna ran down the hall and rifled through her supervisor's in-basket. She removed her daily rounds logs for the week and ran

them through the shredder as she tried to think of an excuse for why she hadn't been in to do therapy with the old lady for a couple days, just in case. Then she reported Elizabeth's death to the receptionist.

Before the sirens from Pequot's ambulance reached Bayside, the staff EMT rushed into Elizabeth's room with LaShawna Jackson trailing closely behind. Elizabeth sat at the table, studying over a crossword puzzle. She turned and glanced at the EMT over her glasses, a look of comic bewilderment spreading across her face. The EMT froze and turned toward LaShawna.

Venom spewed from LaShawna's mouth when she realized the old woman had duped her. "What are you staring at?" LaShawna fired at the EMT. "You see she's fine now. Don't you have something to do?" The EMT shrugged his shoulders and left the room. LaShawna stood before Elizabeth. "Okay, I see how it is now. Look here you old hag. You think that was funny? You mess with me and you will lose!" LaShawna knocked into Elizabeth's chair as she turned and left the room. Elizabeth smiled as she returned to her crossword.

§

Elizabeth continued working on her puzzles. A while later Father Digiacomo tapped on the door. "May I come in?"

"Death takes a holiday Father, didn't you hear?" asked Elizabeth as she removed her glasses.

"No, but I did hear there was some confusion earlier this morning. Something that caused one of the therapists to leave the site terribly flustered," replied the priest.

"Go figure," said Elizabeth. "Anyway, I'm glad you're here. I took your advice and read through my Bible," Elizabeth lied. "I thought maybe I could find some hidden meaning in the Scriptures that I've overlooked the last century. I like anagrams, so I listed the names of all the Books. I took the first letter of each Book and rearranged them until I came up with some words."

Father Digiacomo watched patiently as Elizabeth continued. "I started with the Old Testament. Let's see, there is Genesis, Exodus, Leviticus, Deuteronomy...well, you know the rest, I'm sure. I have to admit, I did find some interesting messages. There was *hopeless, alone, godless, pain, anger, despair, depressed...*"

Father Digiacomo shook his head. "Why do you fuel your bitterness when the answers are right in front of you?"

"Wait, I'm not finished. I thought maybe I'd just gotten off to a bad start. I jumped to the New Testament. That was a little more difficult with Acts and Ephesians providing the only vowels. Try as I might, the word that repeatedly jumped out at me was *hate*. The entire experience proved very disheartening," said Elizabeth shaking her head. "And turn the heat up in here, would you?"

Ignoring her sarcasm, Father Digiacomo crossed the room and examined Elizabeth's Bible. "I heard LaShawna Jackson is suspended. Seems she didn't complete her logs for the last few days. Her supervisor is even questioning whether or not she has been conducting therapy with the residents."

Elizabeth innocently returned the priest's stare.

Father Digiacomo coursed through the heavy Bible's pages. "Life is difficult, Elizabeth. Everyone has events that test their faith. But you should never *lose* your faith. These pages scream with purpose, prophesy, hope. How can you ignore it?"

Elizabeth stared out the window, disappointed with the priest's calm reaction to her blaspheme. The priest's eyes lingered on a page with a handwritten note.

"Daniel, that's a fine Biblical name. What happened to him? It reads here 'Daniel- Father rescued from well.'"

Elizabeth's face contorted with anger. "What happened to Daniel? I'll tell you what happened to Daniel. He fell down a well. Lost his ear and got a bum leg. Had to hide his limp and lie on his enlistment papers so he could join the army. Then he went overseas and got killed. That's what happened to him. So much for your 'purpose for life,' huh Father."

Father Digiacomo continued flipping through the Book in silence. A while later he retrieved an ancient newspaper clipping from between two pages. After reading the article he handed it to Elizabeth. "This is about Daniel Stanton. The Daniel from the well I assume. Have you read it?" he asked.

Elizabeth glanced at the article's bold title, 'NATIVE SON DIES ON GERMAN BATTLEFIELD.' "The headline says it all, doesn't it?"

"No, it doesn't," replied Father Digiacomo.

As Elizabeth pretended to read the article the priest cleared his throat. Elizabeth looked up and saw him holding her glasses out to her. Without speaking, Elizabeth took the glasses and placed them on her head. She read the article for the first time.

With heartfelt sadness this reporter recently received notification that one of our own, Sergeant Daniel James Stanton, son of Wilfred and Betsy Stanton, died a hero's death on a German battlefield last Sunday. Daniel, as reported by his father, stole away from home two years ago and enlisted in the Army in New London. Wilfred and Betsy awoke to find a note from Daniel stating that he would make them proud and do his best to prevent the Germans from stepping foot on our homeland. Daniel quickly advanced from private to corporal and within a year was promoted to sergeant, earning several distinguished medals along the way. Disobeying orders, although at this time it is uncertain whether or not Sergeant Stanton heard the orders above the mortar fire, our native son left the safety of his foxhole and climbed a hill to obtain a vantage point over the rapidly approaching Germans. While Sergeant Stanton slowed the German's advance, the twenty-five members of his squad were able to retreat and join ranks with their platoon. Before Sergeant Stanton was overcome by enemy fire, he radioed the enemy's size and location to his platoon, who in turn requested immediate reinforcements from land and air. The size of the enemy force was previously so underestimated that, if not for the heroic actions of Sergeant Stanton, the members of his squad, and likely his entire platoon, would have been massacred. As it was, our troops suffered only light casualties and beat back the enemy, maintaining their key strategic position. Sergeant Stanton is a hero, and we at the New London Day salute him. Donations in Daniel's honor may be made to the Soldiers' and Sailors' Relief Fund. A Memorial Service will be held at the North Stonington Baptist Church Sunday at seven o'clock.

    Elizabeth turned her head to hide the tears that formed in her eyes.
    Father Digiacomo spoke as he replaced the article between the Bible's pages. "The article said Daniel saved the lives of twenty-five men in his squad. How many men are in a platoon, Elizabeth? A hundred? Five hundred? Do you still think Daniel died in vain? Life is a chain of events that have far-reaching consequences, Elizabeth, not a haphazard collection of isolated, independent experiences. God has a reason for everything, even if we don't always understand it."
    Repressed memories flooded through Elizabeth. Daniel planting Elizabeth's first kiss on her lips, the two of them racing through Beaver Dam Hollow (sometimes with Elizabeth even letting Daniel win), Buckboard nipping at their ankles as they frolicked in the meadows. And of course the morning her father read the fateful headline to her at breakfast. Elizabeth subconsciously began blocking memories of Daniel from her mind the night he told her he was running away to join the Army. A premonition foretold Elizabeth of Daniel's death even before he hopped the train to New London. She had never grieved for Daniel, and the grief now ripped through her in a torrent. Elizabeth's thin body heaved as great sobs consumed her. She knew that she cried like a baby in front of this strange priest, but was powerless to control her emotions.
    Elizabeth did not know how long she laid in bed sobbing. The penalty for eighty-some years of repressed grief proved a heavy toll to pay. When she finally collected herself and turned over, she found herself alone. Father Digiacomo had left during her breakdown, and for that Elizabeth was thankful.

Packer's Tar Soap

Two weeks after strangers took Ethan from his mother, Seth Newton drove Elizabeth and Clara back to Connecticut. Seth received a message from William that his truck was broken and he didn't know when he would be able to get to New York to retrieve his wife and daughter. Elizabeth had been nearly catatonic since learning of her parents' deception and the loss of her child. The betrayal scorched the roots of Elizabeth's heart and soul. At Seth's direction, Elizabeth sat by him during the long drive home.

While driving up the lane to the farm Elizabeth absently noted the peeling paint on the house and a couple shutters hanging askew from their hinges. Elizabeth knew that with summer's arrival her father would be focusing his efforts in the fields. Even so, New England winters were always harsh and her father had never before let the house remain in disrepair. The bed of her father's truck stuck out from the chicken coop, the nose buried inside with the hood removed. Elizabeth assumed her father had built a new coop and moved the chickens.

"Hey," Seth called to Elizabeth when she dismounted from his truck and walked toward the house. "You're forgetting your bags."

Elizabeth returned to the truck and gathered her few belongings.

"You know, Elizabeth," continued her uncle, "people ain't going to look at you the same anymore. They're going to know why you went away. Hell, you might as well brand a scarlet letter right across your forehead. Seems like you and I might have gotten off on the wrong foot, but maybe it would be best for you if you come back with me. Without your mother there, we could, you know, get to know each other a little better. Besides, it looks like hard times have fallen on your father. He doesn't need an extra mouth to feed right now."

Elizabeth turned from her uncle without replying and walked to the house. When she walked up the steps to the house's back door she realized the cause of her apprehension. The fields weren't plowed, the tractor wasn't rumbling, there was no seasonal help milling about. The farm, normally bustling with activity in early June, was shrouded with desolation.

Anxiety over seeing her father twisted Elizabeth's stomach into knots. She loved him and needed him. And hated him. Elizabeth heard her father's voice as she entered the kitchen. He stood over her mother, tears streaming down his face. Her mother's face was buried in her hands, and she struggled for breath through her sobs.

"What's happened?" asked Elizabeth. Neither of her parents acknowledged her. She ran to her father and placed her hand on his shoulder. "What's wrong Father?"

William looked at Elizabeth. His throat quivered and he was unable to speak.

Seth followed Elizabeth into the kitchen and stood beside her. "Lost the farm," said Seth nonchalantly. "He figured it'd be best if he told you himself. Nothing you could do about it anyway."

What little remained of Elizabeth's heart broke. "It can't be. Say it isn't," begged Elizabeth.

Her father looked down at her, unable to collect himself. The harder he tried to speak, the more choked up he became.

"Elizabeth and I were talking, William," said Seth. "Thought it might ease the burden some if she came back with me. Just till you get your feet back on the ground."

Claustrophobia pressed down upon Elizabeth until she thought she would implode.

Clara pressed the balls of her shaking palms into her eyes. "Go to your room," she told Elizabeth. "Now!"

§

The scene became surreal as Elizabeth dropped her arms to her side and left the kitchen. She walked through the parlor and climbed the steps, absently noting the layer of dust coating them. She entered her room and fell into the chair by her bed. She prayed she was having a nightmare from which she would momentarily awake, even though she knew she was not. As her head swam in the room's heavy air she saw a note on her nightstand. Her arm felt like lead as she reached for the note. Elizabeth strained her eyes to focus on the rough handwriting. 'Elizabeth, please forgive me for what I've done. You didn't deserve any of it. All my love, your Father.'

Elizabeth cried and cried as she re-read the note. Memories of the last year converged upon her in a single torrent: the attack, Ethan, her parents' deceit, her uncle's advances, losing the farm, seeing her father cry for the first time. It was all too much for her to bear. She slid from the chair and groped her way to the bed. She reached over and opened the drawer on the nightstand. She rifled through the drawer looking for her letter opener. She would take a deep breath and plunge the letter opener deep into the stomach that recently bore the child that had been taken from her as surely as if it had been ripped from her womb. Her hand kept bumping into something as she fumbled for the letter opener. Praying for the relief that death would provide, she jumped out of bed and stood before the nightstand. She saw the letter opener in the rear of the drawer. As she reached for it, she saw the Bible that prevented her from reaching the letter opener.

The large portrait of Jesus on the Bible's cover stared at Elizabeth. She retrieved the letter opener, but was unable to avert the portrait's eyes. The letter opener stung her hand like a hot iron and she dropped it back into the drawer. She drew her hand across the Bible's grainy cover, gliding her fingers over Jesus' face. She removed the Bible from the drawer and collapsed in the chair, drawing the large book to her chest. She rocked back and forth for hours in a state of emptiness.

Well past midnight Elizabeth lit her lamp and opened the front cover. She read the faded brown ink on the first page. 'This Holy Bible is presented to our son Jedadiah Newton. May God love and bless you as you travel to America. Your loving parents.' Elizabeth stared at the inscription, unable to comprehend all that this Bible had witnessed in her family's history.

Elizabeth turned the first page. 'The First Book of Moses, Called Genesis.' Elizabeth attended church since she was born and stood out in Sunday school for her recitations of the Bible's verses. But it was only a game to her and she never dwelt over the words. For the first time, Elizabeth digested the ancient words as she read them. 'Chapter One. In the beginning God created the heaven and the earth.' Elizabeth turned the pages until roosters from a nearby farm crowed and a soft grayness pushed aside the night. Finally exhaustion overcame her and she slept.

"Rise and shine!" hollered Clara.

Elizabeth stirred in the chair as her hands rubbed the sleep from her eyes.

"Don't think you're going to stay in your room all day. You slept through breakfast so I don't want to hear about it. Now get up." Clara placed a bucket of water on the floor and leaned a mop against the wall.

Elizabeth cleared her mind. "Where is Father?"

"Working," replied Clara. "Now sweep and mop the floors. And do a good job, this place needs it. We've been gone too long."

"Working?" asked Elizabeth. "Where?"

"At the Packer Building in Mystic," replied her mother. "Don't worry about your father's work; worry about your own."

Clara turned to leave the room and Elizabeth called after her. "I understand why you did what you did. I forgive you."

Clara's jaw tightened. She picked up the mop and marched across the room to Elizabeth. "You forgive me?" she steamed. "How dare you! And you wanting to live with your uncle, after knowing how he is! I don't know how you turned out this way, but I mean to save what little dignity remains in this family. You are never to step foot in that man's house again." Clara shoved the mop against Elizabeth and stormed from the room.

Despite Elizabeth's emotionally distraught condition, her uncle's lie infuriated her. She didn't need her mother to order her to stay away from her uncle's house; Elizabeth had that covered on her own. But the fact that her mother believed Seth's lie tore open wounds that Elizabeth thought had already bled dry. She looked out her window and saw that her uncle's truck was gone. For that at least she was thankful.

Elizabeth retrieved the broom and dustpan from the hallway closet and swept the upstairs. When she finished, she mopped the second floor and polished all the wooden furniture. She washed the windows and replaced the linen on the beds. On the couple occasions her mother came upstairs, she marched past Elizabeth without acknowledging her. Morning slipped away by the time she completed her chores. She was tired, but invigorated, from the physical exertion.

Elizabeth carried the bucket downstairs to empty the dirty water. Her mother stood at the counter mixing flour to make bread. "Just set that down, Dear. That's too heavy for you. I made a Shepard's pie for lunch." Clara paused from mixing the flour and turned toward Elizabeth, smiling. "I can't tell you how much it means to me to be spending the day with you. Only a couple weeks left until you start college. You will be the first Newton to ever go. Your father and I are so proud of you!"

Elizabeth stared at her mother in disbelief. "What are you talking about? Classes don't start for three months. Besides, I'm not going. I have to help you and father."

Color spread across Clara's pale face. "Why are *you* talking about college? *Your* type doesn't go to college. Now throw out that dirty water. You can have leftover ham for lunch. I've already eaten." Clara turned her back to Elizabeth and resumed mixing the dough.

Elizabeth stood frozen in the doorway trying to comprehend her mother's bizarre change in behavior. She began to speak, but stopped herself. She went outside and dumped the water, then crossed the yard to the tool shed. She located a screwdriver and an assortment of screws and returned to the house. Her mother knitted in the parlor and didn't look up when Elizabeth passed. Elizabeth climbed the stairs and entered the guest room. She opened the window and sat on the sill. Holding on to the window frame, Elizabeth leaned outside. Hooking her knee against the wall for support, she secured the shutter into position with an oversized screw. After testing the hinges, she latched open the shutter. She climbed back inside and went to her parents' room. She found that the shutter panel had splintered, not merely pulled the screw through as with the previous shutter. Elizabeth unscrewed the hinges and removed the broken shutter.

Elizabeth returned to the tool shed and laid the shutter on the workbench. After clamping it to the bench she knocked off the broken panel with a hammer and looked in the wood bin for a replacement piece.

"What in the world are you doing, Little Me?"

The unexpected voice startled Elizabeth. She turned and saw a smile touch her father's lips.

"Sorry 'bout that, didn't mean to scare you. I've been meaning to fix that myself," said William nodding to the shutter. "We'll have to rip one of those planks in the corner to make a new piece. Mind if I help?"

The man standing before Elizabeth was the father she knew and loved, although he looked a little older and more tired than she remembered. "I don't know," began Elizabeth. "You sure you know how to use that saw?"

William crossed the shed and held Elizabeth tightly. "I've missed you and your mother so much. Are you okay?"

Elizabeth's eyes teared, but the comfort of her father's hug gave her strength. And hope. "Yes. Come on now, we've got work to do."

William measured the broken panel with a carpenter's square and marked the cut lines on the new plank. He uncovered the table saw and told Elizabeth to pull the wood through as he fed it into the blade. He blew the sawdust off the freshly cut panel and applied glue to it. After clamping the piece to the shutter he tapped in a couple finishing nails. "That ought to do it," said William.

Following an awkward silence, Elizabeth asked her father what happened to the farm.

William wiped the sweat from his brow. "We're not the only ones. The Millers sold out. So did the Judsons. Mold ruined most of last year's crop. Debt's been mounting up for the last few years. Besides, the little farmer can't compete with the big farms in the west and south shipping their produce up on trains by the boxcar. They've got longer growing seasons and more land than you can imagine. And labor is dirt cheap in those places."

The incredulity of her father's words cut through Elizabeth like a knife. "But you love farming," said Elizabeth. "It's your whole life."

William smiled at his daughter. "I do love farming. Working the fields, growing something where there was nothing." William looked out the shed's door to the fields he used to own. "But you're wrong about one thing. Farming's not my whole life. You and your mother are."

Elizabeth ran to her father. She buried her face in his shoulder and sobbed, no longer able to control her emotions. William let her get it all out of her system and then patted her back. "We'll hang that shutter tomorrow after the glue sets up. Oh, I brought you something." William fished in his pocket and produced a small box.

Elizabeth took it and looked at her father. "What is it?"

William smiled and told her to open it. "It's Packers All Healing Tar Soap. That's what I do now, over at the factory. They've been making this stuff since eighteen-sixty-nine. It's supposed to clean your skin, clear complexion, help eczema, dandruff and even psoriasis, whatever that is. What do you think?"

Elizabeth removed the soap from the silver foil box. She rubbed her fingers across the sticky bar and then held it to her face. Her nose wrinkled at the pungent smell. "It stinks!"

"Yup," said William. "That's what I thought too. Foulest smelling soap I ever smelled. And you know what else? It doesn't even hardly wash your hands. Go figure! Come on. Let's go see your mother."

Death Incarnated

Breakfast was in full swing when Elizabeth entered the Community Room. Mrs. Nedbetter bounced between tables greeting patrons and relating the day's scheduled activities. As Elizabeth tried to sneak to a small vacant table by the fireplace, Mrs. Nedbetter intercepted her.

"Good morning Elizabeth!" Mrs. Nedbetter placed her arm around Elizabeth and redirected her toward a table in the center of the room.

"I'll be fine over here," said Elizabeth as she attempted to squirm from Mrs. Nedbetter's grasp.

"Absolutely not," replied the hostess. "I'm sure you would be more comfortable with your friends. Besides, you don't want the other guests at your table to think you're avoiding them, do you?"

Elizabeth stared at the hostess and realized the futility of arguing. "Heavens no," she replied. This scenario repeated itself on a near-daily basis. Once Mrs. Nedbetter successfully redirected Elizabeth, she let her go and resumed working the crowd.

"Good morning Bess," said the toothless man who offered to meet Elizabeth by the fireplace. "Ain't you looking mighty spry this morning." He stood and pulled the vacant chair at his side out for

Elizabeth. Elizabeth sat down and the old man helped scoot her chair to the table. Elizabeth returned the greetings offered by the other diners with a nod.

A woman sitting across from Elizabeth snorted and shook her head. "Harry, why do you dote over her like that? She's just a mean old woman who doesn't appreciate anything."

"Now Lucinda, how do you know she doesn't appreciate anything? She keeps coming back here, now don't she?" replied Harry.

"As many times as you've pulled her chair out for her, she hasn't thanked you one time. You never pulled *my* chair out."

The old man sitting by Lucinda yelled. "MEE-OOWWW!" He clawed the air with ancient gnarled fingers. "I think Lucy is jealous!" As his faux scratching subsided, he slapped his knee and laughed so hard he wheezed and gasped for air.

Harry slid his water glass across the table. "Take a drink! For God's sake Jerry, don't die in front of the ladies."

Jerry managed to sip some water and gain control of his breathing. The instant the spell passed, he clawed the air again, igniting a fresh burst of laughter and wheezing. He took another drink and wiped tears from the corners of his eyes until he finally calmed down.

Bart, normally very quiet during meals, spoke. "You know why Harry pays attention to Elizabeth? Because she doesn't feel the need to act happy when she's not. We've all lived long lives. Some of us are happy with the outcome and it shows. Some of us are disappointed, or angry, or confused. But most of us try to act happy regardless. But their discontent reveals itself in other ways. Like gossiping and backstabbing. Elizabeth is genuine. Bitter, but genuine."

Elizabeth listened to the conversation about her unfold around the table. The unexpected seriousness of the man's comment quelled the table's bickering and everyone looked to Elizabeth as if waiting for a response. Elizabeth made eye contact with each of the people sitting at the table. Finally, she said, "I will spit at the next person who talks about me like I am not here."

The table's occupants stared at Elizabeth. Finally Jerry broke the silence. "Oh Lordy, if my old gas tank wasn't sputtering on reserve I swear I'd make a play for you myself. You are the cat's meow!" As the echo of his words died, Jerry clawed the air again toward Lucinda, sending him into another wheezing frenzy. Elizabeth couldn't help laughing. A little.

As breakfast continued, Elizabeth asked, "Where's Ann today?"

"She's with family this weekend," answered Bart. "She has lots of visitors, more than most of us. She should be back tonight."

Bart's words tugged at Elizabeth's heartstrings. *Family? No such luck for her.*

The diners continued their breakfast in silence. When Elizabeth nearly finished her eggs, she felt something rubbing her leg. She glanced out of the corner of her eye toward Harry, whose opposite hand shoveled fried potatoes into his mouth. She turned her head and faced him, but he stared straight into his plate as he ate. "Harry?" she asked.

Without looking, he answered. "Yes, Bess?"

"Please remove your hand from my thigh."

The seniors sitting at the table looked up and saw Harry's hand extending toward Elizabeth until it disappeared beneath the table. Jerry spit out his food and pushed his chair away from the table. "I can't take any more! Are you trying to kill me Harry?" Jerry threw his head back and laughed some more.

Lucinda produced her napkin from her lap and tossed it on her plate. "You are disgusting! Don't expect my company at dinner tonight!" Lucinda stood from the table and left. The other two men at the table grinned from ear to ear.

Elizabeth cleared her throat as she stood from the table and looked at Harry. "So, at the fireplace?"

A toothless smile consumed Harry's face. "Yes ma'am, at ten o'clock."

Elizabeth left her table and crossed the Community Room.

For weeks Elizabeth ate with the members of her assigned table. She initially detested Harry, and then grew to barely tolerate his crudeness and innuendos. Lately however, she awoke looking forward to breakfast and seeing him. Harry's demeanor toward Elizabeth never faltered, despite her singularly sharp responses to his comments. She enjoyed the bantering between Harry and Jerry, and finally allowed herself to venture from the cocoon in which she shrouded herself. Elizabeth hummed to herself as she crossed the room. She navigated between and around the dining tables toward the hallway, the smell of breakfast clinging to the still air.

No longer inhibited or pained by her hip replacement, Elizabeth walked slowly but confidently. As she neared the hallway she approached an old man who could have been ninety or could have been a hundred and ninety. She quickly approached the feeble old man but could not pass him due to the narrow space between the tables. She had seen the man dining many times, but had never been this close to him. He was very tall and gaunt. He hunched over an aluminum walker, clutching the handle with deformed arthritic knuckles. From her vantage point slightly to the man's side, Elizabeth saw his mouth agape, drool coating his pale lips. The man's bobbing head contained eyes that seemed to stare at nothing a million miles away. When he walked, his left foot dragged across the linoleum floor. His right foot shook and pointed inward as it scuffled forward.

Elizabeth's stomach twisted and her body tried to reject her breakfast. The background noise of pots and pans clanking in the kitchen grew louder until it was all she could hear. She had never met the man, but hated him for what he was. For showing her what she would become. Anxiety gripped Elizabeth like a plague. As she tried to pass she couldn't tear her eyes from his face. A single strand of drool clung to his chin and dangled to his chest, dancing with the motion of his bobbing head. The man's own eyes never left the floor directly in front of him.

Elizabeth's heart raced and stabbing pains through her chest constricted her breathing. Her *fight or flight* instinct bore down on her like a press. There was no one or no thing to fight, and the basic instinct of self-preservation caused Elizabeth to barrel through a small space between the man and a chair. Her brief respite from bitterness only a minute earlier blew away like dust in the wind.

She turned sideways, placing her back toward the old man. Her hip banged against a chair and sent it crashing to the floor. Her back brushed against the man first, and then his walker. In the recesses of her mind, Elizabeth hoped she didn't knock the man down. But at the height of her panic attack, her primary goal was to escape. For decades she had condemned life and welcomed the relief that death would afford her. But facing death's incarnation terrified her. The clanking in her head continued to block out everything else. She didn't hear the old man fall and didn't dare look back. Elizabeth dashed down the hall and ducked into her room, petrified that Death followed.

Elizabeth's hair stood on end from her frightful experience as she crawled into bed. Sleep came agonizingly slow and provided no relief from her terror. In her dream she stood alone in a bustling office. There were transparent people sitting at desks and walking back and forth. The silent apparitions didn't acknowledge Elizabeth's presence. The dark room was filled with cigarette smoke that Elizabeth could see but not smell. A teletype machine tapped feverishly in the corner with paper feeding itself through and landing in a heap on the floor. A deafening ticking sound forced Elizabeth's hands to her ears. She searched the room and located the source. An enormous clock with a white face and black numbers was mounted on the wall. The ear-splitting ticking was caused by the clock's second hand as it advanced. Elizabeth studied the clock closer. There were no hour or minute hands, and the clock was numbered backward. The second hand was a quarter way through its rotation, just passing the *nine*.

Elizabeth thought she recognized some of the ghosts in the office. As she concentrated to remember them, their faces faded to obscurity. The teletype continued spitting out paper and the faceless specters continued milling about. The second hand passed the six and the overbearing ticking sound diminished slightly. Elizabeth spun in circles as she looked from one ghost to another trying to identify them before their faces faded. The second hand passed three and the ticking noise in her head dulled even more. Elizabeth became dizzy from spinning and held on to a desk for balance, but her arm went right through the heavy oak desktop. She barely prevented herself from tumbling over when the clock struck twelve. As the twelve chimes enveloped the office, the apparitions disappeared one by one, leaving Elizabeth alone in the room.

The teletype machine *dinged* behind her. Elizabeth turned and saw Tessie gathering up the ribbon from the floor. Tessie neatly folded the ribbon and didn't seem to notice Elizabeth as she crossed the room.

"Tessie," called Elizabeth.

Tessie looked up and then returned to her papers.

"Tess, it's me, Elizabeth."

"I know. I'll be right with you."

Tessie looked satisfied as she completed putting the teletype ribbon in order. Elizabeth read the title at the top of the paper – 'Accepted to Heaven'.

"We're dead, aren't we?" asked Elizabeth.

"Of course," answered Tessie as she ran her finger down the list of names.

"But you're so young. What happened?" asked Elizabeth.

"It seems Benjamin had a bit of a temper," replied Tessie. She turned her head to the side and revealed a bloody mallet-sized hole littered with white skull fragments.

Elizabeth gasped as she placed a hand over her mouth.

"Uh-oh," said Tessie when she got half way through the list.

"I'm not on it, am I?" asked Elizabeth.

"Let's see,' replied Tessie. "Elizabeth Newsome, Elizabeth Newt, Elizabeth Newtown…No, I'm afraid not. But this isn't the final list."

As Tessie spoke, the teletype fired up again and spit out a short list. Tessie grabbed it and a smile crossed her face.

"Am I on it?" asked Elizabeth hopefully.

"No, but look who is." Tessie pointed to Theodore Haas' name. "You remember Theodore, don't you? *Tad* I think he began calling himself. Poor man, he doesn't even know it; he's not scheduled until tomorrow. He's out fishing right now. And at his age, can you believe it? You know you really blew it with him Elizabeth. He fell in love with you that night at Ocean House. He wanted to marry you, even after you…even after what happened. You shouldn't have shut him out."

Elizabeth looked down, no longer hearing Tessie. "Why?" sobbed Elizabeth. "Why can't I go to Heaven?" When Elizabeth looked up, Tessie was gone and her mother stood before her.

"That dress, Elizabeth," answered her mother. "What were you thinking? Huh, what were you thinking what were you thinking what were you thinking what were you thinking…" Clara Newton's words turned into hideous cackling and evolved into heinous laughter. Clara's head tilted back exposing her wide open mouth. Her teeth began falling out, her skin drew tightly across her bones and a repugnant smell assaulted Elizabeth as a half century of decomposition consumed her mother in a matter of seconds.

The final horror of her dream snapped Elizabeth awake. She was disoriented as the objects in her room slowly came into focus. Elizabeth collected herself in short order; such dreams were not uncommon for the old woman. Elizabeth took a deep breath and exhaled the remnants of her nightmare. She glanced at the clock on the wall, relieved to see the hours were numbered correctly. It was Thursday, and Nancy would arrive soon.

Time passed slowly for Elizabeth that afternoon. Her dream didn't disturb her, and she did not believe in signs or premonitions. The dream did however bring forth many memories from a distant past: Tessie, Benjamin, Theodore...the man who attacked her. Elizabeth frowned when she thought that if that happened today the police would catch the man who beat and raped her. Back then of course, there was the supposition that the woman *asked for it*. Not to mention the shame the victim brought to the family, and of course the fact that Elizabeth's family wasn't a contributing member of the Ocean House or the affluent Watch Hill community. Elizabeth wondered how many other "rich whores" had their lives ruined by wandering too far from the herd at Watch Hill.

Hunger gnawed at Elizabeth. Dinner would be served shortly, but she didn't want to miss Nancy. The unexpected thought struck Elizabeth as odd. Surely, Elizabeth told herself, she only feared missing Nancy's visit because she craved a fresh supply of crossword puzzles. The lie quickly revealed itself however. She knew Nancy would leave the magazines on the table even if Elizabeth wasn't in her room. The truth was Elizabeth enjoyed Nancy's company. She was in the Community Room eating dinner during Nancy's previous visit, and Nancy did indeed leave the crosswords on the table. Although Elizabeth told herself she was relieved that she wasn't subjected to the young woman's hard luck stories, she was sullen for the remainder of the evening. She would wait for Nancy.

Not much later Elizabeth heard soft knocks on the door. "Come in," she answered.

Nancy entered the room carrying her backpack over her shoulder and a brown paper bag at her side. "I'm sorry I'm late. I didn't want to miss you again." Nancy unslung her backpack and produced several magazines which she laid on the table. The backpack landed with a thud when she laid it on the floor. She set the paper bag on the table next to the magazines.

Nancy eyed Elizabeth with uncertainty. "Are you feeling alright?" she asked.

"I'm alive, if that's what you mean," answered Elizabeth. "Why are you looking at me like that?"

"When I signed in," began Nancy, "the receptionist told me you had some type of stroke or something last week. Are you feeling better?"

Elizabeth had nearly forgotten about the episode with LaShawna. "I heard about that," said Elizabeth. "I don't know what those people are talking about. I was doing my crosswords when the door burst open. The EMT stood there looking like he was expecting to find a corpse, and the woman, what's her name? Oh yeah, LaShawna. She stood behind him looking like she'd seen a ghost. The entire incident upset me a great deal."

Nancy crossed the room to Elizabeth and sat beside her on the bed. "I'm sorry; there must have been some mistake." Nancy noticed Elizabeth's smile. "What a minute. You did that, didn't you? You tricked her."

"What do I know," replied Elizabeth. "I'm an old woman. What's in the bag?"

"I brought us dinner. I hope you like Chinese. Let me help you up."

Elizabeth allowed Nancy to help her off the bed and they sat at the table. Nancy dug out the tin trays and plastic forks. "I got it from Peking Kitchen. They make the best General Tso's chicken in Groton." Concern crossed Nancy's face. "Can you eat spicy food?"

"What's it going to do, shorten my lifespan," quipped Elizabeth. Elizabeth hadn't eaten Chinese food in twenty years. When she lifted the plastic cover off the tray and smelled the rich aroma, hunger pangs set her stomach on fire. She couldn't get the first forkful into her mouth fast enough. She heard Nancy talking in the background, but intently devoured the meal.

"My mother and I got dinner from Peking every Saturday night for years. Then last year they closed. It was terrible!" Nancy's face wrinkled as though recalling an awful tragedy. "But then they re-opened on Route 12. Thank God!"

"Sorry I missed you last week," said Elizabeth. "I wasn't sure you were going to come."

Nancy looked away from the table. "Yeah, I had some other plans, but I canceled them. Do you like your dinner?"

Elizabeth was going to ask about the bandage that was previously wrapped around Nancy's wrist, but reconsidered. "It's very good. I don't have any money, you know."

Nancy's face flushed. "I don't want you to pay me. I just thought you might like something different."

"That is very thoughtful, thank you. What's in the bag there?" asked Elizabeth, pointing to the floor.

"That's why I've been coming later," answered Nancy. "I signed up for adult education classes so I can get my high school diploma. Then I want to go to college. I want to study nursing, or maybe teaching. I'm not sure yet."

Elizabeth wiped the soy sauce from around her lips and studied Nancy. She wore an attractive button down blouse and a pair of pressed khaki pants. Her hair was pulled back into a pony tail and she wore…

"Are you wearing makeup?" asked Elizabeth.

Nancy's face turned beet red. "Does it look terrible? I'll go wash it off." Nancy pushed her chair back when Elizabeth grabbed her arm.

"Don't be ridiculous! It looks very nice. Why the sudden change in appearance?" asked Elizabeth.

Elizabeth watched with amusement as Nancy struggled for words. "Let me help," offered Elizabeth. "If a decrepit old soul like me who has no purpose for living can still wake up and go on every day, then a young woman such as you has no excuse for quitting. Something like that?"

Incredulous denial crossed Nancy's face. "No, not at all!" But even as Nancy shook her head she saw Elizabeth smile. The two women shared silent understanding and then laughed together as they cleaned up from their dinner.

Descent

Elizabeth trounced through the fallen leaves as she and her father walked to the Packer Building. They began their journey, as usual, about five o'clock in the morning to make the seven o'clock whistle. Still a mile from the plant, Phil Miller slowed his truck as he approached Elizabeth and William. When he was abreast of the two walkers, William waved him on. Phil honked his horn as he accelerated down the dirt road. William set a hard pace to make the six miles in two hours, but Elizabeth never complained. Until today.

"Father," sighed Elizabeth. "Why won't you let Mr. Miller give us a ride to work?"

William pulled up his collar to ward off the increasing wind. "I've told you before you can ride with him any time you like."

Elizabeth shook her head. "You know I'm not going to ride and leave you walking by yourself. You're just being stubborn."

"No I'm not. But it's not Phil's fault that my truck's broken. Besides, I should have enough money to fix it next month."

"I didn't say it was Mr. Miller's fault." Elizabeth leaned forward into the headwind. "If Mr. Miller's truck was broke, and yours wasn't, would you offer him a ride?"

"Yup."

"Would you be offended if he refused?" asked Elizabeth.

"Yup."

"Then why won't you let him give you a ride?"

William considered for a moment and then shrugged his shoulders. "That's just the way I am."

Twenty minutes later the two emerged from the sticks onto Route One in Mystic. William broke the silence. "What do you think of your new secretary job? Beats operating the wrapping machine, don't it?"

Elizabeth smiled. "I'll say! I thought I would lose my mind operating that press all day. It was so boring! I don't know how anyone can-" Elizabeth stopped herself, already ashamed of what she'd said. The lye injection machine that her father operated required as little mental capacity as did the wrapping machine.

Elizabeth's eyes dropped to the ground. "I'm sorry."

William wrapped a large arm around his daughter. "That's okay, don't worry about it. It's not farming, but it's getting us by for now. Something better will come along soon."

Happy to be inside, Elizabeth hugged her father. "See you at lunch?"

William smiled as he punched in. "Wouldn't miss it. Have a nice morning."

Elizabeth had never loved or admired her father more as she watched him walk down the passageway. He never complained about losing the farm, or not having enough money to fix his truck, or working in this sweat shop. He never even complained about Clara's behavior, which had grown increasingly disturbing since returning from New York.

A young man approached Elizabeth as she turned to hang her coat. "Good morning Miss Newton."

Elizabeth turned and smiled when she recognized Toby Garfield. "How many times do I have to tell you to call me 'Elizabeth'? Did you find out if you got promoted?"

Toby blushed and looked at the floor. He couldn't have been more than twenty years old, and traces of adolescent acne still dotted his face. Elizabeth bit her lip to stop from giggling when she thought that the pimples were probably caused by Packer's Tar Soap, the cure-all for skin disorders. Toby was average height and skinny, and always flustered when he entered the administrative office to greet Elizabeth. Elizabeth thought he was cute.

"No, Miss...I mean Elizabeth. I'm afraid to ask about the promotion. I don't want Mr. Shrew to think I'm being pushy."

Elizabeth smiled at the thought of Toby being pushy.

"There's something I've been meaning to ask you," said Toby. The color again rose in his cheeks. "You know I've been stopping in and seeing you for a while now." Toby stammered as he fought to find the words. "Well, you wouldn't want to go to the races with me Sunday, would you? I mean, if you're busy I understand. You're probably busy, sorry I asked."

Although Elizabeth guiltily enjoyed Toby's discomfort, she graciously ended his suffering. "I thought you would never ask. Of course I'll go with you. You can pick me up after church."

"Really? That's great!" Relief and excitement spread across the young man's face.

A voice roared behind Toby as he backed away from Elizabeth. "Are you punched in, Garfield?"

Toby's slight frame jumped as he backed into Mr. Shrew. "Yes sir."

"Then get to work! This ain't the way to get promoted!" bellowed Shrew.

Toby skirted the large man and dashed from the office. Mr. Shrew tipped his hat to Elizabeth and followed after Toby.

Snow flurries dusted the air during the walk home that afternoon. Elizabeth was excited about her date but she was afraid to tell her father. They had grown closer than ever, and she feared that he would not approve.

William finally forced her hand. "You might as well tell me what's got you floating on air, Little Me. I expected you to yell at me the whole way home about the snow. Instead, you're singing and skipping along like a little girl."

Before Elizabeth had a chance to plan her words, she blurted it out. "Toby Garfield asked me to go to the races with him. I hope you're not mad at me." Elizabeth's eyes pleaded with her father.

William's stride didn't skip a beat. "Mad at you? Lordy, it's about time, that's what I say. You've done nothing but get under my feet since you've been home. A man my age needs a little space now and again."

Elizabeth's heart sank and she stopped dead in her tracks. She grabbed her father's shoulder and spun him around. As she looked to his face, his lips and eyes smiled down at her. "I think that's wonderful," said William. He drew Elizabeth to him and hugged her tightly. They embraced for a long minute before he let her go. "I've seen him around, but I don't really know him. Is he nice?"

Elizabeth gabbed the rest of the way home about Toby: how shy he is, how he wants to be foreman someday, how he brought her wildflowers a week earlier, how he makes her feel special. Elizabeth even confided to her father how Toby makes her forget about *what happened*.

As they walked up the lane to the house, William pulled Elizabeth aside. "Maybe it's best if you don't mention anything about the boy or your date to your mother just yet. Let me talk to her first."

Elizabeth nodded and the two hung their coats and entered the cold dark kitchen. "Clara," called William. "We're home." Receiving no response, they walked to the parlor. Clara knitted on the sofa. "No dinner tonight?" asked William. Clara continued knitting without answering. "Clara?"

Clara Newton hurled the ball of yarn across the room at her husband, a trail of twine following in its wake. "I guess you don't consider that turkey in the oven dinner! With you two off all day doing God knows what, I have to take care of this whole farm myself. Milking, feeding. It's too much! And what thanks do I get? You make a joke of me not having dinner on the table when you see it right there when you walked in!"

William nodded to Elizabeth to go up to her room. As Elizabeth crossed the parlor her mother called her. "Good Evening Dear. How was work today? I hate the thought of you working with all those dirty old men, but I'm so proud of you. Do you like the sweater I'm knitting for Ethan?" Clara held up the tiny sweater. "Although I don't know why you're so certain it's a boy. Look how high you're carrying," said Clara as she pointed to Elizabeth's flat stomach. "That's a girl you're baking in there, mark my words. That's why the sweater is yellow and not blue. Did you have enough dinner? You're eating for two now, don't forget."

"Yes Ma'am," replied Elizabeth softly as she climbed the stairs.

William and Elizabeth returned from church services late Sunday morning. Before New York, Clara practically had to pry William from his chores to get him to attend. Since returning however, William hadn't missed a single service. Clara withdrew from society and her family more with each passing week and hadn't attended church in months.

"Clara," called William. "Lorraine Judson sent home dinner for us. Said they had so much left over from Thanksgiving that it would go bad before they could eat it all. She handed out trays of food like they were going out of style."

William and Elizabeth exchanged glances. The food did come from Mrs. Judson, but it wasn't leftovers. People began inquiring about Clara's absences from social gatherings and William took to telling them that she had the flu. *And,* William told them, *please don't be offended, but the doctor said she shouldn't have any visitors. She needs all the rest she can get.* William mentioned to Clara several times that Doc Allyn should swing by and give her a checkup, but she launched into a tirade at the suggestion. William knew the time was quickly approaching that something had to be done. His hope that his wife would snap out of it was quickly fading.

William popped his head into the parlor. "Will you join us for lunch, Dear?"

Clara sat on the sofa holding her knitting needles and staring out the front window. "I need more yarn. The baby will be here soon and she needs more clothes." Clara held up a completed pink booty in one hand and a half-finished booty in the other.

"Clara, you've been on that couch for three days. I told you I can't get more yarn until tomorrow. You have to snap out of it! I can't stand seeing you like this!"

Elizabeth heard the exchange from the kitchen as she set the table. The time spent watching his wife's mental condition deteriorate was taking a heavy toll on her father, but Elizabeth had never before seen him show his emotional stress in front of her mother. When William raised his voice, Clara began hyperventilating and begged him to stop.

"Please don't hit me! I'm sorry, please don't beat me again!" whimpered Clara.

Elizabeth entered the parlor as her father crossed the room to comfort her mother. As he neared her, she curled into a fetal position and tried to ward him off with her hand. "Please, no, I won't do it again. I'm sorry I broke the eggs. The chickens got excited when I was leaving the coop and made me trip. Please don't…" Clara buried her face in her hands and sobbed.

William backed away from Clara with tears in his eyes. Elizabeth patted his back and joined him in the kitchen. "What's wrong with her, Father?"

William fought to control his emotions. After several minutes he said, "I don't know. Maybe guilt. Maybe something I did. Maybe something that happened before I met her. Maybe something that would have happened anyway. I don't know what to do. I can't breathe in here right now; I'm going for a walk. Fix your mother a plate."

Elizabeth's look told her father that she wouldn't eat it. Her father's look told her to do it anyway. "Try to have a good time this afternoon. I'll be back before you get home."

As excited as Elizabeth was about her afternoon with Toby, she had completely forgotten about it since they'd arrived home. She kissed her father on the cheek and asked if he was alright. William nodded and left through the back door.

Elizabeth prepared a plate for her mother and brought it to her. Her mother sat upright, making knitting motions with the needles. "Here Mother, I brought you some food. You have to eat, okay?" Clara continued clanking the needles together without responding as Elizabeth set the plate down next to her. Leaving for work before sunrise and arriving home after dark, Elizabeth rarely saw her mother during the day. But the crisp autumn sun brightly filled the room. For the first time Elizabeth realized how pale and drawn her mother had become. Elizabeth put a hand on her mother's shoulder. "You know there's no yarn, don't you? What are you doing?"

Clara began humming. "Hush little baby, don't say a word. Poppa's gonna buy you a mockingbird. If that mockingbird won't sing…"

Suddenly claustrophobia overcame Elizabeth and she knew exactly how her father felt only minutes earlier. She needed air, needed to escape. She kissed her mother's cheek and bolted outside. Although Toby wouldn't arrive for another hour, Elizabeth walked to the end of the lane and waited for him.

How do we cope when life deals the most dastardly cards imaginable? How do you paint the window trim a week after your son dies in battle? How do you fold laundry after your daughter gets the fever and dies before her first true love? How do you watch your mother's mind deteriorate in front of you and go on a date? How do you bury your bride and go to work the next morning? An outsider looks in and asks "How can he bear that burden?"

You have faith. You have resilience. You have the internal instinct and fortitude to survive. When time distances us from the unthinkable, we say "I don't know how I ever got through that."

But we do.
And we will.

The Races

Elizabeth dwelled over her mother while she waited for Toby. Her father's words haunted her. '*Maybe guilt,*' he said. Elizabeth hated her parents when she found out they arranged to have her child taken from her. She had no hate for them now, however. She still thought what they did was horrible, but she understood their actions and reconciled herself with them.

It was guilt, thought Elizabeth, *but all mine. I did this to her*. Elizabeth walked back toward the house to check on her mother a dozen times while she waited for Toby. To tell her it was all her fault, not her mother's. But invariably she returned to the road.

Elizabeth was relieved that she became excited as each vehicle crested the hill toward her, thinking it might be Toby. She worried that she would not be able to shake her guilt and concern for her mother, and therefore ruin the afternoon. She liked Toby and felt comfortable around him. She knew that she wanted, and needed to get out of the house for a while. She had no friends, and only left the house to go to work, church, and market. Elizabeth grew concerned as the afternoon dragged by; surely Toby should have been there already. She worried that something happened to Toby. She honestly worried that he changed his mind about seeing her.

Just before returning to the house, a horse and buggy kicked up dust at the bottom of the road. As the rig neared, Elizabeth recognized the driver as Toby. "Whoa, Sadie," ordered Toby as he drew up on the reins. "Miss…Elizabeth, I'm sorry as all get-out about this, and I'll understand if you don't want to go. My Daddy told me I could use the truck today, but then something came up and he had to take it to Westerly."

Elizabeth walked up to Sadie and patted the big work horse's cheek. "You're a pretty girl, aren't you? Are you up for the ride to Groton?"

Toby smiled with relief as he jumped down from the rig. He grabbed Elizabeth's hand and, bringing it to his lips, kissed it. "Thanks Elizabeth. Let me help you up." Toby placed his hand on the small of Elizabeth's back as she stepped up to the rig. Toby darted to the driver's side and climbed aboard.

"You're not supposed to make a young lady wait," chided Elizabeth.

Toby blushed as he looked at Elizabeth, uncertain if she was teasing him or angry. "I'm really sorry…"

Elizabeth grabbed Toby's hand and squeezed it. "I'm kidding. It's okay, really. I was worried you weren't going to show up."

Toby looked at Elizabeth and saw the sincerity in her eyes. "Heck, I would have tied the hound dogs to the rig if that was the only way I had to get here. I've been looking forward to this all week."

Elizabeth unwittingly pictured Toby pulling up to her lane with a pack of dogs pulling the rig, and Toby's face beet red, apologizing. She laughed at the mental picture, allowing temporary relief from the heavy cloak of sadness enveloping her. Worried that Toby would be offended by her laughter, she reached over and slid her hand into his. Toby looked at Elizabeth from the corners of his eyes and smiled, clutching her hand firmly.

The two rode in silence through the country roads until they reached Route 184. Elizabeth felt alive for the first time since returning from her uncle's house. She didn't realize the toll the situation at home took on her until she was removed from it. As much as she enjoyed spending time with her father, the dark cloud surrounding him was constant; and it grew more ominous every day. Elizabeth's head never stopped turning. She wanted to burn every moment into her memory, to draw on during bleaker days.

"Will we miss the races?" asked Elizabeth.

Elizabeth's unexpected words startled Toby, causing him to jump. "Some, but this is the last race of the season so everyone will be there. They'll probably race 'till dark. My cousin races there. I want to introduce you to him."

"That sounds fine," replied Elizabeth. "I have something to tell you, and I don't want you to laugh."

Uncertainty crossed Toby's face. "You can tell me anything. I promise I won't laugh."

Elizabeth drew in a deep breath. "This is my first date. Well, since I was in grade school anyway."

Toby snorted and an odd grin twisted his mouth. "Really?" he asked, raising an eyebrow. "This is my first time too."

Elizabeth didn't understand Toby's reaction. "What do you mean? Have you not had any dates before?"

Toby released Elizabeth's hand as he pulled the reins to turn Sadie onto Old North Road. "Have you ever been to the races?" asked Toby.

Elizabeth was uncomfortable with Toby changing the subject so suddenly. Something unspoken had just happened and she didn't know what to make of it. However, she was afraid to do anything that would jeopardize the beautiful day and didn't pursue it. *Besides*, she rationalized, *Toby is very shy. He's probably just uncomfortable speaking of such things.*

"My parents brought me once, when I was very little. I don't remember much about it, except that they raced horses back then, not cars. Oh, and I remember the smell of fried sausage and tons of people cheering and yelling at the horses."

A boyish smile crept back to Toby's face. "Well, except for the cars, nothing else has changed. I come most weeks. So do a lot of the guys from work."

Elizabeth so enjoyed the buggy ride that she hadn't considered who else she might see at the races. She lost contact with her friends from school and didn't socialize with anyone at work. In fact, it almost seemed as though her co-workers made a point of steering clear of her. Perhaps that was one reason she liked Toby so much. Still unwilling to allow anything to ruin the day, Elizabeth shrugged her worries aside.

Toby drew in the reins when they reached Fort Hill Road. Cars and trucks lined the road, and groups of people milled about. Younger children ran around playing tag. Older boys passed footballs; girls huddled around sneaking peaks and giggling at the boys who showed off.

"I think there are hitching posts behind the school," said Toby. He urged Sadie across the street and parked the rig between two other buggies behind Fitch High School. Toby jumped down and tied the rig off, then helped Elizabeth dismount. "Ready?" he asked.

Elizabeth nodded as she stepped off the buggy into Toby's hands.

§

The two emerged from behind the high school, Elizabeth inhaling the afternoon like a breath of fresh air. Toby led Elizabeth by her hand through the crowd of children playing toward the ticket booth. A man greeted them as they approached the roped-off gate.

"Running a little late today Toby?" asked the man.

"Yes sir, Mr. Hauxhurst," replied Toby. "Had to bring Sadie. My father had to take the truck to Westerly to get a clutch for his tractor."

"I see. Who is this lovely young lady?" asked Mr. Hauxhurst, tipping his hat to Elizabeth.

Toby released Elizabeth's hand and let his slide to his side. "Oh, this is Miss Newton, from the factory."

"Well Toby," began Mr. Hauxhurst. "Looks like you've got yourself a fine woman there. Better treat her right!"

Toby looked around nervously. "Don't worry, I will."

Mr. Hauxhurst looked from side to side. "Well kids, the races are almost over. I don't see the need to charge you. Enjoy yourselves now. Oh, Matthew and Lucas said to tell you they'd be at turn three."

"Alright, thanks. Send my best to Mrs. Hauxhurst."

Toby and Elizabeth entered the stands as Mr. Hauxhurst unhooked the chain. Toby scanned the crowd and pointed to a group of people in the stands. "Look, there's the boys!" he exclaimed. Toby jumped up and whistled, waving to his friends. When they saw him and hollered back, Toby made an elaborate pointing motion toward Elizabeth.

Elizabeth pulled on Toby's arm and stopped him. Toby saw Elizabeth's concerned look and the grin left his face.

"Toby," began Elizabeth. "Why did you let go of my hand back there?"

"What do you mean? I didn't." Elizabeth's eyes told Toby she expected an answer. Toby looked at the ground and his face grew red. "Well, I'm just kind of embarrassed. Mr. Hauxhurst is like an uncle to me, and he's never seen me with a girl before. I'm sorry."

Elizabeth kept her eyes fixed on Toby. She knew he was shy and nervous around her at work, but this seemed different. She wanted to tell him that she wanted a man who was proud to be seen with her, but let it go.

Toby reached down and held Elizabeth's hand. As they walked through the crowd she noticed that Toby seemed to hold her hand straight down, not swinging it freely like he did when they left the buggy. *You're paranoid*, Elizabeth told herself. *It's your imagination.*

The infield sparked to life as the drivers started their cars for the final race. The engines revved, blowing carbon from the spark plugs as they jockeyed into their starting positions on the track. Toby said something to Elizabeth, but she couldn't hear him above the roar from the engines. He pulled her along quickly toward the stands where his friends were. They climbed the rows of bleachers and made their way to an open space on the wooden bench. Elizabeth recognized a couple of the men from work, but most of Toby's friends were unfamiliar to her. "Attaboy!" shouted one man as he patted Toby on his back. "Go for it Toby!" yelled another. Toby grinned and stole a look at them out of the corner of his eye but didn't otherwise acknowledge them.

"What's all that about?" asked Elizabeth.

"Aw, they're just being jerks," replied Toby over the din of the engines. "Hey look! They're about to start." Toby pointed to a man carrying a white flag walking onto the track in front of the lead cars. "See the number seven car, that yellow Chevy? That's my cousin Rodney. I'll take you to meet him. You know, *after*."

"After what?" asked Elizabeth.

Toby didn't hear her above the engines and yelling spectators. *Or pretended not to hear*, thought Elizabeth. "Go get 'em, Rod!" yelled Toby.

The man on the track jumped up and down frantically waving the flag, then ran off to the infield as twenty drivers gunned their engines. A massive dust cloud from the dirt track obscured their vision. Elizabeth felt Toby's hand on her back. She looked at him to find him staring at her.

"You are the most beautiful woman I've ever seen," said Toby earnestly.

Elizabeth smiled at him. And felt good.

"You want to get out of here? Maybe take a walk?" he asked.

Elizabeth looked confused. "What about the races? Don't you want to see your cousin?"

"I like the races, but I really just wanted to spend time with you today. Let's go."

Elizabeth was relieved to be leaving Toby's friends. He acted differently around them, and the noise from the cars was giving her a headache. She let Toby lead her from the stands and out of the track area. They walked behind the high school, but circled around the waiting Sadie. "I know a great place we can walk. Ever been to Bluff Point?"

Elizabeth shook her head.

"I'll show you." Toby led her down a dirt road past some marshes. They crossed under a railroad bridge where the marshes opened up to a cove. A large swan flapped his wings and hissed at them when they approached too close to his family. When Elizabeth shied away Toby put his arm around Elizabeth's waist. "Don't worry, I'll protect you," smiled Toby. The dirt road dwindled to a path that veered slightly inland. Large oak trees lined the path, with huge boulders randomly placed along the hillside. The forest was ancient and Elizabeth felt transcended in time. "Look," whispered Toby. He placed his finger over his lips and pointed up the hillside. Elizabeth followed his gaze to a magnificent buck with a full rack staring at them from between two trees. The instant Elizabeth focused on the deer he vanished into the woods like he was never there at all.

Elizabeth fell in love with the area. They walked for another twenty minutes when they began to climb a rocky hill. Toby's hand slipped from her waist and held her hand to help her up. Elizabeth stumbled on the loose rocks, but Toby prevented her from falling. When she regained her footing she looked up. Long Island Sound came into full view and stole her breath. The beauty and expanse of the Sound caused Elizabeth's heart to flutter.

"Nice, isn't it?" asked Toby. "I come up here by myself sometimes and just sit. You can see the New London ferry coming from here, but I don't know when it runs."

Elizabeth inhaled the fresh salt air. The smell attempted to stir painful memories of Watch Hill, but she fought them back. The bluff was so peaceful and sitting so high that Elizabeth felt as though she was looking down on the world instead of being part of it. They sat in silence for several minutes when Toby's hand slid up from her waist to the side of her chest. She absently placed her hand on his to stop him, unsure if he was even aware that his hand came close to her private area.

To Elizabeth's surprise, Toby forced his hand further and squeezed her breast. Her reverie instantly broken, Elizabeth pushed his hand off her and jumped up. "What are you doing?" she demanded.

Toby smiled. "Why are you acting like that? You know that's what we came here for. Everybody knows you're easy and that you went away to have a kid. Come on now, let's do it." Toby stepped closer and shot his arm around Elizabeth. He drew her to him and pressed his lips against hers. Elizabeth felt his excitement against her. Elizabeth brought her hands up between her and Toby and pressed him away. As soon as she had room, she swung her arm back and slapped his face with all her might.

Toby's face turned a deep purple. Not with embarrassment, but with anger. "You little slut, how dare you!"

Elizabeth's heart broke. Her uncle was right after all. She turned to run and heard Toby laboring closely behind her. She felt his breath on her neck. Near the bottom of the bluff she slipped and sprawled face first in the gravel. Toby was on her in an instant and flipped her over, tearing at her dress. Elizabeth turned and twisted beneath him, but the insanity in his eyes gave him the strength to thwart her efforts.

"You're going to make me a man today, everybody knows it!" yelled Toby through his slobber. He tore her dress down the front and pulled it up from the bottom.

As Toby fumbled with the front of his trousers, Elizabeth flailed beneath him. Her hand came across a fist-sized rock. She clutched it tightly and slammed it against the side of Toby's head. Toby cried out and tumbled off Elizabeth. Elizabeth scrambled to her feet and ran down the path. Toby yelled after her. "Come back here! You're dead! We did it, you hear me? You better not tell nobody no different. We did it!"

Elizabeth ran and ran. Her dress was torn and her face and nose were bleeding from the fall, but she felt no pain. She didn't feel anything. It was dark by the time she came to Fort Hill Road. Only a few men from the races remained, huddled in packs and drinking beer. Elizabeth avoided them and, out of breath, began the long cold walk home.

TV Repairman

The table's occupants ate quietly, sullenly as Elizabeth scooted her way through the Community Room toward them. Although Elizabeth felt her bitter edge softening, she endeavored to maintain her harsh external disposition. She no longer needed Mrs. Nedbetter to steer her toward her regular table. She looked forward to Harry and Jerry's bantering, Bart's introspective and unexpected insights, and even Lucinda's haughtiness. Ann bragged about her family although, amidst her bragging, Elizabeth detected a concealed hollowness that she couldn't quite place. Ann never offered much to the conversation, but Elizabeth liked her just the same. Ann was not at the table however, although it was not uncommon for any of the diners to miss a meal now and then, particularly lunch.

Harry did not stand up when Elizabeth approached the table, but slid her chair out from the table for her. "Howdy Bess," he said. "We missed you at breakfast this morning. Is everything alright?"

"Fine," replied Elizabeth. "I wasn't very hungry this morning, and I didn't feel the greatest. It's passed though." The occupants offered greetings without looking up from their plates. Although the diners at the table focused on moving pasta around their plates, Elizabeth noticed that no one had actually eaten very much. She cut her spaghetti, afraid that perhaps it was poorly prepared and that was the cause of the somber tones and lack of appetites. She chewed cautiously, but the food tasted fine. Elizabeth normally ate all three meals every day. Her stomach growled and gurgled from skipping breakfast as she swallowed her first forkful of spaghetti. Distracted by her hunger, she devoured half her plate before she came up for air. She sat back for a moment to let her lunch digest. The black cloud lingering over the table starved the area of air. The other diners placed their napkins and silverware on their mostly full plates. For lack of anything better to say, Elizabeth asked if anyone had heard from Ann. Lucinda and Bart excused themselves from the table without responding, leaving Harry, Jerry and Elizabeth.

"Oh my goodness," said Elizabeth. "Is Ann alright?"

"Not really, Bess," replied Harry. Then, after thinking how that came across, he clarified himself. "Well, she's not sick, or dead. She's...upset, in a bad way.

Jerry piped in. "She's the devil. If I was fifty or sixty years younger I'd take care of her myself. Still might."

Harry saw confusion cross Elizabeth's face. "He doesn't mean Ann, Lord no. He's talking about Dora, one of the orderlies here. Dora is evil! She does things to the residents - unspeakable things. I haven't heard anything for a while, but she got Ann last night. Lucy went to get Ann for breakfast this morning. When she didn't answer her door she opened it and went inside Ann's room. Her bed was empty and Lucy thought the worst. But then she saw Ann curled in a ball in the corner of her room, whimpering like a baby."

Elizabeth shivered at the memory of her own experiences with Dora. "That poor woman," said Elizabeth. "What did she do?"

Harry shook his head and wrinkled his mouth in disgust. "What *hasn't* she done to most of us in here at one time or another? She's *sick*, Elizabeth. Sick, but cagey. She doesn't do things that can come back to her. It's all psychological warfare. Ann told Lucy that she was restless sleeping last night. At one point she opened her eyes. Right in front of her face, so close she could feel the monster's breath, was a hideous face all cut up with blood dripping down and long matted black hair hanging down around its shoulders. Ann said the monster waited a couple seconds for the image to sink in and then started screaming right in her face. Ann was horrified and finally managed to scream in terror. When she did, the monster's screams turned into a cackle – Dora's cackle. Then Dora pulled off her mask and left Ann's room, telling her how much fun it is scaring us old people."

"My God!" said Elizabeth. "Hasn't anyone ever told on her?"

"Of course, at first," replied Harry. "But you see how she does it. No one can prove anything, and then she makes it worse on them that tell."

"Will Ann be alright?" asked Elizabeth.

"I think so. That would be horrifying to anyone, and Ann is more sensitive than most of us. She'll be alright in a day or two I suppose."

Jerry pushed his chair back from the table. "If you two will excuse me, I'm going to my room. I'm in a terrible mood and I'm not very good company."

Harry and Elizabeth bid Jerry well and sat in silence as the cafeteria workers began clearing the empty tables around the room. Elizabeth finally broke the quiet. "How come you stopped asking me to meet you after dinner?"

Harry considered for a moment. "Well, you know I like to joke around and flirt with a lot of the women in here, as ridiculous as that sounds at my age. But it makes me feel good. That's how it was with you, at first. But then I really became interested in you. Not like *that*, but just really interested in what you might have to say. I waited by the fireplace that night you said you would meet me. Waited for hours in fact, and that gave me a lot of time to think. And what I thought was that maybe it's time for me to grow up. You know, time to stop acting the fool. If I ask a lady to meet me once, maybe even twice, and she says no, then I should respect that."

Elizabeth remembered her own encounter with Dora the night she agreed to meet Harry. And felt even sorrier for Ann. "Why don't you ask me one more time. Some ladies don't know when to say yes."

Harry stood and pulled Elizabeth's chair out for her. He locked his elbow with Elizabeth's and escorted her toward the main foyer. "I'd be honored," Harry told Elizabeth. Elizabeth smiled as Harry escorted her out the front doors of Bayside.

§

"Are you cold?" Harry asked Elizabeth as they crossed the parking lot and walked toward Route 1.

Elizabeth shivered slightly. "Yes, but it feels wonderful. This is the first time I've been outside since I've been here."

"Well, we'll have to see that you don't go that long without fresh air again. I sneak out all the time."

"You sneak out? You mean we're not allowed to leave?" asked Elizabeth.

"We can leave anytime we want to, but we're supposed to sign out. I know it's dumb, but it's fun trying to sneak out without them catching me. They didn't even notice us leaving just now. Everyone is busy cleaning up from lunch and getting their afternoon rounds done. They get mad when they catch me sneaking back in and notice I didn't sign out, but what are they going to do to me. Pathetic really, but my entertainment options are fairly limited at this point."

Elizabeth smiled as she pictured Harry waiting for his moment of opportunity to sneak out the front doors. "Harry, I want to apologize for how I acted when I first-"

Harry interrupted her. "No apology necessary. Who has ambitions of living at Bayside when they're young and have the world by the balls...excuse me, by the hair. Most of us are alone in there. Sure, we get the occasional obligatory visit. But for the most part our relatives are busy carving their own way through life. Plus, it scares people coming here. Show's them where they might end up. Can't say I did any better when I was young and my mother was in a home. For me it was worse visiting nursing homes when I was younger than it is living in one now." Harry scratched his chin. "And that's saying something, 'cause it *sucks*!"

Elizabeth smiled. "It really does, doesn't it?" The two walked north on Route 1 in silence. They passed an apartment complex, a shopping center, a large turn-of-the century white church which sat out of place on a small corner lot. Elizabeth breathed deeply, enjoying the fresh air. Walking quickly warmed her and she felt *connected*. "What did you do, before?"

"Before I had no usefulness left in me?" Harry replied with an edge to his voice. Before Elizabeth could respond, Harry continued. "I'm sorry. Being outside today, walking with you, almost makes me forget how old I am and that I really have nothing left to accomplish in my life."

With their elbows still locked, Elizabeth placed her right hand over Harry's. She stopped walking and turned to face Harry. "Don't give up yet old timer. You've accomplished something wonderful for me today."

Harry stared back into Elizabeth's eyes and patted her hand. "Come on now, quit lolli-gagging."

Elizabeth let the moment pass and they continued walking. After a few minutes Harry said, "I repaired televisions. Zenith, Phillips, RCA, all of them, right in Groton City. I was the best around, and I'm not just saying that either. Nowadays televisions are disposable. It costs more to fix them than it does to repair them. That wasn't always the case though. I was the first in the area, back when the sets had transistors, tubes, wiring. And forget about the detailed schematics they have now, shoot! I learned some about electronics when I was in the Army and that's how I got the job down town. I had a knack for it. And you know what? I *loved* it! Back then we knew what customer service was and we went to the houses to make service calls. Now the stores act like they're doing you a favor by taking your money! Every time the owner sent me to a house to fix a TV it was like me and the set going to war with each other. And when I lost, which was only three times, I took it *hard*! Yup, for fifty-two years I fixed TVs.

Elizabeth enjoyed listening to Harry talk so much that she hated it when he stopped. "You know Harry, if I was a younger woman…"

Harry's face lit up like a lighthouse. "That TV repairman line gets the ladies every time!"

Before Elizabeth realized it she looked up and stared right at a large brick building. "The high school," she whispered.

Harry followed Elizabeth's eyes. "Nope, not for some time anyway. It's Fitch Middle School now. High school is up at the top of Fort Hill."

Elizabeth closed her eyes. Whatever the building was used for now, the field just past the building was where Toby took her to the races about a million years ago. Or it could have been last week. Now small slab homes occupied the grounds surrounding the school. Harry's voice brought Elizabeth back from the eighty years she just transcended. "Built all those homes during the Big One, WW-2 that is, to house all the government contractors building ships. Now they're mostly low-income housing." Harry noticed Elizabeth's ominous silence. "You okay? Tired?" Elizabeth shook her head. "Good," said Harry. "I just want to walk a little further to Bluff Point. It's really pretty down there, serene."

Elizabeth's legs began to buckle as she relived Toby's attack on her. From deep in the recesses of her mind she heard Harry calling to her. His voice again pulled her back to the present. Elizabeth's legs regained their strength and she felt the weight borne from decades of resentment and anger lift from her shoulders.

Harry was concerned. "I better get you back, you don't look so good."

Elizabeth smiled. "Don't think you're getting out of it that easily. Let's go." They walked down the sidewalk and under the railroad bridge where the road turned into dirt and gravel. With the murky tidal water on their right, Elizabeth said, "You know, men can be such jerks sometimes."

Harry considered before replying. "Yup. I reckon we can be."

The Explosion

It was after nine o'clock when Elizabeth climbed the back stoop to her house. Her teeth chattered from the freezing cold. Her nose throbbed from the fall at the bluff, and the shallow abrasions on her face screamed like a thousand pin pricks. She knew she would have to face the people at work in the morning, but her thoughts during the agonizing trek home focused on getting past her parents and into bed. Her father expected her home earlier and she hoped he wasn't too worried. She didn't know if her mother would have even realized she was gone all day.

Elizabeth stole through the back door and crossed the kitchen. Her mother sat in the dark in the parlor and didn't look up when Elizabeth told her good night. Elizabeth prayed her father was asleep, although it surprised her that he wasn't sitting with her mother waiting for her to return. She slipped up the stairs and closed the door to the washroom behind her. She leaned against the wall, and although she was relieved at avoiding her father, she sobbed as she relived the day's events. *I should have known*, thought Elizabeth. *I should have known when Toby got that nasty look on his face and told me it was his first time too. I did know! I just didn't want to believe it.* Exhaustion overcame Elizabeth and she just wanted to be in bed. When she reached for a washcloth she heard a knock on the door. "Elizabeth," called her father. "Are you in there?"

Elizabeth froze and didn't answer. A moment later her father knocked again and, receiving no answer, pushed the door open. "I was worried about..." William stopped when he saw Elizabeth's bloody face, torn dress, and blue lips. "Oh my God. What happened? Are you alright?" He stood before Elizabeth and held onto her shoulders.

Elizabeth cast her eyes downward, feeling embarrassed, guilty, and scared. William placed his hand under her chin and held it up to make Elizabeth look at him. Elizabeth couldn't meet his eyes. She shrunk into his chest and cried. William let his daughter finish without rushing her. When Elizabeth finally stopped heaving, William pushed her to arms' distance and looked into her eyes. "Did that boy do this to you?"

William saw the answer in Elizabeth's eyes. "Did he have at you?" he asked.

Elizabeth knew what her father meant. She shook her head. "I'll send your mother up to-" William cut himself off. "Have a seat here, let me see the damage." William took the washcloth Elizabeth still held and wet it. "This is going to sting some." He dabbed at the sand and pebbles embedded in Elizabeth's face. Elizabeth winced as her father cleaned her lacerations. Finally satisfied, William opened the medicine cabinet and produced a small bottle of Mercurochrome. He unscrewed the cap and painted Elizabeth's scrapes with the tiny brush. William apologized when Elizabeth recoiled as the anti-bacterial touched her open wounds. "He hit you in the nose?" asked William casually.

"No, I fell when I was running away," answered Elizabeth.

William grunted and nodded. He rinsed the washcloth and placed it over Elizabeth's nose. "Keep that on there. It probably won't help any, but at least I won't have to see it."

Elizabeth looked up to see her father smiling. "Thank you for everything. I love you Father."

"I love you too Liz. Get along to bed now." Almost as an afterthought, William turned to Elizabeth as he was leaving the washroom. "You're not going back to the plant."

Before Elizabeth could protest, the resolve in her father's voice registered and she recognized the futility in arguing with him. "Yes sir."

William closed the door behind him and walked down the hallway to the stairs. She removed the cloth from her face and looked in the mirror. Despite feeling like she'd been run over by a truck, Elizabeth couldn't help smiling when she saw her reflection. Her face was all scraped up. Her nose was swollen and already turning purple. The generously applied Mercurochrome made the dozens of small abrasions look absolutely ghastly. The smile unwittingly caused fresh ripples of pain to cascade around Elizabeth's face.

The unbearable weight clamping down on Elizabeth since Toby's attack lifted. The guilt about not recognizing Toby's evil designs dissipated. *She* didn't fool herself about Toby's intentions; *Toby* did. And when it got right down to it, she stopped him. She didn't allow history to repeat itself. And unless she was mistaken, Toby had a pretty nasty gash on the side of his head for his troubles. Elizabeth replaced the cloth over her nose and went to bed comforted with a newfound inner strength. And feeling sore.

Elizabeth slept soundly that night but woke the next morning with a start. A few seconds passed before she got her bearings. Although it was still dark outside, Elizabeth knew she had slept past her normal waking time. She jumped out of bed and rushed to her bureau. She pulled her pants up before the previous day's events registered: Toby's attack; her father forbidding her to return to work; her aching head. Elizabeth's shoulders slumped as she sat on the foot of her bed. An ominous feeling invaded her and she grew anxious.

Elizabeth sat in silence. She initially attributed her unease to the incident at Bluff Point. Although she was disappointed with herself for allowing Toby to trick her the way he did, and upset at receiving confirmation that people talked horribly about her behind her back, she dismissed that as the cause of her foreboding. She had come to terms with those issues, and felt stronger because of them. As Elizabeth sorted through her emotions, her thoughts kept returning to her father. Elizabeth assumed her father forbade her returning to work to protect her from the discomfort and embarrassment of facing her co-workers. But the more she thought about it the more certain she became that that was not the case. That was just not the actions of her father, especially given the fact that Elizabeth's wounds were superficial. Her father would never avoid something because it was uncomfortable, and he didn't raise Elizabeth to shy away from difficult situations. He believed in doing the right thing every time. And he instilled that in Elizabeth since she was born.

As Elizabeth recalled the exchange with her father the night before, she marveled at his composure. The reason she attempted to avoid him was to prevent him from getting upset and doing something out of anger that he would regret. Instead, he seemed unshaken by the incident. "That's it!" cried Elizabeth. Elizabeth witnessed her father's great capacity to shroud his emotions during the last few months as he patiently cared for her mother, despite the unbearable heartbreak the situation placed on him. *He did that to me last night*, thought Elizabeth. *It must have taken everything he had to conceal his anger. He's going after Toby!* Elizabeth jumped off her bed and finished dressing, then ran downstairs and out the door to catch her father.

§

Rage consumed William upon hearing of Toby's attack on Elizabeth. His muscles spasmed and he fought with all his might to control the anger that tore through his body. He desperately wanted to race from the house and beat Toby to a bloody pulp. That was not what Elizabeth needed though, and he controlled his instincts. William left Elizabeth and went downstairs, intent on walking to the Garfield's house in Stonington. William attended grade school with Toby's father and knew their house on Pequot Avenue. Rockets exploded in William's head and, now away from Elizabeth, his mind focused on a single thought: *Toby.*

As William crossed the parlor, he recognized a voice in the recess of his mind. His subconscious blocked its origin, and he was nearly out the back door when the voice forced its way through his rage.

"William!" called Clara.

William stopped short and returned to the parlor, not even remembering crossing the room five seconds earlier. He returned to his wife. "Yes Dear?"

"John Amos stopped by today to settle up for the eggs you delivered last week. He said that nearly half the eggs were broken. You have to be more careful packaging them."

William nearly lost his mind. "We haven't had any chickens, any anything, for almost a year! What are you talking about woman?"

A blank look crossed Clara's face. "Don't be so upset, William. I was just telling you. Maybe I could help out more. With Elizabeth going to college you've had to pick up most of her chores. Something's bound to suffer doing all that work."

William's hands flexed and he stormed half-way across the room toward Clara before his sanity returned. He stopped in the middle of the room, trying to recall where he was and what he was doing. Everything quickly filtered in and he looked at Clara. "I'm fine. I'll be more careful with the eggs. Can I help you upstairs?"

"Why William," smiled Clara. "Are you making a pass at me? It's the middle of the afternoon. What if Elizabeth comes home?"

William looked out the front window at the pitch blackness. His chest heaved as he inhaled a deep breath of air and blew it out. His muscles relaxed. He raised his hands to his head and rubbed his temples. He closed his eyes, needing a few seconds to himself.

"You look awful," said Clara. "Are you getting enough sleep?"

William couldn't go to Toby's house. All the stress of the previous year bore down on him at once and he knew if he saw

Toby that night he wouldn't stop until the boy was dead. That wouldn't do Clara or Elizabeth, or him for that matter, any good. He would settle up with Toby in the morning. "Actually," he replied to Clara, "I think I'm going to lie down for a while."

As William climbed the stairs, Clara called after him. "Get some rest. I'll make sure you're up for the afternoon milking."

William shook his head as he lay in bed. His disillusion that Clara would snap out of her condition had long since passed and she grew worse daily. He had no idea what to do for her, but knew the time had come to do something; something that would change their lives forever. William forced thoughts of Clara from his mind. The culmination of his life's recent events consumed him. Tonight broke him and he needed to find peace in his soul if he wanted to continue holding together his family. With remorse he acknowledged that it was only in times of strife he sought the Lord's guidance. Without thinking he went to the bookshelf and looked for the family Bible. After searching for several minutes he remembered they'd given it to Elizabeth years earlier. He walked toward Elizabeth's room to borrow it but reconsidered, not wanting to wake her if she was sleeping. William returned to his room and lay in bed looking at the ceiling. He prayed for Clara. He prayed for Elizabeth. He prayed for himself.

Sleep never came to William that night. He rolled out of bed about three o'clock and went downstairs. Clara slept on the sofa and William drew a quilt over her. He went into the kitchen and brewed a pot of coffee. He drank a cup, and then another. Then a third. He didn't find the quiescence he prayed for that night, but at least his rationality and resolve returned.

William donned his coat and hat and began the long walk to Mystic. The frigid morning snapped William awake and his hands instinctively sought the comfort of his wool-lined pockets. The season's first frost blanketed the rolling hills surrounding the house and the frozen grass crunched under his boots. As the miles clipped by William's thoughts turned to Elizabeth. His blood boiled thinking of the boy attacking her, but even more so thinking of how heartbroken Elizabeth must be. There weren't many secrets in North Stonington and most people knew why Elizabeth went away the year before. William knew people made comments behind Elizabeth's back and saw the way people shied away from her, as though she had some deadly contagious disease. The primary reason William didn't launch much of a protest when Elizabeth suggested she work at the Packer Building was so he could be close to her and protect her. *Well, I failed*, thought William. But Elizabeth was tough and she handled the situation. *She will be stronger for it*. Regardless, William held Toby Garfield accountable for his actions and would send a clear message to everyone else to think twice before messing with his daughter.

Dawn just broke over the Sound when William entered the rear door of the Packer Building. "Morning William," greeted Mr. Shrew. "Where's your sidekick today?"

"Elizabeth won't be coming back," replied William. "Where's Garfield?"

Mr. Shrew jerked his thumb behind his ear. "Back by the furnace," he replied, shaking his head. "He showed up early today. Maybe he's finally growing up."

William walked past the foreman toward the plant's boiler section. He walked past men drinking their final gulps of coffee before the morning whistle blew. The boiler room looked deserted. "Garfield!" yelled William above the din of the room. "I know you're here boy, show yourself!" The high-pitched steam racing through pipes and roar of the boilers drowned out all other sounds. William again yelled for Toby. "I'm not leaving! You might as well get this over with!" William scanned the room searching for Toby. Finally he caught a glimpse of movement from the corner of his eye and turned. Toby stepped from the shadows.

"You don't have to do this!" yelled Toby. "I didn't hurt her none."

William saw the large bandage taped to the side of Toby's head. He actually considered letting Toby go. *Besides*, thought William, *it looks like Elizabeth already taught him a pretty good lesson*. More important, William considered what could happen if he knocked Toby around some. He could lose his job, and that wouldn't do his family any good at all. Things were tough enough as it was.

These thoughts raced through William's mind when Toby yelled again. "Besides, your little whore of a daughter asked for it!"

William's world turned red with rage and he lunged at Toby. Toby's cousin Rodney suddenly emerged from behind a large vat of lye and slammed a heavy iron pipe into William's kidneys. The blow caught William off balance and sent him sprawling to the floor. Rodney jumped across the floor and raised the pipe again. He gripped the pipe with both hands and brought it crashing down on William's side, breaking three of his ribs. William hollered in pain and fury. Anticipating the next attack, William covered the back of his head with his hands. The next blow broke two more of William's ribs. As soon as the third strike landed, William roared like a bear and leaped to his feet. He turned and caught Rodney's arm as it drew back for another swing. With both arms raised above his head, Rodney was caught off balance this time. William grabbed Rodney's wrist with one hand and elbow with the other. William slammed Rodney's arm down across his knee, breaking Rodney's forearm in half. Rodney howled like a coyote as the pipe slipped from his hands and clamored harmlessly against the concrete floor.

Toby jumped on William's back, wrapping his legs around William's waist. He interlocked his hands around William's throat and began strangling him. The pain seared through William's body like a hot iron. Now in a total frenzy, William grabbed Rodney's throat and drew back his mighty right hand. All the grief, despair and anger that consumed William during the previous year manifested in a single instant. With superhuman strength, William punched Rodney so hard that he lost his grip on Rodney's throat. Rodney went flying back into a network of pipes. Rodney slammed into a piece of angle iron that impaled his neck and jutted clear through his throat. Blood burst from the wound and from Rodney's gurgling mouth as he tried to scream.

Sanity returned to William at the sight of Rodney's dying body dangling from the angle iron. As William stepped toward Rodney's suspended body the smell of gas overpowered him. A natural gas line snapped from its coupling when Rodney's head slammed into the nest of piping. William suddenly became aware of Toby still clinging to his throat. William twisted and reached behind him. He grabbed Toby by the throat and threw him across the room. As William reached for Rodney's limp body he heard something behind him. He ducked just as Toby swung the pipe his cousin held only seconds earlier.

The entire scene played in slow motion for William and he yelled. "NOOOO!!!"

But it was too late. The pipe narrowly missed William's head and crashed against a tangle of pipes. The sparks produced by the impact ignited the gas-laden room. The explosion shot a three foot section of pipe through the air toward Toby's head, leaving a baseball-sized hole in the middle of his skull.

The explosion blew William through the back door and everything turned white.

Then everything turned black.

Elizabeth sprinted down the lane to the main road and ran with all her heart toward Mystic. She ran until her sides split and she couldn't breathe. At the point of collapsing, she walked for a minute, and then ran again. She could not shake the terrible premonition that consumed her. Something horrible would happen if she didn't reach her father before he got to the Packer Building. Her blood pounded her head like fists and every second that passed seemed like an hour. She could see Route 1 ahead and felt the first glimmer of hope. *I made it in time!*

Then Elizabeth heard the explosion. Her heart leapt into her throat and she couldn't breathe. Clutching her throat she dropped to her knees gasping for air. After a moment her mind overcame her body's desire to shut down and she forced herself to her feet. She half staggered, half loped the remaining three-quarters of a mile to the Packer Building. By the time she reached the parking lot a huge smoke cloud nearly concealed the building. Workers funneled out every door in the plant as they sought refuge. Elizabeth fought against the tide of people as she tried to access the smoke-filled building. An unseen arm grabbed Elizabeth and yanked her away from the building. The huge hand dragged Elizabeth across the street and she recognized Mr. Shrew's voice calling to her. "…an accident. The boiler blew. Come on!"

Amidst the sirens, soot and screams, Elizabeth knew it was no accident. It was her father.

Fleas

Doc Allyn poked and prodded William. William lay unresponsive on his bed.

"William," said Doc Allyn. "You've been home a month now. Your ribs are healing. We've managed to keep the infection out of your burns. Your broken leg is setting up nicely, and Doctor Hollavan is coming tomorrow to take the bandages off your eyes. We both know there isn't anything wrong with your body that's keeping you from moving a little and talking. Or at least grunting and nodding now and then. Don't forget I put my neck on the line to get you out of Lawrence Hospital so you could lick your wounds at home. You've got to snap out of it. So what do you say?"

Elizabeth stood by the doctor while he examined William. She found her father's hand under the blanket and squeezed it. "I know you can hear me. I love you. Won't you talk to us? Mother and I need you." Tears pooled in Elizabeth's eyes and spilled onto her cheeks. Her father hadn't eaten since the explosion, and only drank the water that Elizabeth dripped into his mouth from a sponge. William was such a burly man that the twenty pounds he'd lost since the explosion didn't stand out as unhealthy looking. But Elizabeth saw the hollowness in his face below the bandages and knew her father was doing this to himself. *No he isn't!* Elizabeth silently yelled to herself. *He just isn't well enough yet!*

"Can I speak to you in the hall for a moment?" Doc Allyn asked Elizabeth.

Elizabeth followed the doctor from the room and closed the door behind her. Doc Allyn placed a comforting hand on Elizabeth's shoulder. "You and I have both known your father long enough to know that once he's made his mind up about something, well, there isn't a man alive that can change it."

Elizabeth's heart sank and her mind exploded with fear. She already knew what the doctor was going to say.

"Your father might be thinking he's not much good to you and your mother in his condition. Maybe he feels he's a burden to you. Do you get my drift?"

Doc Allyn saw by the tears streaming down Elizabeth's face that she did. "So all I'm saying is maybe you should read to him from the Good Book. And when you're not reading, pray for him. Pray that when Doctor Hollavan removes those bandages tomorrow your father's eyes will work."

Unseen hands strangled Elizabeth as she choked the words out. "He...he will, won't he? Be able to see."

The doctor shook his head. "All we can do is pray. If it was just the flash burn, maybe. But the explosion vaporized that tank of lye and your father took the blast full force right in the face. It's a miracle he survived that explosion." Doc Allyn nodded toward William's bedroom door." But...I'm sure he doesn't feel that way. "I'll pick up Doctor Hollavan tomorrow at the ferry. We should be by around ten o'clock or so. I'll see myself out." Doc Allyn tipped his head to Elizabeth and walked down the hallway.

Elizabeth heard Doctor Allyn leave through the front door. She drew her sleeve across her face to wipe the tears and walked downstairs to the kitchen. Her mother sat at the table eating a piece of dry toast.

"I don't know why everyone insists on sending us food. I am perfectly capable of cooking for the four of us. And look at all these notes people keep sending congratulating you on Hester's birth.

Hester is nearly six months old for goodness sakes! I don't know what ails people these days. I'm going to take a nap."

Clara Newton stood up from the table and walked to the parlor. She pulled a quilt from the back of the sofa and draped it over her emaciated frame. She rolled over and seconds later began snoring.

Dozens of get well notes for William and prayers for the family littered the kitchen table. They had all been opened and read by Clara, but the words she read came from her mind, not the printed script. The community bonded together when hard times struck their neighbors and the Newton's predicament proved no exception. The people who cast sideways looks and sneered at Elizabeth since she returned from New York, the people who rolled their eyes and shook their heads when Clara's name came up, the people who spoke ill of William's farming skills when the bank took back the note on the farm, all cast their pettiness aside when it came right down to it. The neighbors brought food in by the basketful. So much food that Elizabeth was forced to throw the majority of it away. Most of the envelopes contained money. Not much, but what people could afford. Twenty-five cents here; a dollar there. The money was enough to keep the electricity on for the time being, but not much more. Elizabeth would go back to work as soon as her father didn't need constant attention. And of course there was the situation with her mother to contend with.

Elizabeth brought herself back to the present. She warmed the plate Mrs. Judson sent over and picked at the leftover turkey. She retrieved the black cast iron jug from the back porch and poured a glass of milk. Elizabeth mechanically ate the tasteless meal. Not hungry in the least, she couldn't remember when she had last eaten and knew she needed her strength.

Despite Elizabeth's efforts to do otherwise, her thoughts wandered back to the explosion. Toby and his cousin were dead. It took a week for the plant to start back up. The investigators determined the cause to be an electrical short that ignited a leaking gas line. *Tragic Mishap at Packer Building* announced the New London Day's headline.

Rescue workers found William lying near the railroad tracks where he landed from the explosion. After the fire brigade extinguished the inferno they discovered two additional bodies. The remains were so severely burned and deformed that they were unidentifiable. Plant management determined that Toby was one of the victims by process of elimination; all the other workers were accounted for. It took a while for the authorities to place Rodney at the plant that morning. It was only after some of Toby's friends confessed that Toby and Rodney planned to gang up on William Newton that morning that they began searching for Rodney. When he came up missing, authorities confirmed that Rodney was the second victim. The smaller set of remains was assigned to Toby, the larger to Rodney. The joint funeral services were held three days later and the two were buried in Elm Grove Cemetery.

The plant physician, Dr. Steelman, raced to William as he lay in the briars behind the factory. A fire brigade member sat beside William as he nursed an arm he singed putting out the fire. "He's gone Doc," said the fireman.

Doctor Steelman gasped when he removed the jacket the fireman draped over William's face. Steam rose from William's clothes. The pungent odor of charred skin caused the doctor's stomach to wretch. Mounds of pink liquid quaked beneath the blackened skin covering Williams' face. The doctor crossed his heart. As he returned the jacket over William's face, the doctor saw, *thought he saw*, a ripple of movement behind William's burnt paper thin eyelids. He removed the jacket and placed his stethoscope on the smoking area over William's heart. Doctor Steelman shouted in disbelief. "He's alive! Get the boat!"

Ten minutes later four men placed William on a travois and carried him to the motorboat the company used to shuttle their employees across to New London. At the doctor's direction, they covered William with blankets. As the boat shoved off from the dock, the doctor yelled to the shore. "Call Joseph Lawrence Hospital! Tell them we're coming!"

Doctor Steelman administered what limited first aid he could as the small boat sputtered across the choppy river.

§

Elizabeth swallowed a few bites of turkey, but mostly just moved the food around the plate with her fork. Finally she scraped the food into the trash and washed her plate. She walked past her snoring mother and climbed the stairs. Remembering the doctor's advice, she retrieved the Bible and entered her father's room. She looked down at his listless form and caught her breath until she discerned his chest rising and lowering. She stood beside the bed and looked at the man who had always been her hero. Doc Allyn instructed Elizabeth how and when to inject morphine to ease her father's pain. She had slowly been weaning him off the medication over the last couple weeks. She hoped it wasn't too soon, but the doctor warned her of greater complications if he became addicted.

Fresh pink skin replaced the charred remnants caused by the explosion. Although the anti-bacterial gel made his face appear ghastly, the skin quickly regenerated. The new skin appeared first as dots, then connected and filled in until William's face, neck and arms were reborn. The multitude of contusions that covered his body faded from purple and red to blue, then green, and now a pale yellow. Doc Allyn told Elizabeth that part of her father's left ear had either been blow or burned off; a fact that presented itself in the form of a small misshapen mound hidden beneath the bandage encircling his head. His body healed well, but it was her father's mind that worried Elizabeth. Doc Allyn was right. If William didn't regain his sight, he wouldn't feel whole.

Elizabeth shouldered the weight of responsibility for Toby's and Rodney's deaths and nearly the death of her father. She felt responsible and would bear that cross forever.

"Doc Allyn says you're doing great," said Elizabeth "Doctor Hollavan is going to remove your bandages tomorrow. I just *know* you're going to be able to see; I feel it. I'm going to give you some water." Elizabeth dipped the sponge in a pitcher of water and let it drip into William's mouth. His tongue gently lapped the water, but Elizabeth didn't know if it was a conscious effort or reflex. Elizabeth continued until her father's face rolled slightly to the side and the water cascaded off his lips and trickled down his cheek.

Elizabeth put away the sponge and pulled a chair to the bedside. She laid the Bible in her lap and ran her thumb down the open edges of the pages. She opened the Bible where her thumb stopped and began reading where her eyes first rested. "Psalm sixty-eight. Let God arise, let his enemies be scattered; let them also that hate him flee before him. As smoke is driven away, so drive them away: as wax melteth before the fire, so let the wicked perish at the presence of God."

A chill ran up Elizabeth's spine. As she read she begged for forgiveness. She begged for redemption. She prayed for her father and her mother. She read for hours until her throat turned gritty and burned. She read until she fell asleep.

Elizabeth awoke with a start when the Bible slid off her lap and landed with a thud on the wide board plank floor. She looked around in the pitch black room uncertain where she was. As she gained her bearings a calming serenity greeted her. The sound of her father's restful breathing sounded like angels singing. She turned on the lamp and prepared her father's injection. "It's time for your shot Father." Elizabeth swabbed his arm with alcohol and slid the needle under his skin and pushed in the syringe's plunger. Her father winced slightly but seemed otherwise undisturbed. Elizabeth turned off the light and felt her way downstairs. She listened to her mother's steady breathing and retired to her own room, hopeful that her prayers would be answered.

Elizabeth awoke early the following morning. She felt refreshed as she washed and dressed. As Elizabeth administered her father's morphine she faintly heard her mother speaking, but it was too early for the doctors to be there. Elizabeth walked downstairs. Her mother sat in an antique Queen Anne chair with her back to the stairs. She wore her favorite dress and her hair was combed and pulled back in a neat bun. Elizabeth couldn't remember the last time her mother wore anything other than her nightgown and house coat. Her head bobbed as she spoke. Elizabeth couldn't imagine who would be visiting at this early hour.

Elizabeth stepped from the landing and faced the parlor. Her mother sat alone in the room. "The eggs have been hatching calves," said Clara. After receiving the unspoken response, she replied. "I can't believe it either. And William is baking cats riding doves. It's the darnedest thing. I've always corned tractors with knives, but now with Satan in the outhouse with Poseidon, the entire factory is full of wishbones."

Elizabeth ran across the room and stood before her mother. She grabbed her mother's shoulders and called her. "Mother. Mother!"

Clara didn't acknowledge her daughter. Her eyes remained fixed on the empty space occupying the sofa across from her. The boniness of her mother's shoulders stung Elizabeth like a bee and she yanked her hands free. Looking down at her mother she saw the full emaciation that encompassed her. Her collar and breast bones protruded through the dress like gnarled branches. Her legs splayed out from the bottom of her dress like dried twigs. Elizabeth stared into the absolute vacancy of her mother's eyes. The full realization of what her mother had become crashed down on Elizabeth like a ton of bricks. She witnessed what her father would never see or acknowledge: the empty vessel that once contained his wife; the mother of his child; the grandmother of his grandson.

Elizabeth replaced her hands on her mother's shoulder and briskly shook her. "Mother! It's me, Elizabeth!"

As gingerly as casting a sideways glance at a lonely mourning dove, Clara looked up at Elizabeth. Looked *through* Elizabeth.

"Dear, ever since Quetzalcoatl sacked the Romans the harbinger has desecrated the sanctity of matrimony. How is your fishing war?"

Elizabeth shook her mother more vigorously. "Stop it! STOP IT!"

Clara's head bounced around on the kindling that was her neck. "Oh, dear me," gasped Clara. "I seemed to have dropped my fireplace in my ear. Can you help me find it?"

On the brink of insanity herself, Elizabeth snapped out of it. She let go of her mother and ran outside. Elizabeth hyperventilated and the freezing air stung her lungs. Lucidity slowly returned. She did not trust herself to return to the house but knew she must. She inhaled the frosty air and entered. She walked back into the parlor. Her mother babbled incoherently and traced circles in the air with her knitting needles.

Elizabeth heard Doc Allyn suggest to William several times that he should consider checking Clara into the Norwich State Hospital. William immediately dismissed the notion every time the doctor spoke of it. But now Elizabeth was positive that she could no longer care for her sick mother. And seeing her mother's skeletal body left no doubt that her mother would starve to death very soon if she did not receive proper care. Attention that neither her nor her father could ever provide. She would talk to Doc Allyn.

§

Elizabeth prayed aloud by her father's side when someone rapped sharply on the back door. Doctors Allyn and Hollavan stood outside, accompanied by a middle-aged woman.

Elizabeth ran downstairs, the anxiety already scratching within her. "Good morning, please come in." Elizabeth held open the door as the three visitors entered.

"Good morning Elizabeth," greeted Doc Allyn. "You remember Doctor Hollavan."

The bald doctor removed his hat and tipped his hand to his brow. "Morning Miss Newton."

Elizabeth returned his greeting. Doctor Hollavan exuded confidence and humility. Elizabeth knew that the gears in the doctor's mind never stopped turning. He was one of the few people Elizabeth ever met that absorbed so much more than everyone around him. His absence of arrogance made Elizabeth appreciate his company, like seeing an exotic endangered species in a zoo. She felt privileged that her father was under his care.

"This is Mrs. Wellington," said Doc Allyn. "Can we speak privately with you before we see your father?"

Elizabeth looked around, suddenly uncomfortable. "Of course. I'll get my mother." As Elizabeth turned Doc Allyn grabbed her arm. "Elizabeth, it's your mother we want to talk to you about." Apprehension quickly replaced the relief that initially spread through Elizabeth at not having to get her mother. The sudden gravity of the situation overshadowed the anticipation of her father's bandages being removed.

"Elizabeth, Mrs. Wellington is the admissions officer at the Norwich State Hospital. I've asked her to come speak with you about your mother's condition and the care that Norwich can provide her. This sickness that your mother has…it's nothing I can care for. I don't even really understand it." Doc Allyn placed his hand on Elizabeth's neck. "Elizabeth, you know your father will never do the right thing for your mother if it involves putting her…putting her where she can be cared for."

Elizabeth fought back the tears that her eyes begged to shed. She won that battle, but didn't dare speak lest her voice belie her bravado. To provide a moment to collect herself, Elizabeth moved behind Doc Allyn and helped him remove his jacket. On her cue, Dr. Hollavan and Mrs. Wellington removed their overcoats and handed them to Elizabeth. Elizabeth steeled herself as she turned and placed the coats on the rack.

When Elizabeth faced the visitors, Mrs. Wellington clasped both of Elizabeth's hands in her own. "I'm not a doctor Elizabeth. But based on what Dr. Allyn told me I believe your mother might truly benefit from our facility. I'd like to meet her and set up an appointment for one of the psychiatrists to evaluate her."

Elizabeth's eyes pleaded for relief. "We can't afford anything like that. I don't even know how we'll be able to pay for my father's care. If it wasn't for the neighbors, we wouldn't even have any food in the house."

Doctor Hollavan interjected. "You needn't concern yourself with that my dear. The factory is paying for all of your father's care, and Norwich is a state hospital. You won't have to pay for any treatment your mother receives. No matter how long she's there."

Elizabeth's desire to retreat within herself was overpowering. How did this happen? When did this happen? How was it that she was the decision maker for her family? Responsible for making decisions that could never be undone. "Thank you. Thank all of you. Follow me."

Elizabeth led the entourage into the parlor. Her mother sat upright on the sofa. When Clara saw Doc Allyn she perked right up.

"Good morning! What brings you out this way Doc?"

"Why, uh, morning Clara." Elizabeth saw the incredulous disbelief spread across Doc Allyn's face. "We just came to see how you're doing today."

Clara smiled. "I've known you for forty years and you've never just "dropped by." You're up to something. Who are your friends?"

Doc Allyn was flustered. "These are two of my colleagues: Dr. Hollavan and Mrs. Wellington."

Clara threw her head back and laughed. "That is so rich! Leave it to you to give your dogs names like that." Clara leaned forward and whispered. "But you'd better not let William see them. He's never liked pets in the house." Clara slapped her leg. "Ouch!" She looked suddenly disoriented. "Ouch!" She slapped her leg again, then her face. "Get them out of here! The dogs have fleas! They're all over me!" Clara slapped herself and feebly kicked at Dr. Hollavan and Mrs. Wellington. "Get them out I tell you!" Clara leapt onto the floor. She writhed and slapped at herself and began barking. "Hellhounds everywhere, *Ruff, Ruff.* Lucifer's fury unleashed on Mount Zion, Mount Lion, HAHAHA, *Ruff, Ruff...*" Clara wrestled with herself, arms and legs flailing, head banging against the coffee table's legs.

Doc Allyn nodded at Mrs. Wellington. As she reached into her satchel, Doc Allyn dove on Clara and pinned the frail woman to the floor. Mrs. Wellington stabbed a syringe into Clara's leg and then stepped back. In less than a minute Clara lay still and the craziness left her eyes. Elizabeth knelt beside her and stroked her mother's hair. Mother and daughter stared into each other's eyes and Clara moved her lips. Elizabeth leaned closer. "What is it Mother?"

Clara's words were barely audible. "How could you hate me this much?" Then Clara's eyes rolled up in her head and she lay limp on the floor.

§

Doc Allyn placed his hand on Elizabeth's shoulder. "Come dear; let's go see your father. Mrs. Wellington will tend to your mother." Doc Allyn turned from Elizabeth and nodded to Mrs. Wellington.

Elizabeth allowed Doc Allyn to pull her from her mother. The two of them, followed by Dr. Hollavan, climbed the stairs to William's room. Elizabeth knocked gently and braced herself as she pushed the door open. The combination of antibacterial lotion, rubbing alcohol and body odor produced a sickly pungent odor that made Elizabeth queasy whenever she entered the room. Her father lay on the bed exactly as she'd left him.

Doc Allyn marched past Elizabeth. "Good Morning William, it's Doc Allyn. Dr. Hollavan is here. He's going to remove your bandages. Can you hear me?"

William remained silent. Dr. Hollavan unbuckled his satchel and produced a folded leather case. He untied the strap and unrolled the case, exposing an assortment of instruments. "Mr. Newton, I'm Dr. Hollavan. We met at Lawrence last month, but I'd be surprised if you remember me. I'm going to put some ointment on your bandage to help loosen it from your skin, but it will still hurt some when I pull it off."

Doctor Hollavan produced a small palate from his bag and applied ointment to William's bandages. The doctor massaged the ointment into the bandage. He let it set in for a few minutes and then selected a pair of scissors from the instrument case. Doctor Hollavan slid the scissors against William's scalp and snipped the dingy bandage. After slicing the bandage in several locations, the doctor returned the scissors to the case and began peeling the bandages. The bandages around William's scalp fell away easily. The bandages on William's face, however, had adhered to his skin. Even with the assistance of the ointment, Dr. Hollavan had to work several minutes to remove those bandages without causing William undue stress. Finally all that remained on William's face were the padded eye covers that the bandages had previously secured in place.

"Elizabeth, pull the window shades closed please," directed Dr. Hollavan. "Too much light could traumatize your father's eyes. Now Mr. Newton, don't expect a miracle when I uncover your eyes. I'm not going to lie to you. I have seen people with worse eye injuries regain their sight, but not many. And if you do, it may not all come at once. You might see shadows at first, or you might see nothing at all."

Elizabeth swore her father flinched when Dr. Hollavan touched the corner of the eye pads. However, he gave no other indication he was conscious of his surroundings. The tension in the room was as thick as molasses. Doc Allyn stood silently as perspiration dripped off the tip of his nose. The doctor's words from the previous day tolled in Elizabeth's mind like a bell tower: *Maybe he feels he's a burden to you.* Elizabeth knew the doctor was right; there was much more at stake than her father's vision. Dr. Hollavan mechanically lifted the pads from William's face.

Elizabeth and the doctors stared down at William. Following an unbearable silence, Doc Allyn spoke. "William, I delivered you an awfully long time ago and my eyes were the first you looked into. I know you can hear me. Now you look at me and tell me if you can see anything."

Elizabeth squeezed her father's hand. Her heart raced and she prayed so hard it hurt. "Please Father," she begged.

William's head turned slightly toward his daughter's voice and then back to Doc Allyn. "William, you tell me now," urged Doc Allyn.

A single tear streamed down William's face and he nodded. Elizabeth threw herself on the bed and wrapped her arms around her father. She sobbed uncontrollably. "I knew you would see! I prayed for you Father; I knew you would see!"

The doctors watched the emotion pour from Elizabeth. She cried so hard that she could barely breathe as torrents of tears flooded down her face. When Elizabeth finally calmed, she lay hugging her father. He moved his lips and she placed her ears by his mouth. "I love you, Elizabeth."

Elizabeth's emotions again took control of her and through her tears she told her father how much she loved him.

Doc Allyn spoke with Dr. Hollavan and then to Elizabeth. "Let's leave the doctor so he can examine your father. Besides, I need a drink."

Elizabeth reluctantly let go of her father and stood up. "I love you Father. I'll be back as soon as the doctor is finished."

Doc Allyn placed his arm around Elizabeth's waist and walked her down the stairs. "I can't believe it!" said Elizabeth. "I prayed all night, but I…I didn't think he would really be able to see. And he talked! He is going to be fine now!" Doc Allyn remained silent. "Doc, he can see, right? I mean, he *nodded*. You saw it! Tell me he can see!"

Doc Allyn breathed deeply. "So it seems. Let's see what the doctor says."

As the two rounded the bottom of the stairs Elizabeth saw Mrs. Wellington lacing the final eyelets on the canvas restraining jacket which she placed around her mother. With all the excitement and emotion concerning her father, Elizabeth nearly forgot about her mother's episode. She ran across the room. "What are you doing? Take that off her!" Mrs. Wellington backed away from Clara. In the recesses of her mind Elizabeth heard Doc Allyn calling her. She looked up at him while she unfastened the laces.

"Elizabeth, come in the kitchen with me. Please."

Elizabeth stood and followed Doc Allyn to the kitchen. He pulled a chair out for her and helped her sit. The doctor held Elizabeth's hand. "Elizabeth, your mother is very sick. You know you can't care for her here; you can't pretend anymore. You don't really have a choice. Not if you care at all about your mother's quality of life. Dr. Freud has made tremendous advances in the field of psychoanalysis. In many cases personal stresses and social dysfunction stem from negative influences of childhood events. There are experts in this field at Norwich that can help your mother."

The fight was gone from Elizabeth. It was all too much for her. Tears streamed down her face as she sat motionless in front of the doctor. Doc Allyn continued. "I brought you and your father into this world. *And* your mother. I only want what is best for all of you. And right now your mother needs to be someplace where the doctors have the training and expertise to care for someone in her condition."

Hearing the reality of the situation spoken aloud forced Elizabeth to acknowledge the denial she had allowed herself to believe. She just wished so much for life to be like it was *before*. Before the explosion, before her mother lost her mind, before the rape. *But wishing is for children*, Elizabeth told herself. *It's time to grow up. This is life.*

Elizabeth heard Doctor Hollavan walk down the stairs and speak briefly with Mrs. Wellington. When he entered the kitchen Doc Allyn stood from the table and greeted him. "How is he?" Elizabeth's eyes were glued to Dr. Hollavan's.

"It's difficult to say. He says he can see shapes and detect movement. But there is substantial retinal scarring and I can't detect any pupil response; it's very strange. I've replaced the bandages. I'll reexamine next week."

The three heard a scraping sound coming from the second floor. "Is he trying to get out of bed?" asked Dr. Hollavan.

Elizabeth's eyes popped wide open and she bolted up the stairs, each step seeming like an eternity. She ran down the hall and slammed open the door to her father's room. The sight that greeted Elizabeth froze her in her tracks. Her father stood on a chair in the

center of the room with a bed sheet tied around his neck like noose. The other end was fastened around an exposed beam in the ceiling.
"Father, DON'T!!!"

William stepped off the chair. The sheet snapped taught and broke his neck, leaving William's dead body dangling before his daughter.

Night of a Blizzard

by Elizabeth Lockett

From out of the depths of some unknown realm
Into a winter's night
Ushered by ever increasing moan
Comes an ominous creature of white.

Obliterating the stars and the moon
Bending the withered trees down
Leaves and dried branches that clung to the end
Are scornfully dashed to the ground.

All night long it wrangles and raves
As here in my bed I cower
Learning that nature is truly supreme
And man must abide by her power.

Then wearied at last by the long travail
And stripped of vengeance and wrath
The winds die down to a funeral dirge
And I dread what they leave in their path

But here, in the light of the winter's morn,
Such majesty greets my eye-
A world transformed by a master's hand
'Neath a cloudless, emerald sky.

The tortured trees are erect once more
In crystalline beauty they stand
The snow has been drifted in measured tiers
And a stillness pervades the land.

Bryan James Lockett

Why do I cringe in the inky black
Of that wild and treacherous night?
When the drabness of winter breaks through again
Please come back and paint everything white.

The Funeral

The days following William's death passed so surrealistically for Elizabeth. She knew her mind snapped when her father hung himself and that Doc Allyn sedated her. She knew that Dr. Hollavan and Mrs. Wellington took her mother to Norwich State Hospital that morning, and that Doc Allyn stayed to care for Elizabeth. She knew that she must have planned her father's funeral, but couldn't remember doing so. Nevertheless, here she stood beside her father's open casket at Nile's Funeral Home. The viewing line formed in the foyer and wrapped around the lobby. Townspeople Elizabeth had known her whole life filled the funeral home. She didn't know if people had been offering condolences for minutes or hours. All she knew was *the line*. "I'm sorry for your loss," "he was such a good man," "if you need anything you let us know." The faceless people whirred past Elizabeth like the wind.

The obnoxious odor of alcohol suddenly overpowered Elizabeth and forced her back to reality. "Too much for him, huh?" slurred the large man. A bear of a hug groped Elizabeth. "Well, looks like you'll be takin' my offer after all." Seth Newton clutched his hands behind Elizabeth's back. "Told you it weren't no good you coming back here. I'll have the lawyer sell his house and he can wire me the money. You're my...what do you call it? Oh yeah, you're my *trustee* now." Spit flew from Seth's mouth as he barked with laughter. "We'll be leaving in the morning."

Claustrophobia devoured Elizabeth. The stench of her uncle's breath made her stomach wretch. She fought to free herself from his grip as her lungs gasped for air. Her uncle laughed at Elizabeth's flailing and pressed himself against her. From the corners of her eyes Elizabeth noticed the other mourners suddenly looking in every direction except hers.

"Come on now; give Uncle Seth a little kiss." Seth mashed his slobbering lips against Elizabeth.

A shadow passed before Elizabeth and she felt her uncle's hands unlock from her back. Like a dream she witnessed a familiar man squeeze her uncle's hand and hold it in front of him. The man twisted the hand unnaturally backward and held it before her uncle's face. Her uncle was a large man, but he had to look up several inches to make eye contact with the intruder.

"I think the lady has been through enough. Why don't you get the hell out of here before you get hurt?" To accentuate his statement, the man bent Seth's hand even further.

Seth cried out in pain and surprise. Then he cried out in rage. His already red face grew violet. "Who the hell..." As drunk as Seth was, he realized the man standing before him meant business. The man was also ten years younger and twenty pounds heavier, and wore a look that promised the subject was not open for discussion. The color faded from Seth's face. "Pshhaw! You can have her. She's damaged goods anyway!" Seth shoved Elizabeth with his chest as he disengaged from her.

Before the echoes from Seth's words died, Jacob Pogsetter landed a crushing blow square against the drunken man's mouth. Seth issued a plethora of curses as he stumbled backward, his hands rising to his broken jaw. A dozen arms reached from the crowd and manhandled Seth out of the funeral home.

"Looks like you've had enough Elizabeth," said Jacob. "Let's get out of here." Jacob ushered Elizabeth out the rear door of the home.

§

Wonderful, innocent childhood memories flooded Elizabeth when she recognized Jacob. Seth's drunken groping was just another notch on life's smoking gun to Elizabeth by that point. But Jacob returned Elizabeth, if only briefly, to days that were carefree and gay. She wrapped her arms around him and cried into his shoulder. Jacob let her cry it all out.

"I wanted to wait until you were alone to offer my condolences. Your father and I had our differences, but I always respected him. But when I saw that man, well, I had to jump in. Who is he anyway?"

Elizabeth shook her head. "My uncle."

Jacob stepped back as though someone slapped him across the face. "You must be joking. But now that you mention it, I can see the resemblance to your father. I'm really sorry that happened. Can I take you home?"

"No thank you," replied Elizabeth. "Doc Allyn..." Elizabeth considered for a moment. She could only remember scattered images of the previous few days, but Doc Allyn was by her side in every one. "Actually, I would appreciate a ride. I'll be right back."

Elizabeth returned to the funeral home. As she parted through the mourners, Joshua Cheseborough stopped her. "Elizabeth, I'm very sorry. But your father put up a valiant fight. No one could have survived that explosion." That's when Elizabeth realized that Doc Allyn didn't tell anyone how her father died. He must have sworn Dr. Hollavan and Mrs. Wellington to secrecy as well. Elizabeth continued searching for Doc Allyn. She finally spotted him standing with his wife. He was speaking with Wilfred and Betsy Stanton. For the first time it struck Elizabeth how old Doc Allyn was. And how *tired* he looked.

Mrs. Stanton intercepted Elizabeth before she reached Doc Allyn. "You poor dear. This must be so hard on you. We know what it's like to lose a loved one so unexpectedly. Ever since Daniel..." Mrs. Stanton placed an already saturated handkerchief to her face and sobbed. Mr. Stanton placed his arm around his wife and excused them.

"She's never come to peace with Daniel passing," Doc Allyn told Elizabeth. "It's eating her alive." The doctor stared into Elizabeth's eyes. "Don't let that happen to you. Make peace with the Lord. Make peace with yourself."

Elizabeth fought back the hot spring of tears that threatened to erupt. "Thank you for everything. Jacob is going to drive me home now."

Doc Allyn's eyes narrowed. "Are you sure? We don't mind taking you home."

"I'll be fine," replied Elizabeth. "I just need some rest. Besides, you've done too much already."

Mrs. Allyn held her husband's arm. "You let us know if there is anything else we can do. This old fool standing beside me needs some sleep also, although he's too stubborn to admit it. Come on, let's go." Mrs. Allyn hugged Elizabeth and then dragged her husband out of the funeral home.

Elizabeth retrieved her coat from the closet and realized that she had not felt the bitter cold when she was previously outside with Jacob. She realized that she had not felt anything for longer than she could remember.

§

Elizabeth returned to Jacob. They ducked their heads into the icy wind as they walked along the Mystic River to Jacob's truck. "Sorry, it's just an old jalopy. But it gets me where I need to go."

Elizabeth hugged Jacob again for what seemed an eternity. The sound of Jacob's teeth chattering brought her back to the present. "I'm sorry Jacob. I just needed someone."

Jacob patted Elizabeth's back. "I'm glad I'm here for you. Ready?" Jacob opened the door for Elizabeth and returned to the driver's side. Neither spoke during the drive to North Stonington.

The farmhouse was pitch black as Jacob drove around back. "Your mother must have turned in early. I don't blame her for not going to the viewing. I don't know how anyone can go to one of those things. You lose a loved one and before you even have a chance to come to terms with it you have people you haven't seen in years telling you how you'll be fine, and how close they were to the one who passed on. Viewings are for folks to catch up with people they haven't seen, and to tell themselves how glad they are it didn't happen to them. That was mighty brave of you to face those lions. How is your mother holding up anyway?"

It hadn't occurred to Elizabeth that Jacob didn't know about her mother. "She's sick. She doesn't even know."

Jacob looked bewildered. "Oh my God. You have to tell her; someone is going to."

"Not where she's at."

Jacob considered for a moment as a look of utter sadness spread across his face. "So you're all alone."

Jacob's words echoed through Elizabeth's mind. She had not considered that fact, but it was true nonetheless. She was all alone.

"Well, I'm staying with you then," announced Jacob.

Elizabeth shook her head. "I'll be fine. I-"

Jacob cut her off. "I'm not taking no for an answer. I wouldn't leave anyone in your situation alone, especially such an old friend. I'll take you to the funeral tomorrow and sleep on the sofa for the next couple nights. That will give you a chance to sort things out by the time I head back home Sunday."

Elizabeth tried to protest but couldn't force the lie from her mouth. She was alone, and suddenly afraid of being alone. Jacob opened the door and helped her from the truck. Once inside, Elizabeth turned on the lights. She retrieved some blankets from the linen closet and placed them on the sofa. She went through her father's bureau and found a set of nightclothes for Jacob to wear. When she returned downstairs she discovered Jacob brewing a pot of coffee.

"I hope you don't mind, but I could use a cup," said Jacob.

Smelling the fresh aroma of the brewing coffee ignited other senses in Elizabeth. She became aware of her exhaustion, hunger, thirst, grief, resolve. "I could use a cup myself."

Jacob smiled. "I didn't figure you for a coffee drinker."

"I'm not." Elizabeth had arrived at a crossroad. Turn left and take the easy road to a bed beside her mother at the state hospital. Turn right and fight every inch of the way. Fight to make some sense of the tragedies levied against her family. Fight to pull herself from the abyss that beckoned her and make her life meaningful. Elizabeth turned right and she smiled. "Thank you for what you did back there. With my uncle."

"He was just drunk. I'm sure he didn't mean anything by it." Jacob considered for a moment. Then he said, "Your uncle - he's a big jerk, isn't he?"

The words cut the tension and Elizabeth smiled. "Yes, he really is a jerk."

Jacob and Elizabeth laughed together. Elizabeth turned off the gas when the coffee percolated and filled two cups with steaming brew. "Cream?" asked Elizabeth.

"No thanks. I take it black and bitter, like my women." Jacob threw his hand to his mouth as soon as the words spilled out. Embarrassment spread across his face like the plague. "Oh my God! I can't believe I said that. It's just that I *always* say that down at the coffee shop. I am such an idiot!"

To Elizabeth's own shock, she answered, "I take mine light and sweet, like *my* women!"

The two stared at each other. Elizabeth's comment melted the final piece of ice and they laughed heartily.

When the laughter subsided, Elizabeth spoke first. "I think there are some leftovers in the ice box. Would you like something to eat?" asked Elizabeth.

"That would be great," replied Jacob. "I'm starving. Now that I think about it, I haven't eaten since this morning."

Elizabeth heated two plates of turkey and mashed. They ate in silence. Finally, Jacob pushed his plate away from him. "I am stuffed! That was delicious, I can't thank you enough."

Elizabeth cleared the table and poured them each a cup of lukewarm coffee.

"What have you been doing since you left?" asked Elizabeth.

"After your father and I parted ways I worked a couple farms. But farming is getting tougher and tougher for the little guys. Most folks have sold off, and the ones that didn't mostly can't afford a permanent hand. Anyway, I got a job at Blakely laundry a few years ago up in Willimantic. It's a sweatshop - dirty and boring work. Plus I do odd jobs here and there for extra money. I don't mind it too much, but it does get lonely."

"You never married?" asked Elizabeth.

"Never figured I had much to offer a woman."

The dimly lit kitchen outlined Jacob's tall muscular frame and square set face. "I don't know about that. It seems to me that a woman would be lucky to have a man that makes her feel so safe." Elizabeth blushed at her own words but there was nothing she could do to retract her brashness.

Jacob fidgeted upon hearing Elizabeth's words. "So...how has your father been getting along with the farm?"

"You don't know? He sold out a couple years ago. All that's left is the house. I don't even know if that's clear. I guess I need to start figuring out what I'm going to do."

Jacob nodded. "You're a strong woman Elizabeth. You'll be fine. But I'll help in any way I can." Jacob pushed his chair from the table and stood. "Well, I guess I better be turning in. Goodnight."

Elizabeth squeezed Jacob's hand. "Thank you for everything tonight."

Jacob patted Elizabeth's hand and left the kitchen. As he made himself comfortable on the sofa Elizabeth bid him good night as she retired to her room.

Elizabeth woke early the following morning and went downstairs to make breakfast. The smell of fried eggs and bacon permeated the house by the time Jacob joined her.

"That smells delicious!" remarked Jacob.

"I hope you're hungry, I made plenty. Did you find everything you needed this morning?" asked Elizabeth.

"I did. How are you feeling this morning?"

Elizabeth pondered the question. The shock of her father's death seemed to have worn off, although the days still possessed dreamlike qualities. She knew that somehow her family could get by even if her father's vision didn't return. But she also knew that her father couldn't get by if he couldn't see, which is why she had prayed so hard for his sight to return. As angry as Elizabeth was at her father for leaving her and her mother, she understood his perspective. She didn't attribute William's suicide to cowardice but rather misguided chivalry. She was glad Doc Allyn didn't tell everyone how her father died. People would only remember that about him, and he didn't deserve that. Elizabeth guiltily admitted to herself that she wasn't that upset by her mother being taken away. She had lived with the twisted shell of what her mother once was. And without knowing how to care for her, Elizabeth uselessly watched her mother starve and mentally torture herself for months. And Doc Allyn did offer some hope that the doctors at the hospital could treat her.

"All things considered, I think I'm doing okay. I have to get up to see my mother soon though. I can't believe she doesn't know about Father. I'm dreading going to his funeral."

"You have to though," said Jacob. "If you don't go you'll regret it for the rest of your life. Besides, I'll be there."

The sincerity of Jacob's voice felt as comforting as her father's hugs. Elizabeth fought back the tears that formed in her eyes. "I hope you're hungry. Oh my, I already said that-I'm sorry." Jacob wrapped his arm around Elizabeth's shoulder and pulled her to his chest. Elizabeth cried into Jacob for several moments before she calmed down. "I'm sorry, I don't know what came over me."

"You don't have anything to apologize for. I can't believe anyone who has gone through what you have could be holding up as well as you are. I'm really proud of you."

Jacob's last sentence fought its way through the muck in Elizabeth's mind and provided a silver lining to the storm cloud that she considered her life. Elizabeth dried her crying eyes with her apron and slid the bacon and eggs onto her and Jacob's plates. The two ate in silence. When Jacob finished he wiped his mouth and pushed back from the table. "That was just fine! A man could get used to eating like that." Jacob stood up and retrieved Elizabeth's coat from the rack. He helped her from the table and held her coat from behind her. "I suppose we'd better get going. Are you ready?"

§

So many people attended William's funeral that Jacob had to park clear at the head of the Mystic River. Elizabeth grew more anxious with each step during the half mile walk to Saint Patrick's Cemetery. Her father was known and loved, and the thousand people crowding the banks of the Mystic River on that freezing morning attested to the fact.

Reverend Lowndes greeted Jacob and Elizabeth as they entered the cemetery through the break in the granite wall. "Come with me Dear." Reverend Lowndes hooked his arm through Elizabeth's. He glanced sharply at Jacob. "Jacob, I hope you are doing well."

Jacob nodded and then shrugged as the Reverend returned his attention to Elizabeth.

"I'm sorry that your mother isn't able to be with us today."

"She wanted to be here. She just isn't feeling well and-"

"It's quite alright Elizabeth. I know about your mother and I am praying for her. Come sit beside me while I speak about your father."

Darkly dressed men and women formed a horseshoe around Reverend Lowndes as he assumed his position beside William's casket. Jacob sat beside Elizabeth and clutched her hand as the Reverend spoke.

"Good morning friends. It is with heavy heart that I speak to you on this somber occasion. We all know of the tragic circumstance that brings us together this morning. But today we are not going to speak of tragedy. Today we will rejoice in remembrance of our brother William. Remembrance of the gifts that William gave us while he walked among us and the legacy that he leaves behind as he joins the Lord to watch over us."

Elizabeth *saw* Reverend Lowndes deliver her father's eulogy, but her mind wandered. She saw the funeral unfold before her as an observer rather than a participant. She witnessed the Reverend conclude his speech, witnessed the pall bearers lower her father into his grave, witnessed people she'd known her entire life toss mementoes into the grave. She watched the procession of townspeople offer condolences to her, and even watched herself thank them for their thoughts.

Jacob bent down and whispered into Elizabeth's ear. "Get away truck is leaving in five minutes. I think we can make it if we leave now."

Jacob's voice was like a life saver in a sea of confusion. Jacob parted the crowd and led Elizabeth from Saint Patrick's. The wind turned gusty and the first pellets of freezing rain splattered Jacob and Elizabeth as they walked along River Road. By the time they reached Jacob's truck Elizabeth's teeth chattered and her body shivered uncontrollably. William noticed as he opened the door for her. "Get inside - you're freezing."

Elizabeth nodded and smiled. "Yes, but at least I'm feeling it. It's been a long time since I've felt anything."

Jacob dropped to his knee in the parking lot of the Old Mystic General Store, still holding Elizabeth's hand. "Elizabeth, I know this sounds crazy. I want you to come back with me. Forget about everything else, we can come back and get your things later. Marry me."

A million thoughts raced through Elizabeth's mind. She became dizzy and the only thing preventing her from toppling over was the steady pressure from Jacob's hand. "Yes. I'll marry you."

Salmon Building

The year following Elizabeth and Jacob's Justice of the Peace wedding spiraled ever-downward, beginning with the consummation of their marriage. Jacob lived in an unkempt row home in Willimantic, which is where they honeymooned. His friend poured him whiskey before, during and after the small ceremony, leaving Jacob drunk and stumbling. When they were finally home in bed, Elizabeth's thoughts were light-years away.

"Time to show you what wives are for," slurred Jacob.

Elizabeth was so distracted that it took her a minute to comprehend her husband's meaning. Jacob crawled beside Elizabeth and pawed at her chest while jabbing his knee between her legs to separate them. Elizabeth's heart raced and a clammy sweat instantly coated her body. She felt strangled from within. "Jacob," she called. "Jacob!"

"That's right Honey, call my name!"

"No, Jacob, stop!"

The words slowly bored through Jacob's dulled senses. "What? Whassa matter?"

"There's something I have to tell you."

Jacob looked bored and annoyed as Elizabeth told him about Ocean House and about Ethan. Tears streaked her face by the time she finished the story.

"Okay," Jacob replied when he was certain Elizabeth was finished.

Elizabeth's sadness turned to anger and hurt. "'Okay?' That's all you have to say after everything I just told you?"

"Well, what I mean is I don't care about any of that."

Elizabeth laid her head back on the pillow as Jacob took her body, his words ringing through her mind. She knew he spoke the truth; *he really didn't care.*

Despite the small income Jacob earned at the laundry, he forbade Elizabeth from working outside the home. In fact, the only time Elizabeth could leave the house unaccompanied was to grocery shop. Elizabeth was certain that if shopping wouldn't inconvenience Jacob too much he would take away that privilege as well. Jacob made it clear that Elizabeth's role was to serve as his home support system. Clean the house, make breakfast, prepare his lunch, make dinner (and it better be warm, whatever time he decides to come home from his post-shift drinks with the boys), and of course be a willing participant in bed whenever the urge struck him. Well, *willing* was optional; denial was not.

Jacob drove Elizabeth to visit her mother on a few occasions, but always remained in the truck. On each occasion, a hospital aid escorted Clara to the visiting room upon Elizabeth's arrival. Although Mrs. Wellington assured Elizabeth that her mother was responding positively to treatment, her mother appeared frail and extremely sedated, and never provided any indication that she recognized her daughter.

To celebrate their first anniversary, Jacob told Elizabeth to invite the Brazzis over for dinner. Sal Brazzi worked with Jacob and Gloria was the only person with whom Elizabeth socialized.

Elizabeth liked Gloria, but Gloria always seemed slightly guarded around her. Gloria was heavy set and a few years Elizabeth's elder. She asked Elizabeth numerous times to attend Sunday services with her, but Jacob wouldn't hear of it. "Ain't no wife of mine going to no Catholic church with a bunch of Guineas." And that was the end of that.

Elizabeth and Gloria returned from market that Friday afternoon. They prepared lasagna with layers of noodles, mozzarella and ricotta cheese, ground beef, Italian seasoning, and some other spices that Gloria wouldn't divulge. They prepared a bowl of crisp salad, loaves of garlic bread, and even bought two bottles of chardonnay for the celebration.

"I'm sure the boys will get a lot of use out of these," said Gloria as she placed the wine in the refrigerator to chill.

Elizabeth smiled as Gloria's sarcasm registered. Neither Jacob nor Sal would drink a glass of wine to save their lives. They would, however, consume more than their fair share of whiskey that night, as well as every other night. "Good point. Maybe we should open one of them now. For cooking, of course."

Gloria giggled like a school girl as she retrieved one of the bottles and poured them each a glass. "I want to make a toast – to good friends."

The women raised their glasses. As Gloria finished her first sip, Elizabeth slapped her empty glass on the table. The wine made her instantly lightheaded and she held on to the wall for balance.

"Oh my goodness, I can't believe you just did that," said Gloria. "Bottoms up." Gloria followed Elizabeth's lead and downed the rest of her glass. She giggled, burped, and giggled again as she finished. She smacked her lips and told Elizabeth that they tingled.

"That must be why the boys always drink more," replied Elizabeth as she refilled the glasses. The ladies polished off the bottle as they set the table.

Elizabeth and Gloria greeted their husbands at the door and led them to the kitchen. They were both giddy and enjoyed their private secret.

"What's gotten into you two?" asked Jacob.

Elizabeth and Gloria exchanged glances and laughed again.

"Whatever it is, I'd like to get me some," commented Sal. "In fact," said Sal as he stared at Elizabeth's chest, "I'd really like to get me some of that." Jacob appeared oblivious to Sal's gesture, but Gloria was not.

Elizabeth's brief respite from the mediocrity of life ended just that quickly. She became instantly uncomfortable and self-conscious. She averted Sal's gaze and prayed that Jacob wasn't aware of Sal's covert flirting. Jacob wouldn't say a word during dinner if he did, but Elizabeth would suffer the consequences after their guests left.

Halfway through dinner Jacob caught Elizabeth's attention and winked at her. Certain that that was Jacob's warning that he caught on to Sal's innuendos, fear shot through her. But instead of growing sullen, Jacob became bubbly and began laughing as though he heard some unspoken joke that kept repeating in his mind.

When they finished eating, a serious look crossed Jacob's face. "That was delicious," said Jacob. "You two outdid yourselves. But I'm very concerned about something." Despite his solemn words, a grin that danced in his eyes. "Isn't today Friday?"

Already toasted from liquor, Sal replied, "Hold on, let me check." He opened up his wallet and checked its contents. "Yup, it's Friday. I still got most of my paycheck."

"Thought so," continued Jacob. "Wasn't that beef in the lasagna?"

The three other people sitting at the table stared at Jacob, not understanding what he was getting at. Suddenly Gloria leapt from the table and ran to the bathroom. Finally Elizabeth understood Jacob's game. Gloria was a devout Catholic and was forbidden to eat meat on Fridays. Jacob's gut splitting laughter filled Elizabeth's ears as she chased after her friend. By the time she reached the bathroom door she heard Gloria gagging. She pushed the door open and found Gloria with her fingers lodged in her throat in an effort to purge the food from her body. In violent waves Gloria expunged her dinner into the toilet. Elizabeth knelt beside her and rubbed her friend's back. When Gloria finished she leaned forward hugging the toilet.

"I'm so sorry," said Elizabeth.

Gloria slapped Elizabeth's hand from her. "Get away from me! You knew it the whole time. When we were shopping, when we were making it. You're supposed to be my friend and you make a joke of me all day. Then you shake your *rump* at my husband like I'm not even there! You think you're so pretty and you have such a handsome husband? You know the only reason Jacob went to your father's funeral? Because he *knew* your mother was crazy and no one any good would want you after what you did, that's why. And let me tell you, he was furious when he found out your father sold the farm. And even madder when there wasn't any money left after you sold the house. He only wanted you for your money, so I guess the jokes on you! It's all true, I heard him telling Sal. You know what else? He told me too, when we were *alone*. So enjoy your perfect little life, but stay the hell away from my husband!"

Elizabeth's body went limp and she slumped against the wall as Gloria stormed out of the bathroom. She couldn't believe the things Gloria just told her about Jacob, but at the same time knew they were all true. She distantly heard Gloria telling Sal to take her home, and heard Jacob's uncontrollable laughter above all else.

Elizabeth awoke the next morning needing to see her mother. She attempted to rouse Jacob but he was incoherent from drinking alone until well past midnight. At one point he mumbled for Elizabeth to drive herself. Elizabeth had never before been behind the wheel of a vehicle, but thought she could manage. On her first attempt she forgot to disengage the clutch, sending the old truck lurching forward when she turned the key. On her second attempt she popped the clutch and stalled the truck. Luckily the truck stalled as it was in first gear instead of reverse and she would have plowed into the garage had the truck continued another five feet. On her third attempt, with much grinding and protesting from the engine compartment, Elizabeth maneuvered onto the street.

Luckily it was early enough that there was little traffic on the roads. Elizabeth stalled the truck six times by the time she got to downtown Norwich. She drove down Washington Avenue and past the head of the Thames River, then headed south on Route 12. A few minutes later she crested the hill overlooking the sprawling hospital grounds. A dozen patients, *inmates* thought Elizabeth, mostly wearing bedclothes milled about the grounds. Most kept their heads bowed and didn't acknowledge Elizabeth when she parked the truck and walked toward the office. As with her previous visits a nauseating odor, which ammonia attempted to subdue or conceal, blasted Elizabeth when she entered the building. When Elizabeth finished gagging in response to the stench she noticed a middle-aged woman, looking equally as foul as the odor, staring at her from behind a desk.

"Visiting hours don't begin until ten o'clock. You'll have to come back."

Elizabeth's hackles stood on end. "I'm not coming back. I'm here now and I'm going to see my mother. Her room is right down the hall, I won't be any trouble."

The woman chuckled. "There isn't anyone down the hall dear. Do you think the patients live in *this* building?"

Heat spread across Elizabeth's face. "I've always visited my mother here, *in her room*!"

"Oh dear me," patronized the woman. She had the attitude of a malicious sister informing her younger sibling that there really isn't a Santa Claus. "This is just the parading grounds. They bring the patients here through underground tunnels from their quarters in other buildings. Go to the Salmon Building and bat your pretty little eyes at Mick. Maybe he'll let you see your mother early." Elizabeth stood dumbfounded. She'd taken comfort thinking her mother was well cared for. Now visions of filthy dungeons filled her mind. "The Sal-mon Build-ing," repeated the woman, speaking as though to a small child. "It's the big building at the end of the sidewalk." The woman flicked the back of her hand toward Elizabeth to dismiss her.

Elizabeth told the woman to go to hell.

"I'm already here, dear, for sixty hours a week. Run along now." The woman returned her attention to the newspaper.

Elizabeth went outside and looked about the complex. There certainly were no signs of underground tunnels, and Elizabeth wasn't certain the nasty woman was telling the truth about any of it. Elizabeth spotted a large brick building with a placard identifying it as the Salmon Building. She entered into a grand foyer with lovely Victorian furnishings. Dark mahogany wainscot lined the walls over half way to the ten foot ceiling. Elizabeth's worry about her mother living in a torture chamber subsided. She felt like she was in a governor's mansion instead of an insane asylum. An enormous marble-faced fireplace with elm trees engraved on both sides dominated the reception area. An intricate coat of arms connected the trees below the mantle, with a banner scrolling beneath it. Elizabeth stepped closer to read the words: *Qui Transtulit Sustini*.

"Beautiful work, wouldn't you say?"

Elizabeth jumped at the words. She didn't hear anyone approaching. "Yes. What does it mean?"

"Dunno, I think it's Latin. Some doctor told me it means 'Those who hold up to carry across,' whatever that means. What are you doing here anyway? The visiting area is -"

"I know, I've been there. The woman told me to see Mick, and maybe he could let me see my mother."

"She did, huh? Well I'm Mick. The thing is, usually the high-ups are the only ones that come to this building. I could get in a lot of trouble if I take you to see your mother." Elizabeth watched the wheels turning behind Mick's eyes before he continued. "But you know the saying, 'you scratch my back, I'll scratch yours'?"

Mick repulsed Elizabeth and she felt like gouging out his conniving eyes. She also wondered how many voiceless patients' backs Mick had scratched during his tenure at the hospital. "Well Mick, let's say you scratch my back first. My mother is Clara Newton."

Mick looked victorious as he strutted behind the counter. He flipped through a large ledger and ran his finger down the page. He removed a set of clanking keys from his belt and told Elizabeth to follow him. Once beyond the lobby the ornate detail disappeared and gave way to bleakness. Halfway down the hall Mick unlocked a door and told Elizabeth to watch her step. She followed him down a set of wooden stairs into a musty passageway. A dull glow illuminated the tunnel and on several occasions rats darted from beneath Elizabeth's feet as she stepped through puddles and debris. Finally Mick fumbled through his keys and unlocked an ancient door. Under normal circumstances Elizabeth would have been much more apprehensive about being isolated with someone as sinister as Mick. However, Elizabeth considered Mick an insignificant minion in the hell through which he escorted her. Unfortunately, things were about to get much worse.

"As many times as I've been through these tunnels, they still creep me out," said Mick.

The words echoed off the walls and sent chills down Elizabeth's spine. The stench of urine and defecation overpowered Elizabeth. She leaned against the wall and vomited. Elizabeth stood up after the initial wave of nausea passed. A catacomb of cages filled the area they entered. Each cage was the size of a small dog kennel and consisted of a hole in the floor in which the occupants could relieve themselves, a box containing personal effects, and a cot. Elizabeth's heart sank. Although she didn't think it possible, her mother's home was even worse than she imagined. Women of all ages occupied the cages. Some lay in bed, some sat on the floor. They rocked back and forth, drooled, yelled, whispered, and stared at nothing. The second wave of nausea attacked Elizabeth without warning and she vomited through the chain link cage beside her. The woman, barely Elizabeth's age, dragged herself across the floor and ran her fingers through the vomit.

"Over here," called Mick.

Elizabeth forced herself from the poor soul drawing in her vomit and joined Mick. Her mother wore a tattered bed shirt and laid on a grimy mattress. "I clean them up before they go to the visitor center. Luckily hardly any of them get visitors."

"Mother. Mother it's me, Elizabeth."

Clara Newton stared at the ceiling. Mick banged his nightstick against the cage. "Hey, wake up! You have company!"

Clara's eyes scanned the cage without moving her head. She rolled onto her side when she spotted Elizabeth. She pushed her spaghetti-thin legs off the cot and slowly stood up and walked to her daughter.

"You've finally come, after all these years."

"I was here two weeks ago, I saw you in the other building. Remember mother?"

"Mother!" seethed Clara. "I don't have a daughter! My *daughter* is rotting in hell! But you Hester, you are my pearl."

Elizabeth's throat constricted in unison with her heart. "How are you? Are they taking good care of you?" asked Elizabeth through her tears.

"Of course, I am fine." Clara stared lovingly at Elizabeth. "How did such a vile creature give birth to such a flower as you? Will I be going home with you today Hester?"

Elizabeth's heartstrings screamed with agony. She wanted to yell: *yes, yes, yes, come home with me*. But before she could reply at all Clara ducked her head. "Look out, they're here!" She bobbed her head to dodge unseen demons.

"Mother, what is it?" cried Elizabeth.

Oblivious, Clara yelled at *them* to leave her alone. "They're inside me!" yelled Clara. She scratched at her face, leaving bright red blood streaks in her fingernails' wake. Clara gnawed at her chain link walls, cutting her lips and gums in the process.

"We'd better go," ordered Mick. "I have to get help and you can't be here when it comes." Mick wedged himself between Elizabeth and the cage and pried her away with his body. "Come on, let's get going."

Elizabeth felt helpless as Mick manhandled her away from the cage toward the subterranean tunnel. Once in the passageway Mick grabbed her hand and dragged her behind him as he ran toward the Salmon Building. When they were upstairs he picked up the phone and called the switchboard. "Yeah, dispatch medical to Building 437, Newton. I saw her freaking out during my rounds. I'll meet them there." Mick hung up the phone. "Stay here," he told Elizabeth. "Better yet, go home!" Mick left Elizabeth and disappeared down the hallway.

§

Twenty minutes later Mick and a sturdy woman dressed in a gray nurse's uniform emerged from the hallway of the Salmon Building. Elizabeth looked up as they entered the lobby. Mick shot Elizabeth a glance that said *I told you to make yourself scarce*!

Elizabeth jumped up. "How is she? How is my mother?"

The nurse was taken aback by Elizabeth. "Your mother? How did you get here?"

Mick jumped in. "She must have been waiting for visiting hours at the other building. Yes ma'am," seethed Mick, "your mother is going to be fine. We had to sedate her."

"When will I be able to see her?"

"Certainly not today," answered the nurse. "Perhaps next weekend, it's too early to tell. You're mother has not been responding very well to treatment."

Elizabeth stood up to leave. "I'd like to speak to you for a moment," said Mick as he nodded at Elizabeth, as if to confirm their prior arrangement.

Elizabeth raised her fist toward Mick and then extended her middle finger, as if to confirm that she had no prior arrangement.

Elizabeth walked back to the truck and fired the old jalopy up. Her nerves jumped as she pulled onto Route 12. The truck bucked and stalled as she headed back toward Norwich. Traffic was much heavier than it was earlier. When she came to the last intersection before leaving downtown Norwich, she popped the clutch. The truck lurched out of control and as Elizabeth fought the steering wheel a telephone pole appeared suddenly in front of her. She turned the wheel at the last possible moment to avert disaster. The truck sideswiped the pole, caving in the passenger side. The intersection was deserted for the moment. She backed the truck onto the road and drove the short distance home.

Jacob flew from the house when the truck pulled in the driveway. He was already enraged, and that was before he saw the passenger side of his truck. "Get out!" he yelled. "What the hell do you think you're doing taking my truck? You can't drive!"

Elizabeth climbed out of the truck. Jacob's ranting momentarily subsided and he stared at Elizabeth. "What happened to you?"

Elizabeth touched her hand to her cheek and smeared a thin channel of blood from her nose. That was when she remembered banging her face against the steering wheel when the truck hit the telephone pole. "I'm fine. There was just a little accident…with the truck."

Jacob tore around the truck. When he saw the caved in passenger side he grew livid. "You stupid *wench*!" He ran back to Elizabeth and grabbed her hair. He spewed profanity at her as he dragged her in the house. While holding Elizabeth up by her hair, he slapped her across the face with his open hand. "Don't you ever get behind the wheel again! Get out of my sight!" Jacob released Elizabeth's hair and shoved her down the hallway.

Elizabeth put her hand to her face as she stumbled to their bedroom, but had no tears. Once her balance returned she opened her dresser drawers and began feeding her clothes into a bag. She didn't know what awaited her without Jacob, but she was about to find out.

That's when the nausea hit. She ran down the hall to the bathroom and made it just in time. She had been there before and recognized it. She was pregnant – and she wasn't going anywhere.

Marian

Following months of ineffective treatment for Clara's psychotic behavior, an ambitious young doctor began insulin shock therapy. Clara never awoke from the induced coma. She was sent to Heaven without the community outpouring of love and support her husband received. Reverend Lowndes delivered the eulogy beside the casket that would soon be buried next to William's. The Reverend thanked the Lord for blessing the world with such a loving wife and mother as Clara, and spoke of God's compassion for relieving Clara's earthly pains and reuniting her with her husband. Elizabeth did not hear the service or condolences or offers of help. Instead she stared at the mound of dirt that would shroud her mother's body for eternity.

As Jacob pulled the truck onto River Road he stated, "I'm glad that's over. I hate those things. Hungry?"

§

Elizabeth gave birth to Marian a month after her mother's funeral. Jacob used Marian as an excuse for his drinking and carousing. "With the pressure of working full time (*overtime, now that there's another mouth to feed!*), raising a family and taking care of the house, I need to blow off steam; so I can be a better *husband* and *father*!"

Elizabeth didn't protest. Her love for Marian filled the void that systematically grew within her like a cancer since her innocence died that night at Watch Hill. She cast no blame for her desolation; merely accepted the numbness as a welcome relief to the reality of life. But Marian sparked Elizabeth's atrophied spirit. The shared love between Elizabeth and Marian fueled that spark into an inferno that completed Elizabeth. Not a night passed without Elizabeth staring at her daughter long after Marian drifted off to sleep. Elizabeth noted every curve of her daughter's face, every unconscious smile or frown. She prayed more than anything that her daughter's innocence would never be stolen. At the end of the day, Elizabeth retired to her room content and excited about waking the following morning.

Elizabeth fretted the year Marian began elementary school. She knew Marian would do well. She could read and write by the time she was four years old, and not only played well with other children but was looked upon as a leader among the other pre-schoolers at the park. Elizabeth prepared Marian well for her debut into the outside world, but worried that she herself would not fare as well. Elizabeth knew that Marian unwittingly carried an enormous burden. Marian's companionship replaced a career, interaction with her husband, friends and any semblance of a social life.

Elizabeth walked Marian to her first day of school. The lump in Elizabeth's throat grew exponentially from the time they left their driveway until they reached the school's entrance. When Elizabeth bent down to kiss Marian and wish her luck, she could not speak. Marian understood and hugged her mother. "Don't worry Mommy, I'll be fine. So will you."

Elizabeth patted Marian's back and turned away, not wanting her daughter to see her cry. And she did cry. Elizabeth cried and sobbed the entire half mile walk home. Her face glistened with tears and snot as she returned home. Being alone for the first time in years provided an opportunity for all her repressed sorrows to emerge; and they came forward with a vengeance!

Elizabeth's body shook from the anxiety that sacked her. She rose and poured a tall glass of Jacob's bourbon. She clutched the glass with her trembling hands and raised it to her lips. The smell of the hard whiskey caused her to gag and she slammed the glass on the table. Next to the glass sat the paper on which she'd made Marian write (and re-write and re-write) her name and address the night before. Elizabeth stared at the paper for what seemed like an eternity, but was actually no more than a minute. Elizabeth turned the paper over and retrieved a pencil. She sat at the table and stared at the blank page. Guided not by her mind but by her soul, Elizabeth began writing. "Ode to My Parents – Loving Mother and Father, here no longer yet always with me…"

Elizabeth wrote for hours. When the sheets of paper were filled she retrieved the grocery bags from the garbage and wrote on them. A decade of heartbreak and sorrow poured from Elizabeth as fast as she could put pen to paper. When at last Elizabeth looked at the clock panic struck: school would be dismissed in ten minutes! She dumped her day's work in the trash and ran the five blocks to meet Marian.

Out of breath and sweating, Elizabeth arrived at the school with five minutes to spare. She joined a herd of mothers waiting for their children outside the school doors. The bell rang and a moment later an elderly teacher opened the doors. Young children funneled through the doors searching for their mothers. Tears of joy replaced the morning's tears of anxiety when Marian finally emerged from the school. The other children ran full steam toward their waiting mothers, those emerging behind Marian quickly passing her. Marian spotted Elizabeth and walked purposefully toward her, studying her. When she reached Elizabeth, she grabbed her hand and stared into her mother's eyes.

"How are you Mommy? I was worried about you today."

Elizabeth smiled. "I had a wonderful day," she said honestly. "How was your day?"

Relief spread through Marian and a wide smile made her own face glow. "I love school! It was so much fun! First, Mrs. McNair, that's my teacher, assigned our seats. And she made *me* sit between two boys! That's okay though because …"

Mother and daughter glided home as Marian described her first day of school in giddy detail. She was so proud of Marian and happy for her daughter's happiness. And Elizabeth no longer worried about herself. That day was one version of perfect for Elizabeth.

§

"Why the big deal, she's had eleven other birthdays. It's not like this is her first one," noted Jacob.

"You might want to brush your teeth before Marian's friends arrive. You smell like last night's gin," replied Elizabeth. "And, not that there has to be a special reason to have a birthday party, but if you need one this is her first birthday as a *woman*."

Jacob scoffed and headed down the hallway toward the bathroom. He hollered over his shoulder. "You better tell the *birthday girl* to hurry up. I'm meeting Sal at Sully's at noon and I don't want to hear you nagging if I leave before the party is over."

Elizabeth had been so busy preparing for the party she had not noticed Marian's absence since her daughter helped bake her birthday cake earlier in the morning. She walked to Marian's room and tapped on the door. "Marian. Marian?"

When her daughter did not reply, Elizabeth pushed the door open and entered the room. Marian lay sleeping on the bed with her arms wrapped around her old teddy bear. Elizabeth did a double take and then smiled; Marian hadn't slept with Teddy in years. Elizabeth knelt beside Marian and stared at her beautiful resting face. They were closer than ever, although the two were no longer inseparable. Marian had a cast of friends and played sports in school. Elizabeth had her writing. She didn't even know if Jacob knew she wrote; and didn't really care. Elizabeth placed her hand on Marian's shoulder and gently shook her. "Honey, it's time to get up. The guests will be arriving shortly."

Marian's eyes opened momentarily. Her pupils fluttered and then rolled up behind her eyelids and disappeared. Marian's eyes closed as quickly as they had opened.

A horrible premonition hit Elizabeth. Marian's face felt unnaturally cold against Elizabeth's hand. "Marian! Wake up! Do you hear me?"

Marian's eyes fluttered again, but this time focused and remained open. "What time is it?"

Elizabeth stared at her daughter. "Are you alright? Say something!"

"I'm fine. What are you doing?" asked Marian.

Elizabeth's rapid pulse and breathing slowed as relief spread through her. "Nothing dear. Ready for your party?"

Marian stared at her mother. "Sorry, I must have fallen back asleep. I'll be right out."

"Alright. I could use some help getting the prize bags together." Elizabeth stood and walked toward the door. As she crossed the threshold, Marian called after her.

"I love you."

Moisture filled Elizabeth's eyes. "I love you too. Let's get going now." Elizabeth hurried down the hall before her daughter saw the tears streaming down her face.

Elizabeth returned to the party preparations. She fished a pink streamer from a grocery bag. She tied one end to a kitchen cabinet and unrolled the streamer. She looped it around a lamp, over a ceiling light, through the curtain rod, and finally tying the other end to the coat rack in the living room. Next Elizabeth retrieved a blue streamer and criss-crossed the pink streamer wherever she could. Elizabeth was excited about the party. Excited for Marian, but admittedly for herself as well. Elizabeth enjoyed seeing the young girls playing together and giggling, exchanging secret glances, talking about boys. She loved seeing Marian happy with her friends. She shuddered suddenly at the scare she had just experienced in Marian's room. She quickly shook it off however and removed the cover from the new record album she bought especially for the party. Marian would love it! She was setting up the phonograph when she heard it: "Pshhht!" Jacob just opened a beer bottle.

"Jacob, come here right now. We need to talk!"

Jacob sported a wide grin as he crossed the room holding his freshly opened bottle of Milwalkee's best.

"I mean it! Come over here and sit down for a minute."

Jacob shuffled his feet across the floor as he joined Elizabeth on the coach. "Yes, *mother*!"

"Mock me all you want, but listen up. It's not even ten o'clock! You agreed not to drink until after Marian's friends left. Do you want to embarrass her at her own party?"

"It's just that I'm not used to all these kids that are coming over. Figured a cold one would take the edge off. I'll behave, I promise."

Jacob and Elizabeth's attention was drawn to Marian as she entered the living room. Marian crossed the room in a daze. She didn't respond to her mother. When finally Marian stood before her mother she placed a hand to her head and said, "I don't feel very well."

Marian spun half around and collapsed into her mother's lap. Her eyes rolled into the back of her head and her young body convulsed a half dozen times before sprawling lifelessly across Elizabeth's legs.

Elizabeth and Jacob stared at their dead daughter for several seconds. Elizabeth reacted first. She jumped off the couch, launching Marian's body onto Jacob. Elizabeth shrieked insanely as she ran to the kitchen. She opened the oven door and stuck her head all the way in as she fumbled with the switch trying to ignite the pilot light. Jacob was seconds behind her. Hollering at Elizabeth to stop, he wrapped his large arms around his screaming wife and yanked her from the oven just as the gas ignited. The fireball blew from the oven's face. The explosion blackened Elizabeth's face and set her hair aflame.

Jacob batted the flames scorching Elizabeth's skull. The explosion temporarily blinded him and he could barely breathe. He felt for the counter and supported himself against it. He grabbed

Elizabeth by the throat and dragged her to the sink. He opened the spigot and shoved Elizabeth's face into the sink while splashing the water over her burning hair. The stench of burning hair permeated the room and caused Jacob to gag. Elizabeth fell unconscious as the first alarm sounded at the Cohanzie Fire Department.

Elizabeth never remembered the week following Marian's death. The seconds before and after the tragedy, however, haunted her soul with unyielding clarity forever.

Word Games Part II

"I hope they hurry up," said Ann. "My daughter and her husband are going to be here soon."

"Patience," said Harry. "You see they're teaching a new gal this morning."

Harry, Jerry, Ann, Bart, Lucy and Elizabeth all watched an unfamiliar young lady accompany Daphne as she waited on Bayside's breakfast crowd. Finally the two women arrived at their table. "Good morning everyone," said Daphne. "I want you to meet Beth. Today is her first day so I'm introducing her to everyone. Please join me in welcoming her to Bayside."

"Good morning Beth, and welcome," said Bart. Harry, Jerry, Elizabeth, and Lucy joined Bart's greeting. Beth fidgeted, obviously uncomfortable being the center of so many people's attention.

"You're going to have to pick up the pace if you want to work here," said Ann. "Some of us have family coming. Running late with meals isn't going to cut it around here."

"I'm sorry Ann," said Daphne. "It's my fault. I just wanted everyone to meet Beth on her first day. We'll get breakfast right out." Daphne taking responsibility for the delayed breakfast did nothing to prevent Beth's face from turning beet red.

"Don't mind Ann," stated Harry. "She just gets jealous every time a pretty young thing shows up here. She's afraid I'll get the hots for you. And she's right, you're one hot tamale!" Harry sensed Elizabeth glaring at him. "You'll have to excuse me, Miss Beth. I forgot to take my medication this morning. Welcome to Bayside."

Beth peeped a meek "thank you" and followed Daphne to the serving window. Within a few minutes everyone in the Community Room had their breakfast. Ann made a production of shoveling down her food, ensuring everyone knew the reason for her rush. Once all the meals were served, Beth separated from Daphne and began refilling drinks at the tables.

"She seems like a nice enough gal," said Harry.

"Nice, but nervous," replied Elizabeth. "She'll do fine once she gets over her first day jitters. For years I worked serving meals. I saw tons of people come and go when I worked there."

"Well she better catch on quickly," stated Ann.

Jerry grew irritated at Ann's nagging. "Get over yourself already. You know right darn well that-. Well, never mind what you know. Just give the poor girl a break." Elizabeth stared at Jerry. Ann's nagging and bragging did grow tiresome, but she'd never seen Jerry snap like that.

Mrs. Nedbetter made her first appearance of the day. She normally fluttered around the room like a butterfly during breakfast, relating the activities planned for the day. With breakfast running late and everyone watching Beth, no one at the table had noticed Mrs. Nedbetter's absence. She entered the room from the administrative office area and crossed to the front of the room. "Excuse me. Excuse me! May I have everyone's attention?" Mrs. Nedbetter had never before made a public announcement during meals, and everyone provided their full attention. "I'm sorry for the interruption, but I have terrible news that I feel compelled to relay." The clank of knives and forks being laid down on ceramic plates peppered the room as everyone awaited the announcement. "There's been a tragic accident. Most of you know Dora Blackmoor. She's been an orderly here for many years. Last night her dog apparently went berserk and attacked her. She didn't survive. I'd like to observe a moment of silence in remembrance of Dora and her contributions at Bayside."

Not many of the four dozen or so diners at breakfast that morning didn't have their own tragic memories of Dora Blackmoor, and shivers went up their spines as they relived their horrifying experiences. The room became so quiet that a pin dropping would have reverberated like a baritone. No one bowed their heads; they just stared at Mrs. Nedbetter. Finally Jerry pushed back his chair and stood up. All eyes were on him. He stared at Mrs. Nedbetter and clapped his hands together once. Then twice. As he continued clapping, the residents who could stand joined Jerry. Those that couldn't clapped from their chairs. The Community Room sounded as though a thunderclap exploded. People clapped and whistled as relief spread through the crowd. Before she knew it, Elizabeth stood and joined the applause.

Mrs. Nedbetter became flustered and begged everyone to sit down. "Stop that! What's *wrong* with you people? One of our own has died a tragic death! Did you hear me?" Mrs. Nedbetter's face grew crimson as she finally stormed out of the Community Room.

Through the crowd Elizabeth spotted Beth frantically untying her apron. She threw it on the floor and ran out of the Community Room toward the exit, not making eye contact with anyone. Even amidst the ruckus and the horrifying events leading to people applauding such a violent death, Elizabeth smiled when she thought of what poor Beth must think of the people behaving so callously. *Okay*, thought Elizabeth. *So I was wrong about the new waitress working out.*

The days at Bayside turned into weeks, the weeks into months. Elizabeth lay on her side as she blinked the remnants of sleep from her eyes. She awoke to sunshine in full bloom cascading throughout her room. Through her window Elizabeth spied on the red-breasted harbinger of spring methodically plucking worms from the hill outside her room. The sounds of little brown birds happily chirping lifted Elizabeth's spirit like cotton candy at a summer carnival. Father Digiacomo's booming voice abruptly ended Elizabeth's solitary reverie.

"Wonderful morning, isn't it Elizabeth?"

Elizabeth's slight frame jumped beneath the covers. "I swear to Christ Father! If I ever considered becoming religious you'd scare me right out of it! " Elizabeth rolled over to look at her visitor, who couldn't fully conceal his smile.

"I'm sorry. I thought you heard me come in."

"How in the world would I hear you sneak in like a ghost when I'm sleeping? How would you like someone doing that to you when you're my age?" asked Elizabeth.

"I'll never be your age," said Father Digiacomo.

"I don't have much time left," replied Elizabeth. "You'll have your chance to catch up, don't worry." The reality of her words sunk in even as they left her mouth.

"We all have a certain time on earth, Elizabeth. Then our spirits ascend and we live on. So you see, I really never will be as old as you. But enough sparring. Did I see you and a friend walking down the road last week?"

'Enough sparring?' thought Elizabeth. *I have not yet begun to spar.* "Maybe you did. I have to get out of this hell-hole sometimes. Why do you keep coming back here? Haven't I made it clear that I'm not looking for salvation?"

"We all have a purpose, Elizabeth. I'm not trying to save you. I'm trying to help you find peace with yourself. You should rejoice in the life you've given others." Father Digiacomo surveyed the crossword magazines littering the small table and night stand. "I see you've been keeping busy. Have you looked at *the* Word, or pacified yourself only with these puzzles? If you just open your mind you'll see that you already have the answer to a much greater puzzle. But if you want a refresher you need only open the Bible laying by your bedside."

This should be fun, thought Elizabeth. "Actually I have perused the Good Book," Elizabeth again lied. "I don't think I was playing fairly last time we chatted. I didn't look at the big picture. I limited my search for the meaning of life to either the Old Testament *or* New Testament. So I combined them to see if perhaps I overlooked something." Father Digiacomo patiently waited as Elizabeth continued. "I must say Father; I uncovered some fairly disconcerting messages. Let's see, taking the first letter from all the Books I came up with *spite, desolate, desperate*."

Father Digiacomo shook his head. "You're not ready yet. Please don't wait until death knocks to realize your purpose. Your life's purpose lies right before you Elizabeth."

Unphased, Elizabeth continued. "But there is more, Father. I looked harder, like you suggested. Let's see…what do you get when you rearrange the first letters from Acts, Timothy, Hebrews, Isaiah, Exodus, Samuel, Thessalonians, Ephesians and Nehemiah? I'll tell you Father. You get *atheist* and *heathen*. So you see, the more I look in the Book the further I get from religion. It's very disheartening, I must admit." The more Elizabeth spoke the humbler she became. She actually wanted nothing more than to kneel before the holy man and ask forgiveness, but couldn't. Instead she turned over and stared back out her window.

Father Digiacomo studied Elizabeth for some time before responding. "This burden that you've carried for so long Elizabeth, this *guilt*, is not your cross to bear. Life is full of trials and tribulations. But the glory of God overshadows all of it! Open your mind, Elizabeth. Open your *soul*."

Father Digiacomo rose from his chair and engulfed Elizabeth's head in his large hand. He squeezed her head firmly and softly prayed aloud. Elizabeth felt her soul melting into his palms and tears streamed down her face. After an eternity the Father removed his hand from Elizabeth. A million images flashed before Elizabeth. When she finally had the courage to face Father Digiacomo, she turned over and found herself alone.

Irene

"I can see you're upset," said Dr. Rogers. "But maybe you could take a different perspective. Don't look at it as though you wasted ten years. Try taking the approach that you've finally found the solution and you won't have to live like that anymore. You should be excited about this."

Elizabeth exhaled a stale yellow stream of cigarette smoke. "Excited? I'm knocking on middle age Doctor. I don't think I have much more *excitement* in me. I'm going to ask you one more time. Are you *positive* that my problem is an underactive thyroid and not pernicious anemia?"

"I am absolutely certain. You'll take one pill a day to control your condition. No more weekly B-12 shots, no more prune juice with desiccated liver. Unless of course you've grown fond of the blend, in which case you may continue drinking it."

Elizabeth inhaled deeply on her Pall Mall, disregarding the doctor's attempt at lightening the conversation. "So my yellow flaking skin that always itches, my lack of energy will go away just like that? I haven't been able to walk up stairs without gasping for air for longer than I can remember."

"I know it's hard to believe right now. But within a week you will feel twenty years younger. You will be able to enjoy life again."

Elizabeth took another drag on her cigarette and exhaled. She had been smoking since Marian died and couldn't get enough. She prepared to vent more to Dr. Rogers, but as the words fought their way to her mouth her throat constricted. The doctor's words registered: "*able to enjoy life again.*" The gravity of the statement hit Elizabeth like a ton of bricks. She hadn't enjoyed life, or a single day, since her daughter collapsed with a brain hemorrhage in her arms so many years before. She tried to speak but again was too choked up. Instead of words coming from her mouth, tears erupted from her eyes. Jacob's doctor diagnosed Elizabeth with pernicious anemia a year or so after Marian's death and her well being had declined steadily since then. The weight of the world crashed down upon Elizabeth and she sobbed into Dr. Roger's shoulder. When Elizabeth could finally speak she said, "I'm sorry I've acted like such a…well I guess I wasn't acting. I'm sorry I'm such a witch."

"Don't worry about it. Everything will be fine now. Start taking these pills today and come see me next week. I expect a different person will be standing before me next time we meet."

During the walk home the overwhelming claustrophobia Elizabeth experienced at the doctor's office subsided. She put her faith in the doctor's word: *absolutely*, he had said. Against her better judgment Elizabeth began envisioning life without pain, without hopelessness. She relished the prospect of freedom from her bodily prison. As she turned onto her street however, the reality of life clawed back into her mind. Jacob provided room and board for Elizabeth and normally (thank goodness) only one drunken conjugal a week. Due to whiskey most of those visits did not result in Jacob's climax. That fact, however, did nothing to lesson Elizabeth's revulsion. That was the extent of their relationship and Elizabeth had long since stopped considering doing anything about it. Rather, she patiently served her sentence on earth in anticipation of reuniting with her family in Heaven when she was released.

Elizabeth entered the house and sat at the kitchen table. Over the years Elizabeth filled and discarded reams of paper laden with bitterness. That day however, she didn't scribe words of death and despair. Instead she recounted the beauty of nature and the purging of dark with light. The words did not come as fluently as usual but they were *right*. Elizabeth wrote for hours, and actually thought she could feel the medicine stimulating her body's chemistry into alignment. She knew she imagined it, but took relief from the feeling nonetheless.

The sound of footsteps and conversation at the front stoop caught Elizabeth's attention. Jacob burst through the door and strutted across the living room like he was king of the world. "I brought us dinner, and a guest," he said. "Writing about dying again, what a surprise! Anyway, I want you to meet my cousin. Irene, come on in and meet my...meet Elizabeth."

Elizabeth set down her pencil and watched a young woman enter her house. Her clothes were tattered and she didn't look up to meet Elizabeth's stare. Elizabeth's eyes shifted from Irene to Jacob. "You don't have any cousins around here. And she is young enough to be your granddaughter."

"Ma'am, we're not really cousins-" began the girl.

Jacob interrupted. "Well, not blood cousins. She's Vinnie's niece. You know, Vinnie from Sully's. Anyway, she's *like* family. I've known her since she was a child."

"She *is* a child," stated Elizabeth.

Jacob ignored her. "Like I was saying. Vinnie's brother is going through a rough time right now and Irene needs a place to stay for a little while. He'd do the same for us if the tables were turned. Besides, I thought it might be nice to have another girl around. You know, since-"

Fury racked Elizabeth's body. She jumped up from the table and stood before Jacob, cutting him off before he could use her daughter's name as an excuse to bring this homeless girl into their house. "What the hell are you doing? You think you can just bring this tramp into our house and I won't say anything about it? I know you don't have any respect for me, but I didn't know I sunk this low!"

Irene began sobbing. "Ma'am," she said. "I'm not a, not what you said. Vinnie really is my father and he's in lock up. Jake said I could stay here, but I didn't think it was a good idea. I'm sorry for the trouble." Irene turned and left the house.

As disgusted as Elizabeth was with Jacob, her heart wept for this stranger she just turned out to the streets. "You will rot in hell - *Jake*!"

Elizabeth chased after the young girl. "Wait! Irene, wait up." Elizabeth caught up to Irene. "I'm sorry for what I called you. I didn't mean it. You have no where to go? No friends or family?"

Irene shook her head.

"Come back with me then. We have a room you can stay in." Elizabeth held the girl's hand and walked her back home.

"Now that's better," said Jacob when the two entered the house. "I'm starving, let's eat."

As Jacob pulled a chair out from the table Elizabeth grabbed it. "Thank you so much for dinner, Irene and I will enjoy it. Now go to Sully's, or wherever else you go every night."

"But we have a guest, we should eat like a family," protested Jacob. The venom in Elizabeth's eyes caused Jacob to flinch. "Yeah, fine, great," he stammered. "You two get to know each other. I'll be home later."

Connecticut turned hot and steamy as spring ebbed and summer came into its own. Jacob spent more evenings at home. Elizabeth remembered how handsome he was at her father's funeral. Still, something dark festered underneath the façade.

"Rummy!" shouted Irene as she laid down three kings on the table.

Elizabeth slapped her palm on the table. "Darn you! I was one card away! We need to think of a different game to play."

Irene smiled as she collected the cards and began shuffling. And shuffling. And shuffling. Elizabeth watched patiently and finally asked, "Is something on your mind?"

Irene's face flushed. "Well, I want to ask you something but I don't know how."

Elizabeth smiled and waved at Irene to spit it out.

"Remember when you came after me when Jake, Jacob, first brought me? Well, I feel bad saying it, but I was scared of you. Your skin was yellow. And you only ran a few seconds but you were out of breath and wheezing and kind of wobbling." The words seemed to sting Irene's face as they left her mouth. "But now, your skin is fine and pale. And when we go for our walks I can barely keep up with you sometimes."

Elizabeth nodded. "It's a long story, but I was sick. I just didn't know with what. To tell you the truth, I think I owe as much to you for getting me better as I do my medicine."

Irene didn't know what to say and she bowed her head. And shuffled some more.

"There's more?" asked Elizabeth.

"I owe you so much Elizabeth. You have too much class to ask about my family, but my childhood wasn't the greatest. I quit school early and could barely read or write. Now I write every day with you and read everything I can get my hands on. And there's so much more than that! Sometimes when I'm laying in bed at night I could just burst thinking of all the things I want to thank you for. You're like the mother I never knew."

Elizabeth clasped Irene's hands in her own and looked into her eyes. "The feeling is mutual dear. You're welcome here as long as you like." Following an awkward silence Elizabeth asked, "So, ever hear of pinochle?"

The two women played until midnight, when once again the student bested the master. "I'm done," stated Elizabeth. "I know when I've been beat. Actually I knew it about six hours ago, but I'm ready to throw in the towel." Elizabeth kissed Irene on the cheek and retired to bed.

Following a delightful day with Irene, Elizabeth crawled under the covers. The hot stale air did not move in the bedroom and sweat coated her forehead. She lay with only a light sheet covering her body. "Dear Lord," Elizabeth prayed aloud, "I know it's been a while since you've heard from me. I want to thank you for my health. And I really want to thank you for sending Irene to our house. I pray that I am doing the right thing for her because of all she has done for me. I've strayed from You for so long, but maybe there is a reason for everything You do after all. In Jesus's name I pray, Amen."

§

"Come on, I need some loving," slurred Jacob as he tugged the sheet off Elizabeth.

Elizabeth awoke to Jacob's rough hand shaking her. The foul stench of liquor caused her stomach to wrench. She turned on her side away from her husband. "Not tonight. You're drunk." She covered her body and drew the sheet around her neck.

"So I had a couple beers. A man has certain needs. Come on now." Jacob grabbed Elizabeth's shoulder and pulled her to him. "Don't make me ask again."

Elizabeth shot out her hand to stop Jacob's advance as he hooked his leg over her waist. "Get off me and go to sleep!"

Jacob outweighed Elizabeth by a hundred pounds and she couldn't prevent him from rolling on top of her and pinning her to the mattress. To no avail Elizabeth struggled to free herself. Jacob ran his hand up Elizabeth's nightshirt and roughly grabbed her breasts, squeezing and tugging them. "Stop it, you're hurting me!"

"You like to play rough, huh? You like it, I know you do!" Jacob kicked Elizabeth's legs apart and fumbled with his zipper.

Finally Elizabeth freed her arm and let is dangle off the side of the bed. Before Jacob entered her she bared her claws and swiped at his face with all her might. Jacob hollered like a jackal as he jumped up clutching his face.

"You're gonna pay for that!" Jacob socked Elizabeth with his backhand and nearly launched her off the bed. With his left hand still covering his wounds, Jacob fully extended his right over his head. In the dull moonlit room Elizabeth's last conscious vision was Jacob's mighty fist plunging toward her face.

§

Unconsciousness claimed Elizabeth and rescued her from the initial pain of a broken cheek and nose. The tide of darkness soon receded and left in its wake memories that the trials of life had long since eroded.

Sunlight streamed through her bedroom window at the farm. She rubbed the sleep from her eyes and got dressed. As she went downstairs the smell of bacon and eggs generated a gnawing sensation in her stomach. By the time Elizabeth sat at the kitchen table her mother set down a steaming plate that Elizabeth jumped into. She saw her father working in the fields swinging a scythe. Her mother poured a tall glass of freshly squeezed orange juice and told her to hurry so she wouldn't be late for school. Elizabeth had just recently been allowed to help with the chores and cut through the woods instead of going to school with her mother. Elizabeth kissed her mother and darted out the back door toward the chicken coop. A voice startled Elizabeth as she scooped the grain into an old metal bucket. She turned as Jacob stepped directly in front of her. To the little girl Jacob stood as tall as an oak tree. 'Elizabeth,' said Jacob. 'I have a secret. I want you to be my special friend. You can't tell anyone though, you have to promise.' Elizabeth was excited at the offer a special friendship from an adult.

Those two words, *special friend*, bombarded Elizabeth's subconscious. They repeated time after time and grew louder and more ominous with each recitation. Accompanying the phrase were memories of Jacob patting her behind, giving her "horsey-rides" on his lap, games of "you show me yours and I'll show you mine," long stares that Jacob stole at Elizabeth when William and Clara weren't watching. Even as these dark suppressed memories fought their way to the surface Elizabeth felt guilty about the hatred she felt toward her parents when they sent Jacob away so many years before.

The truth of her childhood relationship with Jacob proved too much to bear and blackness fought to regain its foothold on Elizabeth's mind. An instant before darkness again consumed Elizabeth, thoughts of Jacob's prolonged looks at Irene, casual pats on her back which sometimes were too low for comfort, and comments about what a fine woman she's turned out to be came crashing to the forefront.

Elizabeth clawed her way to consciousness. The side of her face pounded like a drum and her left eye was swollen shut. When she pushed herself off the bed she drew her hand away wet and sticky from the pool of blood that recently poured from her nose. When she first stood she lost her balance and stumbled backward against the bureau. The corner stabbed Elizabeth's back and made her cry out. She closed her good eye until the room stopped spinning. Shrieking from across the hall urged Elizabeth forward. Using the wall for balance Elizabeth navigated out of her room into the hallway. The cries were louder and more insistent. Elizabeth forged ahead and opened the door to Irene's room

The streetlight illuminated the small room. Irene curled in a ball in the corner of the room with a sheet wrapped around her. Blood smeared the girl's face and Jacob grabbed the sheet and tore it from Irene. In one swift movement Jacob tore off Irene's underpants. He flipped her over and shoved her head against the wall. As Jacob positioned himself behind Irene, Elizabeth grabbed the lamp from the dresser. Holding it by the light fixture she swung it as hard as she could. The ceramic base shattered over Jacob's skull. The room turned deathly quiet and all movement ceased. Suddenly Jacob jumped up and charged like a bull toward Elizabeth. As Elizabeth turned her head to avoid direct impact from Jacob's fist, Irene caught his leg. With his footing lost, Jacob tumbled forward. His head smacked against the corner of Irene's dresser and he collapsed to the floor.

Elizabeth screamed. "Get out of here! Go get help!"

Irene scrambled to her feet and slipped out the door, urging Elizabeth to follow.

Elizabeth pushed Irene out and ordered her to hurry. She stood before her husband, expecting his arm to shoot out at any moment and grab her leg. But Jacob lay still. Elizabeth tipped his face upward with her foot. Jacob's unseeing eyes were wide open and a small stream of blood trickled from his ruptured temple. Elizabeth felt no remorse staring down at Jacob's dead body.

§

Jacob was well known by the police, many of whom were his drinking buddies. However, one look at Irene and Elizabeth made their decision to determine Jacob's death "accidental" very easy for the investigator.

Jacob's life insurance policy and his modest annuity from the laundry permitted Elizabeth to keep the house and send Irene to college. Irene took a position in San Diego and established herself as one of the country's first credible female journalists. Elizabeth flew to California for Irene's wedding, and years later Irene and her husband visited Elizabeth with their three children. They never lost communication, and Elizabeth was eighty years old when Irene's husband of forty years called her to tell her Irene passed away peacefully in her sleep.

Dawn

by Elizabeth Lockett

Skies aglow from an unknown torch
Amber and russet and gold
Dawn is the bridge between night and the day,
A span of a million years old

Purple and blue and black is the night
But sunrise brings new hope restored.
Go-fears and tears and sorrow of night
Each dawn is a tryst with the Lord.

Victor

"I know you're not going to put that pot away like that. I don't care if you are on community service. Would you put it back in your mother's cabinet like that?" scolded Elizabeth.

Juan Esposito returned Elizabeth's stare. "My mother is a crack addict that's been locked up in prison since I was three. She wouldn't care."

"What's that got to do with me?" asked Elizabeth. She yanked the six gallon pot from the counter and shoved it into Juan's midsection. "Get a spatula and scrape the burnt sauce from the bottom, then show me."

As Elizabeth walked to the serving line, Juan called after her. "You're sexy when you're angry."

Elizabeth left the kitchen and walked back to the serving line at Thames Valley Senior Center. "Bess," called Janice. "You better be careful talking to him like that. You know why he's here."

"He's not really a bad kid. Maybe if he'd had someone to tell him what to do when he was growing up he wouldn't be here now. Besides, he thinks I'm *sexy*." Elizabeth gyrated her seventy year old hips and smacked her bottom. It took a moment for Janice to connect Elizabeth's words and actions, but when she did an asthmatic cackle erupted from her wrinkled lips and she began wheezing. "Stop it! You're-killing-me!" Janice produced a brown lunch bag from her apron pocket and lifted it to her face. The bag inflated and collapsed as Janice's breathing returned to normal.

"You can't blame me for that," replied Elizabeth. "I think it might have more to do with the two cartons of Winston's you suck down every week."

"Look who's talking! You smoke like a chimney," countered Janice.

Elizabeth smiled. "That's not true at all. I haven't smoked in…days. Three, to be exact."

"No wonder you say whatever you want to Juan, you're probably going loco quitting cold turkey like that! 'Suicide by Criminal' they'll put on your death certificate. You ought to just keep on smoking, you'll probably last longer."

Elizabeth smirked. "As enticing as living as long as humanly possible sounds, I think I'll just do it my way."

Janice shook her head. "Besides, why do you waste so much time trying to help these thugs when there's a real man right in front of you?"

"You are not a man," replied Elizabeth.

"You are impossible Bess! You know who I mean. Victor has been interested in you since he started coming here. That's why he's always the last person to leave, just so he can offer to drive you home. Which, by the way, you've never accepted. I heard he has a lot of money too; he was a doctor or something. And he's not even on the rebound; he's been a widower for ten years."

"I'm leaving," stated Elizabeth. "Make sure Juan cleans those spaghetti pots good." Elizabeth went to the bathroom and hung her apron on the hook behind the door. As she washed her hands she hesitantly looked at her reflection in the mirror. Brown dye disguised the gray, but there was no hiding the sparse straw-like hair that eventually covered her head following the oven explosion decades earlier. Following her release from the hospital after Marian's death, fresh pink skin replaced the singed skin that sloughed off her face. Although she didn't scar from the explosion, she was wrinkled even beyond her years. Elizabeth thought her reflection a ghastly sight and left the bathroom.

She patted her hair in place and walked through the dining area of the Senior Center toward the front door. Despite what she told others, and herself, it was more convenient for her to leave through the back door. Still, Victor *would* be waiting to offer her a ride.

"Excellent pasta today Elizabeth," stated Victor as Elizabeth walked toward the door.

Elizabeth stopped. "Why do you call me Elizabeth? Everyone else in here calls me Bess."

"I know they do. But my first day here I read the "Book of Poetry" that the Center published. You have three poems in there, and each one says by "Elizabeth Newton." I figured if you wanted to be called Bess, the poems would have said by *Bess* Newton."

Elizabeth had nearly forgotten about "Book of Poetry: A Gift for the Generations." Years earlier the director of TVSC launched an initiative to publish a book of poems written solely by staff and patrons of the Center. After much prodding, mostly by Janice, Elizabeth agreed to submit a few poems.

"I can't believe you read that," said Elizabeth. "To be honest I'd nearly forgot about that book. I haven't even seen the Center's copy of the book for quite some time."

Victor looked away. "Well, the thing is, I have it at home. I read the other poems, and some were really good. But when I read yours, especially "Journey Through Time," well, it really moved me."

"You *stole-*"

"*Borrowed*, Elizabeth. I'm going to return it, just as soon as I'm finished with it. So, can I give you a lift home?"

Victor interpreted Elizabeth's slight hesitation as acceptance. He stood from his chair and hooked his arm through Elizabeth's. As the couple left the Center, a round of applause erupted behind them. Above the clapping of the six staff members and final four diners, Elizabeth heard Juan holler, "I guess the best man won. You go girl!"

§

Except for her telephone calls from Irene and the interaction with people at the Center, Elizabeth was alone. She had long since sworn off pets to avoid the inevitable heartbreak that accompanied their passing, and her life was routine. Her crosswords and game shows kept her mind active and sharp, but her heart was cynically tainted. Victor drove her home and escorted her to her apartment door. Elizabeth's discomfort was obvious and manifested in her silence.

"Are you going to invite me in?" asked Victor.

"I'm tired, but thank you for the ride."

"Alright then. I'll see you tomorrow at the Center." Victor turned to go, but called after Elizabeth. "You know, a lot of us have loved and lost. I have. I was ready to give up hope, give up everything. Until I read your poems, that is. Your words jumped off the pages at me. For the first time since my Millie passed on I understood that I wasn't alone in my desperation; the pointlessness of life, the feeling that I alone suffered unbearable loss. Your words provided me solace that people can endure heartbreak, and yet carry on with grace."

Emotions boiled within Elizabeth as she stood speechless before Victor. *Could it be true? Did others bear calluses as thick as she did where hope and dreams once lived?* "Come in, please. And tell me about Millie."

The two sat on the sofa and spoke for hours of their lives, each drawing tears and laughter from the other. As the final wisps of light from outside faded, Elizabeth asked, "Can I get you another cup of tea?"

Victor shook his head. "Thank you, no. As it is I'll be going to the bathroom all night. I suppose I should be getting along. Will I see you tomorrow?"

"Lord willing," replied Elizabeth. "One never knows at this age."

Victor smiled and clasped Elizabeth's hands in his own. "This afternoon has been wonderful. I hope there will be another verse to "Journey Through Time," an ending with a more hopeful outlook."

Victor drew Elizabeth's hands to his lips and kissed them. "Good night Elizabeth."

§

As the days following Elizabeth's first afternoon with Victor quickly turned into weeks and months, Elizabeth's heart smiled for the first time in years. Victor somehow slipped past the concrete walls behind which she barricaded her emotions. They enjoyed each other's company naturally; no awkward silences, no pussy-footing around issues. They communicated as though they had been together always. On the Saturday that Victor planned on taking Elizabeth to Devil's Hopyard State Park, Elizabeth awoke as the first rays of sunlight crept through her blinds. When she blinked her eyes a gray cloud veiled her sight. Elizabeth blinked again and rubbed her fists in her eyes to clear her vision. Elizabeth looked around her bedroom as though through cell block bars, with rows of black and gray lines running vertically down her eyes. *Oh my God*, thought Elizabeth, *I've had a stroke!* She closed and reopened her eyes, but experienced the same occluded vision. She concentrated and methodically wiggled the toes on each foot, then her ankles, legs, fingers, hands, arms and head. Satisfied that she still possessed motor function, she spoke out loud to test her speech. "How do I sound?" Elizabeth asked herself. Again satisfied, Elizabeth breathed a sigh of relief. She resigned herself to going blind, but could not accept immobility. Elizabeth slid her legs over the edge of the bed and stood. She obtained a towel from the bathroom and wrapped it around her face, tying the ends behind her head. She spent the morning navigating her small apartment, preparing for her impending blindness. She counted the number of steps from the television to the sofa; bathroom sink to the tub; kitchen table to the cabinets and refrigerator and microwave. She noted the height of door knobs, light switches and closet hangers. By the time Victor rang the door bell at eleven o'clock Elizabeth was comfortable that she could get by without vision. The assimilation so absorbed her that she didn't think to remove the towel before opening the door.

"Victor, is that you?" asked Elizabeth.

"Yes Dear, but you might be able to see better without that towel around your face."

"Dear Lord!" shouted Elizabeth. She yanked the towel from her face and pulled her bathrobe closed as she ran into her bedroom. "I'll be right out!"

Twenty minutes later Elizabeth joined Victor in the living room. "Are you ready?" she asked.

Victor stared at Elizabeth. "I am, but is there anything *you* would like to talk about?"

"Not at all. Why do you ask?" replied Elizabeth.

"No reason I guess. The facial wrap was a nice effect. Shall we?"

Elizabeth accepted Victor's hand as he escorted her to his Lincoln. She observed the bursting autumn foliage during the drive to Hadlyme when it struck her that this would most likely be the last season she would be able to enjoy the colorful display. Although Victor knew something distressed Elizabeth from the moment he arrived at her apartment, he gave her time to tell him herself. Elizabeth finally reached out.

"Victor, it's my eyes. When I woke up this morning there were lines running through my vision. I think I'm going blind." Elizabeth's eyes teared up as the sudden images of all the things she would never see again flashed across her mind.

Victor reached across the seat and held her hand. "I'm sure it's not that serious. My nephew is an optometrist. Let me call him." Victor pulled the long car to the side of the road and keyed numbers into his cell phone. After a brief conversation he told Elizabeth that they were driving to his nephew's in Groton Long Point. Victor drove back through Norwich. Through her obscured vision she observed the state hospital straddling Route 12. Memories of her mother in that hideous cage in the bowels of the hospital slapped Elizabeth across the face. She pushed the image from her mind and took no solace in Reverend Lowndes' graveside assurance that her parents are now reunited in Heaven. Self-pity snuck its meddlesome nose in and replaced Elizabeth's sad reflections of her mother. She tried to burn every image into her mind as though she was seeing it for the last time. As if reading her mind, Victor squeezed her hand and assured her everything would be alright.

The two drove briefly through Preston and Ledyard and entered the northern tip of Groton. Elizabeth was amazed at the sprawling submarine base. The last time she had seen it there was a single guard out front and a couple barracks located within. Elizabeth marveled at the non-stop strip malls, stores and traffic they passed driving through Groton. As they left the business district and approached Fort Hill, Victor nodded outside Elizabeth's window. "That's where I went to high school. A *very* long time ago, of course." Elizabeth looked at the old brick building which now indicated *Fitch Middle School* and saw the densely packed houses that crept right up to the school yard perimeter. "I remember when this was all open field," she said. "They used to race-" Memory of Toby Garfield's attack on her suddenly flashed before her eyes. Then she remembered clocking him with the rock and she smiled. "They used to race cars here."

Victor smiled. "Well, not to give away my age, but I remember watching horse races here. What I wouldn't give to have those days back."

Elizabeth's smile faded as thoughts of Toby triggered thoughts of her father's confrontation and the explosion at the Packer Building...and her father's death. "Not me. Good riddance to them, I say."

Victor drove up Fort Hill and turned past the police station toward Esker Point. They entered Mumford Cove and passed million dollar waterfront homes by the dozen. Finally Victor turned into a circular cobblestone driveway with an enormous fountain in its center. He escorted Elizabeth up the steps to the entryway and rang the bell. A moment later a handsome young man answered. "Hi Uncle Vic, come on in. I'm Preston, and you must be Elizabeth. I've heard so much about you, I'm glad we finally get to meet." Preston hugged Elizabeth. "You've given new life to Uncle Vic. He walks on air ever since you two have been together. We were really worried about him after Aunt Millie passed."

"Mind your business," ordered Victor. "Can't you see Elizabeth is concerned about her eyes?"

"Oh, right. Follow me." Preston took Elizabeth's hand and led her to an office. Floor to ceiling cherry wainscot lined the walls. An enormous King Louis desk occupied the center of the room, and pedestals containing very uncomely sculptures occupied the corners of the room. Preston caught Elizabeth scrutinizing a particularly disproportionate bust. "I know," he commented. "They stink, I know. But sculpting is my hobby and I spend so much time working on them I can't bear to throw them out. This is the only room in the house my wife lets me keep them. Anyway, what's going on with your eyes today?"

Preston retrieved a flashlight from an ornate wooden case as Elizabeth spoke. When she finished he tilted her head back and examined her eyes for several minutes. He placed the light back in its case and spoke to Elizabeth. "I can't be one hundred percent certain, but I'm pretty sure you have a case of Spider Eye."

Elizabeth clenched the arms of the chair. "Good Lord! What is that?"

"No, no, no, don't worry; it sounds a lot worse than it is. It's called Spider Eye because in most cases the patient's vision is obscured as though looking through a spider's web. It's a temporary condition that should last a few days and then gradually fade. I'd be glad to see you in my office next week, but I think by Monday your vision should be returning to normal."

Elizabeth closed her eyes and drew in a deep breath. As much as she convinced herself that life without vision would be palatable, the instant she realized she wasn't going blind she thanked God. And then chastised herself for the hypocrisy of thanking the same God that she denounced only an hour earlier when they passed the state hospital. "Thank you Preston. I am so relieved."

The doctor patted Elizabeth's shoulder. "No problem! It's the least I can do for the woman who made an honest man out of Uncle Vic. Can I get you two something to eat or drink?"

"No thank you Preston," replied Victor. "If my lady friend is still up for it we have a date."

Elizabeth nodded and thanked the young doctor again as they left the house and began the drive back toward Hadlyme.

§

Unsuccessfully Elizabeth fought to deny her feelings for Victor: her *love* for Victor. She felt that Victor returned those feelings. As much time as they spent together, and as openly as they shared their most intimate and personal secrets, the *four letter word* never crossed their lips. Elizabeth thought that denying the word would deny the heartbreak that inevitably accompanied it.

"Why so glum today, Elizabeth?" asked Janice. "He'll be here, don't worry."

"I'm not worried about that," replied Elizabeth. "I'm just upset that the lettuce isn't very fresh."

"The lettuce is perfectly fresh and you know it. Call him if you're worried about him."

Elizabeth's throat constricted. "I tried, but there's no answer."

"I'm sure he's fine. But if he doesn't show up I'll drive you to his place when we're finished cleaning up from lunch."

"Janice," began Elizabeth. "Today is our one year anniversary – from the first time he drove me home." Elizabeth's eyes began tearing.

Janice placed her arms around Elizabeth and patted her back. "Don't worry. He probably lost track of time."

Janice's words provided Elizabeth no comfort. Victor never lost track of time.

"Uh-oh Bess, I didn't know you swung that way," said Juan as he entered the kitchen and observed the two women hugging each other. "I could handle losing you to Mr. Moneybags, but not to another woman. That's hard on a man's ego."

Janice broke her embrace with Elizabeth and shoveled Juan from the kitchen. "What are you still doing here anyway? Your community service was up three months ago."

"I know," answered Juan. "But you two are like the great-great-great grandparents that I never knew." Juan shielded himself from Janice as she stormed up to him.

"Great-great-great...? I'll give you a great-great-great whipping! Get out of here!"

"Okay ladies, I'm going. But if you ever decide to give men another chance, don't forget the great Don Juan. I'll be here waiting!" Juan dashed from the kitchen just in time to dodge the hamburger that Janice threw at him.

An hour later Janice, Elizabeth and Juan left the Center. As they crossed the parking lot a police cruiser pulled beside them and stopped. Elizabeth's heart skipped and her legs threatened to give out. She was certain the police brought news of Victor. As the cruiser's window lowered Janice observed Elizabeth's pale complexion and placed her arm around her for support.

"Good afternoon. I'm here to pick up Juan." The officer nodded at Juan. "Get in."

Juan circled behind the cruiser. It took Elizabeth a moment to realize the officer didn't come to relay terrible news about Victor. "Juan, what's this all about?" she asked. "I thought you were doing so well."

Before Juan could reply the officer spoke. "Oh, it's not like that. Juan is an auxiliary officer with the Norwich police. He didn't tell you? A couple months after he started doing his community service at the Senior Center he came to the station and said he wanted to be a cop. We all thought he was busting our balls...oh, excuse me...giving us a hard time. But he's been riding with the officers for a few months now. I think he's going to be an excellent officer one day. Something about working here really turned on a light switch for Juan. Have a nice day ladies." The cruiser pulled away from the Center leaving Janice and Elizabeth speechless.

Elizabeth's happiness for Juan ebbed and trepidation about Victor returned. The ten minute drive to Victor's home in Bozrah seemed an eternity to Elizabeth. As they approached Victor's house the City Coroner's van pulled onto the street from Victor's driveway. Janice pulled to the curb and looked at Elizabeth. "Just drive," whispered Elizabeth. Before Janice placed her Impala back into drive, Victor's nephew Preston approached the car and tapped on Elizabeth's window. When Elizabeth didn't respond Preston opened her door and knelt before her.

"Elizabeth, I'm really sorry. I only just got here myself a few minutes ago. Is there anything I can do for you?"

Elizabeth's heart felt like someone wringing a wet cloth to squeeze the water from it. Through short gasps, she asked, "Did he go quietly?"

Preston clasped Elizabeth's hands. "I believe he went in his sleep." Preston hesitated before continuing. "But I think he knew he was going. He left this for you." Preston reached into his shirt pocket and produced a sealed envelope with Elizabeth's name written on it. She folded the envelope in her lap and closed the door. "Take me home, Janice."

Despite Janice's insistence, Elizabeth refused her offer to accompany her inside. She braced herself for the torrent of tears that would erupt once safely isolated in her apartment. Surprisingly, no tears came. She dropped the envelope into the trash can and turned on the television. She didn't hear the answers Alex Trebek provided, nor did she hear the questions offered in response. She boiled water and didn't feel the scalding tea she poured down her throat. She fell asleep on the sofa and didn't notice the darkness that pushed aside the light. She awoke before night fell and methodically boiled more water. Almost as an afterthought she retrieved the envelope from the trash can and read the note inside.

Dearest Elizabeth,

I don't have the gift for words that you do, so I know I can never do justice writing about the gift of life you have given me. I was so distraught upon losing my Millie that I tried to take my own life twice. I devised a fail-safe plan and was going to do it after one nice final meal – my first time at the Senior Center. While waiting for lunch I read your poem in "Gift for the Generations." Instead of performing the ultimate sin, not to mention dying a bitter, hopeless man after living such a blessed life, I connected with you. I clung to your words. I am dying tonight a happy man and cannot wait to bask in the Glory of God. This I owe to you. Please do not mourn me, Elizabeth. Rejoice in the soul you breathed life back into. Until we meet again. Love, Victor.

Elizabeth tore the note in two and threw it back in the trash. And then the tears came.

Seaside Gardens

The icy wind whistled through the windows as Elizabeth sped through her crossword puzzle. The words methodically poured from her fingers as she tried in vain to ignore the fact that it was Christmas. The sharp rap on the door startled Elizabeth. She peeked through the peep hole and recognized Alberta. Elizabeth opened the door. "I told you I'm not going," replied Elizabeth to the unasked question.

"I know what you told me, but it's Christmas and you're not going to stay here all alone. A local family is making everyone breakfast at the Hall and you are coming."

Elizabeth had lived at Seaside Gardens for nearly a decade. She kept to herself, and the few acquaintances she made over the years passed on regularly. She seldom ventured to the Hall at the senior citizen complex. The only resident she had any communication with was Alberta, although Elizabeth didn't understand Alberta's persistence. Elizabeth was old and bitter; and she knew it. It wasn't a cute act; Elizabeth had no use for life. She closed the door on Alberta and returned to her puzzle. Elizabeth grew tired and set down her paper and pen. She placed her glasses on the coffee table as her head drifted down against her chest. As Elizabeth slipped from consciousness violent colors bombarded her, signaling the entrance of another bizarre dream. Elizabeth did not care and she let herself sleep.

A shimmering mass sped across the room toward Elizabeth and stopped a few feet before it reached her. "I'm the Tick-Tock Man, remember me? It's been a while since we've chatted." As the words registered, the shining ball transformed into the face of a giant schoolhouse clock. As stoically as Elizabeth confronted life, her nightmares elicited terror within her. She shielded her face from the giant clock. The slow methodical ticking produced by the second hand barely registered. The clock's glossy bloodshot eyes glared at Elizabeth as Jacob's voice howled at her from an unseen mouth. "Don't ever drive my truck again!" The clock screamed and opened its mouth to emit drunken laughter. The Tick-Tock Man moved closer as the ticking intensified. "Look at me when I'm talking to you!" Elizabeth peered through her fingers. The clock's eyes closed. When they reopened the clock's face was thinner and Toby stared at her. "Look what you did, you little whore!" As Tick-Tock spoke, a large hole grew in the middle of Toby's face where the pipe had blown through it seventy years earlier. "All I wanted was a little kiss and you killed me!" Elizabeth cowered as Tick-Tock moved closer still. The ticking sound reverberated in Elizabeth's ears. When Elizabeth next looked back she faced that man that attacked her at Watch Hill. "I get one of you rich whores every year. Come on, you know you want it!" The ticking turned into a deafening roar. Elizabeth's hands went to her ears and she screamed. The instant before terror forced her awake, the Tick-Tock Man retreated from Elizabeth and transformed ever so briefly into her father. "Don't let them do this to you, Little Me. You are better than that." Tick-Tock disappeared and Elizabeth snapped awake, sweat coating her face.

Elizabeth's breathing returned to normal and she collected her thoughts. Her furniture took shape, colors restored themselves, and memories of her childhood forced their way past Elizabeth's fortified psyche. Each nightmare was unique, but every one left in its wake horror and loneliness. Never before had her father accompanied her nightmares. *Why this time?* Elizabeth asked herself. She put on her glasses and drew a cup of water from the tap. Without thinking she went into her bedroom and dressed. Before she knew it she left her house and walked toward the Hall. The day was crisp and bright, and several times during the short walk across the street she contemplated returning home. Elizabeth entered the Hall and joined about twenty other residents of the Gardens with no family, or with family who didn't care enough to spend Christmas with them.

A large smile grew across Alberta's face when Elizabeth entered. "I was hoping you would come," said Alberta as she approached Elizabeth. "Follow me." Alberta grabbed Elizabeth's hand and escorted her across the room. A man, woman, and three children stood behind a banquet table adorned with a Christmas table cloth. At one end of the table sat a coffee decanter and pitchers of juice and milk. Lining the rest of the table sat stainless steel trays warmed by propane burners. The trays contained eggs, waffles, sausage, bacon and toast. "Grab a plate before it's all gone. Most of these people usually eat like birds, but when it's free, look out!" Alberta handed Elizabeth a plastic plate.

"Can I get you something to drink?" asked the man at the head of the table. "I'll bring it to your table."

"Why are you doing this?" asked Elizabeth. "Are you on Community Service?"

The man smiled. "No, I'm afraid not. This is actually my wife's idea. Honey, come over here." A young woman with dark hair joined her husband "This is my wife Elena, and my children: Beth, Jacqueline and Carolin. What can we get for you?"

Before Elizabeth could answer a short wiry old man approached the table and butted in. "Elena, did you say? I'm Sal, recently from the Hawaiian Islands."

Elena smiled. "Really?"

"Oh yes," winked Sal. "Do you know ComeonIwannalaya? Or perhaps Wannaknockyersocksoff?"

Alberta jabbed Sal in the ribs. "You'll have to forgive Sal. He even gives dirty old men a bad name. Sal, go sit down and quit bothering these people!"

"Oh, jealous, huh Berta? Don't worry, there's plenty more where that came from!" Sal dished some scrambled eggs onto a fresh plate and returned to his table.

"Juice would be fine," Elizabeth told the man. Elizabeth helped herself to eggs and toast and followed Alberta to her table. The man placed the juice in front of Elizabeth and rejoined his family. With the diners occupied for the moment, the family piled food on their own plates and sat at a small table behind the serving table. When they finished eating the children each picked up a pitcher and worked the room, filling empty glasses as requested.

As everyone finished eating, an elderly woman crossed the room and stood behind a podium. "Good morning everyone, and Merry Christmas! I'm Natalie Schaeffer, as most of you already know. I hope everyone has had enough to eat?" A chorus of *Heavens yes* and *oh Lords* filled the room as the residents patted their stomachs and shook their heads. "I want to thank the Eugenes for treating us to this wonderful breakfast." Natalie turned toward the Eugenes. "I can't tell you how much it means to me that people would take time from their own lives and do this for total strangers. Some of us are going to dinner later with family. But I don't think it's any surprise that many people in this room would have spent Christmas alone if not for you." Natalie clapped her hands and was quickly joined by the other seniors. Natalie smiled as the youngest daughter, Jacqueline, bowed her head as her face turned beet red at the attention. "I don't want to take too much of your time. But there is one more item. A lot of you have donated items for the rummage sale to raise funds for…" Natalie clutched her throat and coughed into her hand. "To raise funds for-" Natalie stood speechless.

After a moment Alberta joined her at the podium. "Thank you Natalie, and thanks again to the Eugenes. As many of you know we are collecting items for the rummage sale next weekend to raise funds for Natalie's great-granddaughter Isabella. Isabella was born with Leukemia and is really struggling right now. She is six years old and has been receiving chemotherapy for years. Unfortunately it isn't working anymore. Without a bone marrow transplant things don't look very good for Isabella. Her mother quit working to care for her and stay with her at the hospital. Natalie's grandson is working two jobs just to try to get by week to week because of the mounting medical bills, and his medical insurance has long since exceeded his maximum benefits. They've sold their house and live in an efficiency motel. Every dollar helps so please pass the word to all your friends and relatives to donate items and to stop by the sale."

The door opened and a young couple entered the Hall. All eyes turned to the frail pale-faced girl accompanying the couple. When the girl spotted Natalie at the podium she strutted up to her and held her hand. The man spoke up. "Sorry Nana, we got here a little sooner than I expected. When you weren't at your place I thought I'd try over here. Sorry for the interruption."

Everyone's eyes in the room locked on Isabella. Finally Alberta broke the deafening silence. "Not at all, and welcome. You must be Justin. We were talking about the rummage sale we are planning. Your grandmother was just leaving, perhaps you could help her."

Justin joined Isabella and took his grandmother's other hand. "Come on, Nana, I'll help you. We still have quite a ride to get to Mom and Dad's by dinner." As Justin, his wife and Isabella escorted Natalie from the Hall, Isabella turned to the residents. "Merry Christmas everyone." And then the family disappeared outside, closing the door behind them.

The light buzz that permeated the open room dissipated by the time Isabella and her parents left. All thoughts were on the young girl who never had a chance for a normal childhood. The residents of Seaside Gardens silently pushed their chairs from the tables and donned their coats and hats. A few solemn exchanges of Merry Christmas occurred as the seniors departed the Hall.

Alberta joined Elizabeth. "I'll walk you home."

"If you must." Elizabeth's thoughts were still on Isabella. "Where does Natalie live?" she asked.

"Unit twenty-four, right behind the fire house. But she's not home. You just saw her leave with her grandson."

"Don't worry about what I just saw. I'm not blind," replied Elizabeth. "Not yet, anyway." The two walked to Elizabeth's unit.

"I'm glad you came to breakfast," said Alberta when they reached Elizabeth's front door.

"Me too," replied Elizabeth. "I feel so much merrier now." She entered her apartment and pushed the door closed on Alberta. Guilt sacked her and she opened the door to invite Alberta in for tea, but Alberta had already disappeared. Elizabeth returned to her chair and resumed her crossword puzzle. She couldn't focus and the words did not come. Finally Elizabeth turned on the television and agonized through the day. She was still full from breakfast as lunchtime came and went. For dinner she poached two eggs and toasted a slice of bread. Although it was only just past five o'clock, soft darkness blanketed Groton. Elizabeth walked to her bedroom and turned on the light. She slid open her closet door and knelt down. She tugged open the lid of a cardboard box and withdrew an old pillow case. She took a quick look inside and stood up, holding the pillow case at her side. She scribbled a note on an envelope and placed it inside the pillow case. She walked to the living room and put on her coat and scarf, then ventured outside. She looked left, then right, and proceeded down her walkway. Her teeth chattered in the freezing cold. As she walked past the Hall a car turned into Seaside Gardens, its headlights pointing toward Elizabeth. She felt ridiculous as she darted off the sidewalk and hid behind an old pine tree for cover. Once the car passed she continued her journey. She walked past the fire house and found unit twenty-four. As she approached the apartment she slid on a slick piece of sidewalk. Her feet flew out from beneath her and the pillow case sailed threw the air. Pain seared through her hips and back when she landed on the hard cold ground. Elizabeth lay still for a few minutes before trying to move. She didn't appear to be injured and slowly stood up. She found the pillowcase lying a few feet from her with some of its contents spilled out. She crawled to the sack and replaced its contents. She stood and walked to Natalie's front stoop. She tied a knot with the corners of the pillowcase and left it inside Natalie's storm door.

§

Two days later Elizabeth answered a knock at her front door. She greeted a smirking Alberta. "Good morning, would you like to come in for tea?"

"Tea would be fine," replied Alberta. She sat at the small kitchen table as Elizabeth boiled water.

"What brings you out so early," asked Elizabeth.

"Oh, no reason in particular. I just finished reading the paper and thought I'd take a walk. Why the sudden hospitality? You've never invited me in before."

Elizabeth nodded. "You are right, and I'm sorry. I was going to invite you in the other morning but-" When Elizabeth turned toward Alberta she saw her guest smiling like a Cheshire Cat. Alberta removed the newspaper from her purse and unfolded it on the table. "Could you take a look at this, Elizabeth? I'm having trouble reading this morning."

Elizabeth crossed the room and looked at Alberta like she was daft. Alberta pointed to a bold headline in the Region section that read *"Anonymous Samaritan Donates $200,000 to Leukemia Victim."*

Two-hundred thousand dollars? thought Elizabeth. She knew she pocketed a nice chunk from the sale of the house in Norwich in addition to squirreling away a couple thousand dollars a year since Jacob died, but she didn't realize it was that much. "So, what's that have to do with me?" asked Elizabeth. The two women stared at each other for a moment, and then laughed aloud simultaneously.

"Elizabeth, you *do* have a heart hidden away somewhere in there. You didn't have me fooled, I *knew* it!"

The smile left Elizabeth's face. "Don't you say a word to anyone. Do you hear me?"

Alberta reached across the table and held Elizabeth's hand. "I don't understand why the big secret, but of course I won't tell anyone if you don't want me to. I think the water is boiling. How about that tea?"

§

The years at Seaside Gardens passed slowly for Elizabeth. Natalie died, and so did Alberta. Isabella received her bone marrow transplant and fully recovered. Elizabeth followed Isabella's life through The Day. She was the first sophomore to be captain of the girls' volleyball team at Fitch High School and was turning into a beautiful young lady.

The bright spring sun glared through Elizabeth's kitchen window as she finished her tea. Although it was already the end of May, it was the first time that it felt like spring. The warmth filtering through the window cast off the final chills of winter and took the edge off Elizabeth's stiff bones. As she looked across the Gardens, she thought that a million years ago her father would be sowing his fields on a day like this.

Elizabeth pushed her chair from the table and went to her bedroom and dressed. She applied makeup and pinned her hair. She put on her wig and, and after scoffing at her own reflection in the mirror, walked into the kitchen and retrieved a loaf of bread from the cabinet. She sat at the table and tore several slices of bread into small pieces and placed them in a plastic bag. She placed the bag into her purse, donned her coat and walked outside. Other than her crossword puzzles, Elizabeth looked forward to taking the SEAT bus to Mystic Village once a week to feed the ducks that swam in the small stream in the middle of the Village. The morning's warmth felt even better outside and Elizabeth inhaled deeply, savoring the fresh spring smells of honeysuckle and wild grapes. She walked to the bench alongside Old North Road to await the bus. After a short while Elizabeth heard the low groan of the bus and looked toward Route 12. A young man jogging caught Elizabeth's attention and memories of running through the woods with Buckboard flashed before her. The bus eclipsed the jogger and Elizabeth grabbed her purse. She pushed up with her hands, but instead of standing erect she actually rolled forward in slow motion; melting rather than falling onto the concrete.

Panic and confusion consumed Elizabeth as first the jogger, then emergency medical personnel huddled around her. Almost before she knew it her hip was replaced and she was en route via ambulance to Bayside a week later. No surprise to Elizabeth; the beginning of the very end was finally at hand.

The Ride

"Moving a little slow this morning, ain't you Daphne?" commented Harry. The table's occupants had not yet been served their drinks, and their eggs had nearly cooled.

"Mind your business Harry," scolded Elizabeth. "You can see how busy she is."

"Thank you Elizabeth, but it's quite alright," replied Daphne. "The last time I tried to get help in here you scared her off. I heard she's in therapy, the poor child. What a *vile* crowd you are!"

Harry's face instantly turned deep purple. "Daphne, I've always liked you, and you know we don't normally behave like that. But that Dora…!"

Daphne winked at Elizabeth as a smile stole across her face. "I know about Dora. What's the matter boys, can't take a joke?"

Jerry guffawed and slapped his knee. "Lordy girl, you been spending too much time with Elizabeth. There's hope for you yet!"

The color receded from Harry's face as he struggled to overcome Daphne getting his goat. "I was just saying that my breakfast is getting cold and-"

"For God sakes," piped in Ann. "Let it go. My niece and nephew are going to be here soon and I don't want to be late just because

Daphne got the best of you. Run along now dear, won't you?" Daphne disappeared in the crowd, promising to return shortly with their drinks.

After a moment Bart said, "Ann, I think it's wonderful that you have such a supportive family. But since they take you three or four days a week, wouldn't it make sense for you to live with them? Seems like an awful lot of running back and forth on their part. Then maybe you wouldn't have to be so inconvenienced by those of us who aren't as blessed with loving relatives."

Despite the low buzz in the room, dead silence hung over the table. "I don't believe I like the tone of your voice Bartholomew. In fact," said Ann, "I think I've suddenly lost my appetite." Ann folded the silverware across her plate and stood up.

Harry, Jerry, Bart, Lucy and Elizabeth watched Ann wind her way through the tables and exit the room. Lucinda finally broke the silence. "If I knew that was all someone had to say to shut Ann up I would have done it long ago."

Without hesitation, Jerry clawed the air. "Mee-oowww! You're a feisty little kitty cat, ain't you Lucy!" Jerry slapped his knee at his own comment and laughed so hard that his breath became wheezes. He continued clawing the air and, when his breath allowed, he issued more broken cat calls.

Elizabeth shook her head and excused herself as well. "I'm afraid I'm also done. I can't bear the thought of watching Jerry give himself a stroke right in front of me. Besides," said Elizabeth in her most haughty, unpracticed voice, "my extended family is taking me out on the town today, and I can't be distracted by such aberrations of humanity. *Quite*!" As Elizabeth stood and turned to exit the room, she heard Jerry wheezing, cat-calling and slapping his knee behind her. She smiled and couldn't help tilting her nose toward the air, certain that Jerry would recognize her faux aristocracy and give himself a heart attack before she reached the hallway.

Elizabeth returned to her room and bathed. She spent considerable time applying the makeup and wig that Nancy Nichols brought on an earlier visit. Although far from satisfied at her appearance, Elizabeth did take consolation that she made the effort - an effort she hadn't made since arriving at Bayside nearly a year earlier. Elizabeth had given up pretenses that she didn't look forward to Nancy's visits. She longed for them, and certainly not just for the puzzles Nancy brought (although she did love them!). As the minutes crept by, Elizabeth worried that Nancy would not show up. After an eternity Elizabeth heard a knock. She opened the door and was awestruck. Nancy stood before her, a total vision of beauty and self-confidence. She wore hip-hugger jeans, a white button down blouse, and black flats with no socks. Her hair was medium length, styled chicly to one side with the tips ever so slightly highlighted. She applied just enough makeup to accentuate her features, but not enough to even make it apparent she even wore any. A sleek red valise draped over her shoulder, a far cry from the paper grocery bag in which she initially brought Elizabeth her goodies.

Nancy's face lit up at Elizabeth's reaction. "Good morning Elizabeth. How are you doing today?"

"Not nearly as good as you are, I can tell you that!"

Nancy smiled. "Are you still up for our ride?"

Elizabeth answered by stepping into the hallway and closing the door behind her. She hooked her elbow into Nancy's and allowed the young lady to escort her through Bayside's front doors. Elizabeth and Harry had taken several walks around Groton, but this was Elizabeth's first ride in a vehicle since the ambulance carried her to the facility - and her first real outing since her weekly trips to Old Mystic Village to feed the ducks a lifetime ago. The weather was unseasonably mild for March, with just enough chill in the air to make the day brisk. Elizabeth basked in the fresh air, and knew before the trip began that she would never want it to end.

The two crossed the parking lot and walked toward the visitor parking section. They passed car after car. They circled around the rear of an enormous fire engine red Cadillac that stuck out eight feet further than any of the SUVs in the lot. Nancy turned Elizabeth in between the Caddy and the next car, which was previously concealed by the car's tail fins. Next to the Cadillac sat an older model four door sedan with peeling green paint and sagging head upholstery. As Nancy withdrew a set of keys from her valise Elizabeth protested. "You're *not* my chauffer. I'm not going to sit in the back seat and have you drive me around all day."

But as Elizabeth spoke Nancy inserted the key into the passenger door of the Caddy. "I wouldn't think of it! Here you go." Nancy opened the door and helped Elizabeth into the passenger seat. Elizabeth surmised the car to be older than Nancy, but in showroom condition. As if the sun bouncing off the bright red paint wasn't enough to force Elizabeth to shield her eyes, the seats were pure white leather with an equally bright and flawless red dashboard and carpet. When Nancy disappeared behind the car to go to the driver's side, Elizabeth tweaked her neck looking at the vehicle's expansive cabin. When Nancy climbed in and turned the ignition, the Caddy's huge eight cylinder engine jumped to life and sounded like a jet.

"I've been in smaller buses than this," exclaimed Elizabeth.

Nancy flushed. "This was my mother's car. My father bought it new for her in nineteen-seventy-two. She only drove it on special occasions. I just thought-"

"I love it," interrupted Elizabeth. "I feel like a princess! Let's go!"

Nancy smiled and backed the Fleetwood out of the parking space. "Are you hungry? I have something special planned, but we have time."

Elizabeth's growling stomach reminded her of her pre-empted breakfast. "That sounds fine. Do you have any place in mind?"

"As a matter of fact I do." As Nancy drove toward Mystic, Elizabeth took in the sights, equally looking out the window and inside at the enormous interior of the Caddy. Nancy continued on Route Twelve, which became Route One as they left Groton and began the descent toward Mystic, passing the dominating white Union Baptist Church on their left. As they passed Water Street a clanging sound erupted from outside the car. "Great," said Nancy.

"The drawbridge is going up. Guess we're stuck for a little while." As Nancy eased the car to a stop, Elizabeth relished the forced delay and watched the people entering and leaving the quaint shops and staring as the hulking cams lowered to lift the antiquated drawbridge. Dozens of spectators crowded the bridge as the turn-of-the-century whaling ship *Charles Morgan* headed up the Mystic River toward its berth at the Mystic Seaport. Elizabeth thought of her parents laying in rest at the head of the river. When the gate lifted and traffic resumed, Nancy continued driving up Route One. As the Caddy turned toward Stonington the looming Packer Building assaulted Elizabeth without warning and stole her breath. Nancy asked Elizabeth if she was alright. Elizabeth assured her she was.

A moment later Nancy turned onto Route Twenty-seven at Angie's Pizza. They drove past more shops, old sea captains' homes, and the Mystic Seaport. After another minute they entered the Old Mystic Village parking lot. Nancy parked the Caddy and escorted Elizabeth into Go Fish, a trendy little restaurant. After being seated and provided menus, Elizabeth commented that the restaurant was the fanciest she had ever eaten at. Nancy replied that she must not get out much, and they both laughed. Sipping tea following a light lunch, Nancy glanced at her watch and told Elizabeth they had to get going. She paid the check and escorted Elizabeth from the restaurant.

Once outside Nancy said, "We still have a little time. Are you up for a walk around the village?"

They walked between the dozens of small shops, ice cream parlors and coffee houses. Nancy walked Elizabeth to the very stream-side bench from which Elizabeth fed the ducks hundreds of times during her years at Seaside Gardens. Once seated, Nancy unzipped her valise and produced two small bags of breadcrumbs. She handed one to Elizabeth. As a brown duck and her new family slowly paddled their way toward the two new marks, Elizabeth stared at Nancy. "How did you know?"

Nancy smiled at Elizabeth. "Know what?"

§

Nancy and Elizabeth tossed bread crumbs to the feathered family for a half hour. By the time two Canadian geese bullied their way into the mix, the women's feed bags were empty. Nancy called Elizabeth twice before she responded. "Oh, I'm sorry. I was lost in thought."

"Are you ready to go?" asked Nancy.

Elizabeth was certainly *not* ready to go. In fact, she would have stayed on that bench all day. "I suppose we should be going."

Nancy helped Elizabeth up from the bench and held her hand as they walked to the car. Still shaking off her walk down memory lane, the red Cadillac snuck up on Elizabeth and made her smile again at its enormity. "Promise me you will always keep this car," she begged Nancy. Nancy promised and helped Elizabeth inside. Nancy started the vehicle and headed back toward Groton. Elizabeth grew anxious thinking that the day with Nancy was nearing an end. She didn't want to seem ungrateful, but finally couldn't help herself. "So...you said you had a surprise planned?"

The nearly constant smile on Nancy's lips never left. When she finally answered, Elizabeth's heart sank. "I thought you enjoyed the Village?" asked Nancy.

Elizabeth wished she had never opened her big mouth. "I'm sorry, I loved it. I just...I just don't want today to end."

Nancy reached over and squeezed Elizabeth's hand. "Don't worry; today hasn't even begun for us."

"You are very special Nancy."

Nancy held onto Elizabeth's hand. "Thank you. So are you."

The Fleetwood veered slightly off the narrow road and Elizabeth returned her eyes to the front of the car just in time. "AAAHHHHH!"

Before she even knew what Elizabeth was screaming at, Nancy screamed too. "AAAHHHH!" She jerked the wheel and returned the enormous vehicle to its lane just before slamming into an empty garbage can that rolled partially into the street. "Okay Elizabeth, we'd better save our sentimental moments for when I'm not driving!" With both their hearts still lodged in their throats (and *both* of Nancy's hands gripping the steering wheel), the two women drove in silence for the next ten minutes. They drove on Route One back toward Groton and were within a half mile of Bayside. Elizabeth worried that Nancy's statement about their day just beginning was an arbitrary comment. But a quarter mile from Bayside Nancy turned left. A moment later they passed under a railroad bridge. When they emerged the back field of the Groton-New London Airport came into view. Private planes sputtered along the tarmac jockeying for takeoff position. Nancy drove past a couple corporate hangars as Elizabeth watched the planes in turn accelerate down the runway and go airborne. Nancy entered the main terminal and parked.

Nancy helped Elizabeth from the car. "Let's go inside."

"We can see fine from here, unless you're chilly," said Elizabeth.

"A little maybe, come with me." Nancy led Elizabeth inside the small terminal and found two seats by a plate glass window overlooking the airfield. They watched the planes for about ten minutes before Nancy excused herself. She returned five minutes later accompanied by a tall young man wearing a jacket and tie. "Mrs. Newton?" said the man. "I'm Glen Kirk, I'll be your pilot today. Can I escort you to your plane?"

Elizabeth jumped up from her seat as she realized what Nancy had planned for her, ignoring the searing pain that shot through her hip at the sudden movement. "You certainly may!" Elizabeth felt like a princess for the second time that day as the handsome young man escorted her to "her" plane. Elizabeth walked on cloud nine. Suddenly a thought struck her and she turned to Nancy, who trailed closely behind. "I can't do this! This must be costing you a fortune!"

Nancy glanced downward, her eyebrows lifting and her lips crunching up like a child who "forgot" to tell her mother she'd spilled milk all over the kitchen floor. "I don't know if I ever mentioned this, but my mother was filthy rich. Actually, this is her plane. Well, I guess now it's my plane."

Elizabeth placed her hand on her hips and stared at Nancy, shaking her head. "Child, you never cease to amaze me! Pilot, can you please get me in the air?"

The three crossed the tarmac to a waiting Cessna. The pilot helped the ladies into the cabin. As he closed the door behind them, Elizabeth asked, "So then, you're Captain Kirk, like on Star Trek?"

"Yeah, about that," said the pilot. "Glen will work just fine. Okay ladies, buckle up. We'll be airborne in five minutes."

The pilot flipped a couple switches and a low vibration consumed the cabin. A moment later the twin propellers began rotating slowly enough for Elizabeth to count the blades as they turned outside the window. As the large engines barked to full throttle Elizabeth thought for a moment she would pee herself. The propeller blades become a blur. Elizabeth couldn't hear the pilot's words as he talked on the radio, but a minute later they taxied the runway. The plane felt like a go cart to Elizabeth as it slowly lumbered to the end of the runway. The pilot turned to the ladies and told them they were third in line for takeoff. One by one Elizabeth observed the other two planes accelerate down the runway and lift off to points unknown. Glen told Nancy and Elizabeth to sit back and hang on. Elizabeth thought this to be the finest moment of her life. The plane picked up speed. Bluff Point to the left went by faster and faster until Elizabeth could no longer discern individual trees. Suddenly the momentum from the acceleration pinned her against the seat and she screamed. "AAHHHH!"

Nancy snapped her eyes at Elizabeth. "You okay?"

"I'm fine! AAHHHH! I'm okay, don't worry! AAHHHH!!"

The pilot and Nancy glanced at Elizabeth and smiled. "Hang on," Nancy told her.

The plane climbed and climbed. Elizabeth watched the smaller boats in Long Island Sound disappear, the larger boats become dots, and finally the dots become wakes.

"How we doing back there?" asked the pilot.

Elizabeth couldn't yet speak, but waved the pilot on. Once at cruising altitude the pilot told Nancy and Elizabeth that he would take them for a tour around the Sound. He pointed out Block Island,

Plum Island, the tower at Millstone Power Station and Martha Stewart's mansion on Long Island. For Elizabeth the entire adventure tasted the first bite of sweet chocolate. They were airborne for a half hour when Elizabeth turned to Nancy. "I love you." Nancy smiled back and patted Elizabeth's leg.

"There's some cloud cover ahead," said the pilot. If you ladies don't mind a few seconds of turbulence, I want to show you something." Without waiting for an answer, the pilot pulled back on a lever and the plane climbed. As the first wisps of cumulous clouds masked the previously unencumbered view, the plane rocked back and forth. Transiting the cloud cover took about fifteen seconds before the ride smoothed. In an instant bright yellow sun filled the cabin. The sky all around was the most magnificent blue Elizabeth had ever witnessed. The clouds below them formed a bed of the softest cotton, accented with spiraling mountains and glaciers of pure white moisture. Elizabeth had no doubt that that was the most awe-inspiring sight she had ever laid eyes on. Heaven could not be more splendid. The vision stole Elizabeth's breath. She placed her hand over her heart and gently shook her head back and forth at the sheer wonder of such beauty. "I wonder if Father Digiacomo has ever seen this," Elizabeth said aloud.

"Why would you think of him?" asked Nancy. "Whenever you talk about him you tell me what a 'pain in your backside' he is."

Elizabeth held Nancy's hand. "Maybe it's never too late to teach an old dog new tricks. Maybe I'm not as smart as I thought I was."

The pilot turned to Nancy. "You said about an hour. Are you ready to return Miss Nichols?"

"'Miss Nichols' is it?" chided Nancy. Yes Captain Kirk, I think we're ready."

"Yes ma'am, uh, I mean Nancy, right. Okay hang on, we're going down."

The plane bumped and rocked for a few seconds as it drove through the clouds. A moment later the green and blue earth returned. "There's Watch Hill to our left," announced the pilot. "Home of the richy-rich. And there's Point Judith. We'll hug the coastline until we get home. Enjoy the ride Elizabeth-and *Nancy*."

Not without satisfaction, Elizabeth noticed Nancy's cheeks grow bright pink. *Wouldn't they make a lovely couple?* Elizabeth sensed the electricity between the two young people. She wondered if it was as obvious to Glen and Nancy as it was to her. Fifteen minutes later the plane began its descent toward Groton. The plane flew over Bluff Point, made a U-turn and began its approach toward the runway. The plane slowed and the nose tipped up slightly. Halfway down the runway the tires first contacted the ground. "Ohh!" shouted Elizabeth as the plane bounced off the ground. A second later the tires touched again. "Ohh!" And again. "Ohh!" Finally the plane taxied across the tarmac and came to a stop. The pilot opened the door and helped Nancy and Elizabeth to the ground. Once Elizabeth's feet were firmly planted, she wrapped her arms around the pilot and thanked him. Then she whispered into his ear. "Don't miss your chance with her. She is *very* special." Glen patted her back and walked the ladies to the terminal.

Elizabeth's spirits still sailed as high as their flight as they walked through the terminal. The airport was small and primarily used for white collar commuters to Boston and New York. There were only a few dozen seats for waiting passengers, and they were all empty save one. An elderly woman sat facing the runway, her head buried in a book. A small McDonald's bag sat on the floor next to her. She looked familiar, but with her head down Elizabeth could only see the woman's hair and forehead. Then she recognized the woman. "Quick," Elizabeth told Nancy, "hide me!" Nancy didn't understand, but let Elizabeth jump on the other side of her, placing Nancy between Elizabeth and the woman. Confident that the woman could not see her, Elizabeth told Nancy to walk closely behind her. Elizabeth walked to the nearest counter. A woman promptly asked if she could help. "Yes," replied Elizabeth. "That woman sitting alone over there," Elizabeth motioned with her head. The receptionist looked toward the woman reading. "Don't let her see you looking at her. Who is she?"

Uncertain, the woman turned back toward Elizabeth, sneaking a sideways glance at the woman. "I don't know her name. She's been coming here for years. She comes a few times a week and sits there all day. She reads, watches the planes, drifts off to sleep. It's against regulations to loiter here and security used to make her leave. I won't let them anymore though. She never bothers anyone, so I say leave her be. Do you know her?"

"No," replied Elizabeth. "No, I guess I don't know her after all."

Elizabeth knew that if it had been Lucy that discovered Ann's sham she would race back to Bayside and blab it all over the place. Elizabeth would never say a word.

§

Nancy and Elizabeth walked in silence back to the Cadillac. Once inside, Nancy asked, "Who was that woman?"

Nancy was pulling out of the parking lot before Elizabeth answered. "Ann."

"Ann from Bayside? The one who is always with her family?"

Elizabeth considered for a moment. "Apparently not. Maybe sometime you wouldn't mind asking her out to lunch?"

Nancy finally connected the pieces. "Sure, I could do that."

"Nancy, you have just given me the happiest day of my life and I feel like a scoundrel for asking. Would you mind terribly driving me to North Stonington?"

Nancy glanced toward the sky. The sun had past its crest, but there was still plenty of daylight left. "Your wish is my command. Just point the way."

"Well, that could be a problem. It's been eighty years since I've been there, but I think if you get me to North Stonington I can find it." Elizabeth beamed with renewed excitement, but worried that she wouldn't be able to find her old home.

Nancy didn't seem concerned in the least. "No problem, let's go!" Nancy turned right onto Route Twelve, and then left on Old North Road. They drove past Seaside Gardens, and Elizabeth frowned at the sight of the bench from which she fell and broke her hip. A couple miles later they turned north on Route One-Eighty-Four and drove for several miles. The shopping plazas, gas stations and convenience stores gave way to forest and two-hundred year old homes. There were no cars behind them, and Nancy slowed as much as she could to allow Elizabeth to gain her bearings.

"There!" shouted Elizabeth, pointing to a canopied road jutting off the two-lane highway. The two women looked on either side of the road. They could have just stepped back in time a hundred years, or three hundred for that matter. The roads cut slim black swaths through the dense forest, and appeared to be losing their struggle for existence. They passed horse farms, ponds, even a winery. Elizabeth recognized the roads and landmarks, but as though from a dream. "Pull over here!" ordered Elizabeth. The sudden outburst startled Nancy and she glided the Cadillac to the side of the road. Barely visible through the forest Nancy spotted a dilapidated old farmhouse and a couple small outbuildings. Mother Earth was reclaiming her own. Trees, weeds, ivy and brush nearly enveloped the structures. What few windows remained were broken. A few shards of paint remained, but the buildings were for the most part bare rotten wood. Elizabeth's mind transcended nearly a century. She saw Buckboard running after the chickens, and her father chasing after him yelling at the top of his lungs. The smell of her mother frying bacon permeated Elizabeth's senses, and Daniel's freshly planted first kiss lit up Elizabeth's lips like holiday sparklers. Tears streamed down Elizabeth's face as her childhood of yesterday danced before her mind's eye. Elizabeth closed her eyes and leaned back against the headrest as the tears fell in buckets.

"Elizabeth. Elizabeth, are you alright?" Nancy reached over and patted Elizabeth's leg. After an eternity for Nancy, Elizabeth clasped the young woman's hand. "I'm fine dear. And I'm ready to go."

"You mean you're ready to go back to Bayside?" asked Nancy.

"Yes," replied Elizabeth. "That too."

Epiphany

After returning to Bayside and walking Elizabeth to her room, Nancy asked, "Are you alright? Elizabeth…?"

Nancy's words finally registered and a slight smile touched Elizabeth's lips. "I'm fine dear. Come here please." Nancy pulled the door closed behind her and crossed the room. When she stood before Elizabeth the older woman wrapped her arms around her and laid her head against Nancy's shoulder. Nancy returned Elizabeth's hug and the two women embraced for several minutes before Elizabeth pushed Nancy away. "Thank you for everything," said Elizabeth. "I'm going to rest now."

"Maybe I should stay with you for a while," said Nancy. "I don't mind if you rest. I've been meaning to start doing crossword puzzles anyway. I could start today." Elizabeth's look answered Nancy's question.

"Alright, if you're sure you're okay. I'll see you Thursday?" Nancy turned to leave the room. When Elizabeth didn't reply she looked back.

Elizabeth stared right through Nancy. "Don't you have a handsome pilot to meet someplace? Get along now."

Nancy's feet shuffled backward like bricks as she forced herself from the room. Alone in her room, Elizabeth sat on her bed. With the vibrant images of her childhood freshly blazed in her mind, she lay back and slept a dreamless sleep.

§

A booming voice blasted Elizabeth from her innocent sleep. "I hate to wake you Elizabeth."

Elizabeth's bones jumped in her skin. "I swear to Christ, Father! Why do you do that to me?" As apologetic as Father Digiacomo always claimed he was when he startled Elizabeth, she was certain she always detected an ill-concealed smile. The Father bore no such playfulness this time.

"Have you read your Bible? I mean really *read* it, not just recite verses and chapters to antagonize me."

Elizabeth felt very small hearing the Father actually confront her with her games. The quip that bubbled in her throat died. "I'm sorry Father, I haven't."

The Priest stood from the chair. "I have to go. The words are there for you. Do this for yourself."

Elizabeth closed her eyes in humility. When she again opened them she was alone in her room.

§

The endless stream of red ambulance lights bounced around Elizabeth's room like a uni-colored kaleidoscope, signaling another arrival or departure from Bayside. The lights awoke Elizabeth and she lay in the absolute silence of her room. Her throat was parched but she was exhausted. She tried in vain to ignore her thirst and return to sleep. Finally acknowledging that sleep would not return without getting a drink, she swung her legs over the side of the bed and switched on her light. She walked to the bathroom and filled a cup with water. She was so dehydrated that the first couple swallows scratched her throat. She stared at her reflection in the mirror. Elizabeth reflected on her life. Even as a child she knew she had a wonderful life. *But why all the rest? Why all the heartache, sorrow, disappointment, loss, loneliness? What was the point?*

Elizabeth set down her cup and left the bathroom. She noticed something on the table and initially assumed it was the fresh supply of crossword puzzles Nancy left for her. But then she remembered she had moved them to her nightstand. She approached the table and saw a medium-sized manila envelope. She carried the envelope to her bed and sat down. She picked up her glasses from the nightstand and put them on. Her name was written on the front of the envelope. She fumbled with the tiny clasp and finally opened it. Elizabeth upended the envelope and tapped it on the nightstand. A small picture and a handwritten note spilled out. The note read, "Elizabeth, there isn't much time. Search your soul and read the words in the Book and play your game one more time. Have Faith." The note was unsigned, although Elizabeth had no doubt that Father Digiacomo wrote it. The picture was old and she held it up to the light. It was a picture of her and her baby right after Ethan was born. Elizabeth didn't understand. She turned the picture over. Written in a child's hand were the following words: **The only picture of me and my birth mother.** The photograph was signed: **Ethan Digiacomo.**

A prickly sensation enveloped Elizabeth as she realized the implication of the picture and the words on the back. "Oh my God," she whispered. "It can't be." Elizabeth scrambled across her bed and opened the box containing her few possessions. She removed the large Bible and set it on the floor so she could rummage through the rest of her belongings. She quickly perused the contents and discarded them. Near the bottom of the box she retrieved a time-yellowed envelope. She opened it and pulled out the small photograph contained inside. She rolled back across the bed and picked up the picture Father Digiacomo had left her. She held the two photographs side by side under the light. They were nearly identical, but there were subtle differences. In one picture Elizabeth faced the camera, in the other her head was turned to the side. Her mother's arm was visible in one picture, but half of her body in the other. Ethan's eyes were wide open in one, nearly closed in the other.

Emotion racked Elizabeth's body. Great sobs came in huge torrents that stole her breath. "Ethan, *my son!*" she cried. "Why didn't you *tell* me?" But even as she cried she understood that her son had provided the answer in his note to her. "*Have faith.*" *Faith* demanded no proof. "Read *your* words in the Book," Elizabeth repeated aloud. Through tears she crawled back across the bed and lifted her family's ancient Bible from the floor. She opened the Book arbitrarily and began reading from Judges. But even as she read, the Father's note played across her mind: "Your words." Elizabeth finally understood. She began turning the pages looking for notes she had written over the last century. The pages flew by as Elizabeth read a lifetime worth of notes: 'Daniel- Father rescued from well', 'Irene gave birth to David today', 'I finally let Victor drive me home', 'Isabella had her surgery today', 'I have a new friend-Nancy'. Thousands of memories of those people close to Elizabeth flooded her mind like a whirlwind. Elizabeth retrieved the pen from her nightstand and found a page in the Bible on which she hadn't written. In the margin she wrote: 'Ethan came back to me.'

Suddenly the memory of Father Digiacomo's sense of urgency earlier that day and the words in his note confirmed to Elizabeth that she would not see him anymore. At least not in this lifetime. Elizabeth was equally elated and fatigued. She turned off the light and laid back. Memories of the people she just read about continued bombarding her. In a state that wasn't a dream, but also wasn't consciousness, countless blurred images played out before Elizabeth. Thousands of people across the globe that wouldn't be alive except for Daniel's heroism, and therefore wouldn't be alive except for Elizabeth helping her father find Daniel in the well that night so many years ago. An image of Irene shooting herself up with heroin and selling herself for her next fix was replaced with the successful businesswoman, wife and mother of three that she had become. Elizabeth recognized these images as those that *would have been* without her intervention, and those that *were* because of her. Victor lay alone with a bottle of rum and an empty bottle of sleeping pills beside him. A paramedic stood before him and told his partner 'this ain't the first time he's tried it. Guess he finally got it right.' This image was replaced with Victor writing his final note to Elizabeth stating that, *"I am dying tonight a happy man and cannot wait to bask in the Glory of God."* In her trance-like state Elizabeth was forced to bear witness to Isabella dying from cancer at the tender age of nine years old, her parents distraught at her bedside. Thankfully the image was quickly replaced with a photo shoot of Isabella after leading Fitch High School's volleyball team to the state championship. Next Elizabeth witnessed Nancy slice not one, but both her wrists and laying down for her final long sleep as the blood drained from her young body. Next she saw a long white trail behind Nancy as her and the handsome pilot walked down the aisle together. Elizabeth was forced to relive the anguish she experienced when her baby was taken from her arms. That memory, that *vision*, lingered forever to Elizabeth. Finally the images of people Elizabeth had never seen flashed before her mind – thousands of people that Father Digiacomo, her son, had helped find peace and salvation during his lifetime.

Elizabeth closed her eyes and prayed in humility. *Did I really cause all those positive changes?* She certainly didn't have any intention to, nor did she understand the impact of her actions. Still, she couldn't deny their outcome. Then she remembered one section of Father Digiacomo's note: *'play your word game one more time.'* Elizabeth initially thought the Father chastised her for her blaspheme and she felt even smaller than she had. With her eyes still closed she repented. All of these people so important to Elizabeth's life again flashed before her. Daniel, Irene, Victor, Isabella, Nancy, Ethan. Their faces came one right after the other, again and again and again. Daniel, Irene, Victor, Isabella, Nancy, Ethan. And Elizabeth got it. DIVINE! Her son helped answer her question, '*Why all the heartache, sorrow, disappointment, loss, loneliness? What was the point?*' "That *is* the point!" cried Elizabeth aloud. "It *is* Divine. *Everything is Divine!*"

The passage from Isaiah 53:6 shot into Elizabeth like a thunderbolt. "All we, like sheep have gone astray; we have turned – every one – to his own way; and the LORD has laid on him the iniquity of us all." Elizabeth rolled off the bed to her knees and bowed her head in humility as she spoke aloud. "Dear God," began Elizabeth through streaming tears, "I am an unworthy sinner who has turned her back to you my entire life. You sent your only son to die a horrible death on the cross for me and I have done nothing but scorn you. Please forgive my sins and use my life for Your purpose. In Jesus' name I pray, amen."

As the echo from her words died, the room brightened. Elizabeth's mind brightened to the point that she was forced to shield her face from the light even through closed eyes. All of Elizabeth's weariness departed. Her aching body rejuvenated and ached no more. She felt only euphoria and she opened her eyes. Everything was pure and she understood how *wrong* she was when she thought that Heaven could not be more beautiful than the clouds. Holy Paradise opened its gates for Elizabeth, and it was *infinitely* more wonderful than anything Elizabeth could ever have imagined. As Heaven's light beckoned Elizabeth, her Mother and Father appeared together before her. They extended their arms and held onto Elizabeth's hands. "You are ready, Elizabeth," said her mother. "It's your time now." Elizabeth's father smiled and squeezed her hand as the three turned and entered the Kingdom of God.

Epilogue

The attractive young woman entered the foyer at Bayside and proceeded to the front desk. The receptionist hung up the phone and scribbled a note. "Can I help-" As the receptionist glanced up from her desk she recognized Nancy. "You're Elizabeth's friend. I am so sorry, but Elizabeth passed away last night."

"It's alright, I know."

"You know? Did they call you?" asked the receptionist.

"They didn't have to," replied Nancy. "I'm taking care of all the funeral arrangements. But you could help me. Elizabeth spoke highly, in her own way, of Father Digiacomo. I want to ask him to deliver the eulogy."

The receptionist's face turned pale and she sat speechless. "What's wrong?" asked Nancy.

The receptionist regained her composure. "I'm sure he would be honored, but that's not possible. Father Digiacomo was a saint, but I don't think even he could pull that one off. He passed away last year."

"That's impossible," said Nancy. "Elizabeth told me of all their conversations. When did he pass?"

The receptionist banged away on her keyboard as she studied the computer monitor. "Looks like last April. Easter Sunday as a matter of fact." The receptionist's fingers returned to the keyboard and pecked some more. "Wow, this sure is a big coincidence," she said. "Father Digiacomo passed away the same day Elizabeth arrived at Bayside. They could have crossed paths the day Elizabeth came here."

Which they did.

Journey's Destination

The empty canvas of life lay before me - my own clay to mold
With me, for me, and by me nature's blessings abound
My mother, my father, my God to love and to hold
The absolute silence of winter's night creating a miraculous sound

One by one all things good departed
Their voids filled with bitterness, loneliness, disillusion and fear
A century later I exist, bitter and empty-hearted
Expunged of hope, devoid of cheer

Through life I stumbled, deaf and blind
Oblivious to the work of Master's Hand
No longer looking, and therefore never to find
My purpose in life designed by His command

As twilight descends upon me, He has not despaired
His messenger He sent to me
An injured soul not yet repaired
With long shadows, still there is time to see

Night falls as Death cloaks my eyes
Awakened from dormancy is this soul of mine
I leave this world free from self-imposed doubt and lies
Content for eternity that Life is blessed, pure and Divine